THE PARIS CHAPTER

VICTORIA WALTERS

Boldwood

First published in Great Britain in 2025 by Boldwood Books Ltd.

Copyright © Victoria Walters, 2025

Cover Design by Alexandra Allden

Cover Images: Shutterstock

The moral right of Victoria Walters to be identified as the author of this work has been asserted in accordance with the Copyright, Designs and Patents Act 1988.

All rights reserved. No part of this book may be reproduced in any form or by any electronic or mechanical means, including information storage and retrieval systems, without written permission from the author, except for the use of brief quotations in a book review. This book is a work of fiction and, except in the case of historical fact, any resemblance to actual persons, living or dead, is purely coincidental.

Every effort has been made to obtain the necessary permissions with reference to copyright material, both illustrative and quoted. We apologise for any omissions in this respect and will be pleased to make the appropriate acknowledgements in any future edition.

A CIP catalogue record for this book is available from the British Library.

Paperback ISBN 978-1-83518-970-2

Large Print ISBN 978-1-83518-969-6

Hardback ISBN 978-1-83518-968-9

Ebook ISBN 978-1-83518-971-9

Kindle ISBN 978-1-83518-972-6

Audio CD ISBN 978-1-83518-963-4

MP3 CD ISBN 978-1-83518-964-1

Digital audio download ISBN 978-1-83518-966-5

This book is printed on certified sustainable paper. Boldwood Books is dedicated to putting sustainability at the heart of our business. For more information please visit https://www.boldwoodbooks.com/about-us/sustainability/

Boldwood Books Ltd, 23 Bowerdean Street, London, SW6 3TN

www.boldwoodbooks.com

For Paris

1

I weaved through the passengers, my suitcase squeaking as I walked towards the waiting Eurostar train, wondering why I had let my best friend Carly talk me into this.

I had only made the final decision to come this morning, so I hoped I'd remembered to pack everything I needed. After leaving without it, I had rushed back to my flat to grab my passport, but I had made it and before I could chicken out, I climbed onto the train and found my seat, stowing my case nearby.

As I collapsed into the seat, I had a moment of thinking that what I was doing was a stupid idea and would never work in a million years. I wondered if it was too late to get off the train and run back home, but then the doors closed.

I took a deep breath to steady my nerves. As we moved away from St Pancras towards Paris, all I could do was hope that this trip would be the healing balm I desperately needed it to be. Because my career, and all future happiness, depended on it.

No pressure or anything, Paris.

I hadn't been to Paris before and never expected to be going there solo today. I rested my head against the back of the seat with a sigh. The conversation I'd had with Carly two days ago flashed back through my mind.

'The Airbnb emailed me to remind me of my booking,' I had said to her on the phone. 'The romantic trip to Paris that Joe got me for Christmas. Except he asked me to book it as he was waiting for a new credit card,' I added, bitterness tinging my voice. 'Now, of course, I know it was because he didn't want Rachel to see the booking and find out about me.' I couldn't believe that only two months ago I'd had no idea about her; I'd thought me and Joe were madly in love. Turns out, he had been cheating on me for the whole of our six-month relationship with a woman he worked with called Rachel.

'The utter bastard,' Carly replied, her voice spitting venom through the phone.

'Yep,' I agreed, but I couldn't be as enthusiastic. My initial rage had dulled to sadness and bitterness. 'I completely forgot about the trip with everything that happened.' I paused before delivering the worst part of it all. 'It's non-refundable.'

'It sucks to lose the money but it would suck more if Joe was still in your life,' Carly replied. 'I still want to cut off his balls.'

I snorted despite my melancholy. I knew that feeling well. My imagination had run wild about how I could get revenge on my ex. That was the problem with being a writer. Your mind was always overthinking. But in reality, I'd never have the guts. 'It's just brought it all back, you know?' I sighed and closed the email but then a worse one appeared in my eyeline. 'Oh God, Gita has sent another one.' My editor at my publishers, Turn the Pages, was increasingly getting panicky as I ignored her asking about how my new novel was coming along.

That makes two of us.

'What are you going to do?'

'Pay back my advance?' It was a flippant suggestion because I'd already spent most of it – first, on booking the aforementioned trip to Paris, and the rest on a deposit and the first few months' rent on a new flat. An expense I certainly hadn't been planning on. 'How am I supposed to write a happy-ever-after romance after my boyfriend cheated on me? I don't think I'll ever believe in love again,' I declared, dropping my head down dramatically onto my desk.

Carly tutted. 'Look, Tessa, you picked a wrong-un, yes, but you believe in love. You always have. Remember when we were teenagers and you wore your mother's wedding dress for our Halloween party? And what about your Pinterest board?'

I sighed. It was full of wedding inspo. 'I can't believe I thought Joe might actually propose on this trip to Paris.'

'Well, you do have rose-tinted glasses on when it comes to boyfriends,' Carly said softly. 'But that's why I love you. You are so optimistic.'

'Not any more. I've learnt my lesson.'

'I hate to hear you talking like that. You just haven't found your person. If I can, so can you.'

'You found him when we were fifteen; it's not a fair comparison,' I said, but I wasn't bitter about that. Carly and her husband Luke had been at school with me and once they'd started dating, that had been it for the both of them. I don't think either had even looked at someone else. Their love used to give me hope; now I just felt like I'd never find it.

'It's Tessa.' Carly muffled the phone. 'She's okay…'

'You can tell him,' I called out. Luke knew pretty much everything in my life, like Carly. If I was honest, he was the only man, apart from my father, that I trusted now.

I could hear her telling Luke about the Paris reminder email and how it had sent me spiralling. 'Okay, so Luke has an idea. I'm putting you on speaker…'

'Tessa,' Luke said, coming on the phone. 'Why are you talking to Carly instead of packing?'

'Huh?' I said, confused.

'Paris!' Luke cried. 'Why don't you still go on your own?'

'Oh my God! That's genius,' Carly said. 'You should do that!'

'No way,' I replied firmly. 'Walking around the City of Love by myself? Sounds depressing with a capital D.'

'But you need to write your next book,' Luke insisted. 'Where else can you get that kind of inspiration?'

'If anything can make you believe in love again, it's Paris,' Carly agreed.

And that phone call was the reason I was currently on the Eurostar.

All by myself.

I picked up my Kindle and opened up the new romance novel I was reading. *First Impressions* by Liv Jones. She was best friends with my publicist at Turn the Pages, Stevie, who had told me I would love this book. But I tried and failed to even read the first page. I closed my Kindle case quickly. Not only could I not write about romance, but I also currently couldn't bear to read it either. But I still hadn't been able to bring myself to admit that to anyone at my publishers. My editor Gita had no idea I hadn't written a word of the novel that was due in only three weeks' time. I'd never missed a deadline before. That just wasn't me.

But then Joe had screwed me over.

Gazing out of the train window, I watched as St Pancras faded away and we headed towards the City of Love. I regretted letting Luke and Carly talk me into this, but I was desperate. I needed inspiration. Something to pull me out of my hating-love mindset. Otherwise Joe would not only have taken my heart and trampled on it, but he would ruin my career too.

Please, Paris, work your magic.

2

Gare du Nord was hectic when I got off the Eurostar, dragging my suitcase behind me. I hadn't slept well last night and was too keyed up to snooze on the train, so I fought off weariness and made my way outside. It was February and London had been grey, miserable and cold so I was happy to see Paris was bathed in wintery sunshine instead. The bright day gave me some hope that this trip might not be a complete disaster. I walked out of the station and hoped the crisp February air would help to wake me up.

The Airbnb that Joe had chosen was only a ten-minute walk from the station, so I set off in the direction I'd memorised from Google Maps. As I made my way through the winding streets, I looked up at the Parisian architecture that couldn't fail to thrill even the most cynical Londoner. There was something about Paris. Even though Carly accused me of having rose-tinted glasses when it came to romance, she couldn't say the same about this city. It was beautiful. I held back from calling it romantic, my heart was firmly closed against all of that, but it did help to lift my sprits just a little bit.

I soon reached the apartment building and stared up at it in awe. Joe, I hated to admit it, had chosen well. It was a Haussmann-style building with a cream-coloured stone façade, a steeply sloped roof, and ornate black balconies that were charming. I typed in the door code the Airbnb host had given me and walked through the main door. I then had to walk up to the second floor, the building having been constructed before lifts were a thing. Luckily, I'd packed light, my mind only half on the job, so it wasn't too hard to get my suitcase up there.

Outside the front door was a key box. I put in the code the host had given me and took out the key to open the door. I was surprised to find only one key but as I'd come alone, it didn't matter. Letting myself in, I stepped into the apartment and forgot everything that was wrong for a moment.

After walking through the tiny hall, I found myself in the living room. The light was glorious as the sunshine beamed in through the huge windows, displaying the balcony and then the city beyond. The floor was shiny wood and there was a stunning fireplace in the corner. The furniture was antique and so Parisian, my heart sung.

I shrugged off my leather jacket, left my suitcase and hurried towards the window, stepping out onto the balcony, the smile wide on my face. Then I actually gasped out loud. Because to my right, peeping through a gap in two buildings opposite, was the Eiffel Tower. This Airbnb was a dream. I wasn't grateful to Joe for much but I was for him finding this.

Maybe, just maybe, this will be good for me.

I walked back inside from the balcony and looked across at the kitchen in the corner and then as I stepped towards where the bedroom and bathroom were, I frowned. I could hear running water nearby. I spun around but then told myself not to be so jumpy. The walls were likely just really thin.

I grabbed my suitcase and wheeled it with me towards the open bedroom door. I was just about to walk through when the sound of water abruptly finished and there was a click, and to my shock and horror, the door next to the bedroom opened and out walked a man wearing the skimpiest of white towels around the middle of his body, shaking his damp hair all over the wooden floor.

'Oh my God...' I cried, and acting on impulse, I pushed my wheelie suitcase at him.

'What the actual fuck?' the man cried, jumping back just before it hit him, crashing into the wall instead. Then things got even worse and his towel slid down his body. I yelped as I caught a flash of flesh while he hastily grabbed the towel and pulled it up to cover himself.

'Who are you? What are you doing in my Airbnb?' I demanded, hiding my eyes behind my hand in case I saw more than I should again.

'Hang on... Tessa?'

I took my hand away in surprise. Now the man had the towel firmly back in place, I looked at him properly. His cheeks were bright red and he was staring at me, confused. His blonde hair flopped over his face and when I looked into his eyes, they were a startling blue. 'Sorry, I...'

'Oh, yeah, I guess you probably don't remember me,' he said uncertainly. 'It's Ethan. I'm Joe's...' He trailed off as recognition sunk in.

'Best friend,' I finished for him, staring into his frankly terrified-looking face. I had only seen him twice, both fleeting meetings, and obviously he had been fully clothed as expected. This was most definitely unexpected. I shook my head. 'But what are you doing here?' I repeated, marginally more calmly than I had squealed at him a minute ago. At least he wasn't a stranger about to attack me. But I wasn't sure Joe's best friend being here was much better.

He raised an eyebrow. 'I could ask you the same thing.'

I realised I was still staring at him. And he was still in a tiny towel with most of his body on show. He had a more muscly, defined chest than I would have thought based on the fact he equalled my five-foot-eight frame. I looked away quickly, desperately trying hard not to think about the glimpse I'd had of what was underneath that towel. Thinking about the word 'hard', I blushed instantly and coughed, thanking God that people couldn't hear each other's thoughts. I took a breath and tried again. 'Please tell me why you are in my holiday flat. The one I've rented for the next five nights.'

'You haven't rented it, I have,' Ethan said slowly, as if mulling over what I was saying. I saw out of the corner of my eye he was shaking his head. 'Joe said...'

I breathed in sharply. Of course this was Joe's fault. And it explained me finding only one key in the box outside. I held up my hand. 'How about you get dressed and I sit down and then you join me and we can talk about this without you being in a towel and me hyperventilating from the shock?'

'That sounds like a plan.' He sounded amused now. Of course he did. He was probably loving every minute of my panic attack, poised to tell Joe all about it.

I quickly spun around and went back into the living room. I heard Ethan walk into the bedroom, closing the door behind him. Collapsing onto one of the sofas, I shut my eyes and put my head back against the soft, cream fabric. I couldn't believe that this trip was already turning into a disaster. Then again, it just topped off the past couple of months really.

After what felt like an hour but in reality was only ten minutes, the bedroom door opened again and out came Ethan, no longer half naked. I opened my eyes as he edged towards me cautiously. He had pulled on jeans and a black jumper that looked really soft. His blonde hair was still damp and his feet were bare. I caught the scent of something oak-y and warm. His whole presence was calm, the complete opposite of mine.

'How about a coffee?' Ethan suggested, walking towards the kitchen. 'I feel like we both need one. I went to the shop on the way here.'

'Uh, I don't drink coffee. Did you get any tea by any chance?' I asked, taken aback by his very normal suggestion.

'Of course, I'm British,' he replied. Again, I caught amusement in his tone. 'Milk? Sugar?'

'Just milk. Uh, please.' I followed him with my eyes as he busied himself in the kitchen as if he made me tea every day. Which Ethan definitely had never done before. I remembered Joe telling me, 'Don't be offended by him not wanting to meet you, he hardly likes anyone,' when I questioned why he wasn't introducing me to his friends. I'd only seen Joe's best friend twice on nights out. His words had hurt. And they made me feel even more awkward now. Ethan must be pissed off to see me here.

Finally, he returned with two cups, passed me one, and sat on the sofa opposite.

Unsure how to begin, I took a sip. 'It's nice.'

'Surprised?'

'Kind of. Joe couldn't make a hot drink for shit.' My eyes widened. 'Sorry, I...'

Ethan waved a hand as he propped his leg on his thigh. 'It's true. I think he just can't be bothered to try. Whereas I would hope I can make a decent coffee or tea in my line of work.'

'Oh, yeah, sorry, I forgot you're a chef,' I said, relieved he didn't call me a crazy ex-girlfriend for my Joe comment. 'So, shall we address the elephant in the room?'

His lips twitched again. 'Go ahead.'

I took another sip of the tea to fortify me. 'Well, I'm confused. I booked this apartment for us at Christmas and, obviously, now that I'm no longer with Joe, I decided I'd come by myself. Instead of letting my money go to waste.' There was no way I was admitting I was currently in the midst of crippling writer's block. I didn't want Joe to ever hear about that.

Ethan frowned. 'You booked it? With your money? I thought Joe paid for this.'

'Uh, no. It was meant to be my Christmas present but he said he was waiting for a new credit card. Now I realise it was so Rachel wouldn't know... Anyway, I said I'd pay. But then we broke up so...' I trailed off, feeling even more stupid than I already did for how I'd let Joe treat me.

'Seriously?' He coughed and quickly took a sip from his coffee cup. 'When I told Joe I was coming to Paris to do a cookery course for two weeks, he said he had this apartment going spare. He told me he'd paid and asked me if I wanted to use it before I stay with friends for the rest of the time. He never mentioned you might be here, Tessa.'

'And he didn't think to check with me whether that was okay or not?' I closed my eyes and took a breath. I was feeling very murderous towards my ex all over again.

'I'd call him but he'll be at work; this is a better conversation for this evening,' Ethan said after a moment. He was still remarkably calm.

'This is a nightmare! I thought I was coming for a relaxing, inspiring solo break away, to try to put that...' I trailed off before I called Joe all the bad names under the sun. I sensed that wasn't a good move in front of his best mate. 'Look, Ethan, I know this isn't your fault but this was my holiday, I booked it, and after Joe did what he did... I need this.'

Ethan swallowed visibly and for a moment seemed lost for words. I couldn't quite bring myself to say it out loud but I was sure he knew what Joe had done and why I'd left him. And no doubt he didn't care about it as he hadn't wanted to get to know me. But I hoped he just might possibly understand why I wanted this break.

Finally, Ethan nodded. 'I'll see if I can find somewhere else to stay, okay?' He pulled out his phone.

I breathed a sigh of relief. 'Good idea, thank you. I'll just, uh, freshen up.' I drained my tea then put the cup on the side table before fleeing to the bathroom. Once in there, I leaned against the basin and glanced at the mirror above it. I looked rough. The lack of sleep, train journey and shock of seeing Ethan made me look tired and puffy, there were dark circles under my green eyes and my winter skin was paler than ever. To top it all off, my shoulder-length highlighted hair was a frizzy mess from rushing this morning and not having time to curl it. I also had on a loungewear set for travelling, so it certainly wasn't the best I'd ever looked. I really hoped Ethan wouldn't tell Joe I had fallen apart without him. I splashed water on my makeup-free face, as I hadn't had time to do that either, and could only be relieved I'd at least had a shower and put on deodorant before I left the house.

'Tessa?' Ethan's deep voice came through the closed door.

I looked up at the mirror again. 'Yes?'

'I forgot – it's Paris fashion week. Everywhere is completely booked up.'

You have got to be kidding me.

3

'I'll keep trying to find somewhere else to stay.'

Ethan's promise echoed in my ears as I walked alone along the Seine. After he'd dropped the bombshell reminder that the city was full to the brim for one of its biggest events of the year, I had told him I needed some air and left the apartment abruptly. He had been on his phone attempting to find another place to stay, but it was looking like a fruitless search. And I had no idea what to do about it. It had taken a lot to get me on that Eurostar and now I might have to just go back to London again. Or face living in a one-bed apartment for five nights with someone who hadn't even wanted to meet me a few months ago. Not only that, but who was best friends with the man who had betrayed me.

Does the universe actually hate me?

I spotted a crepe stand and knew if anything might help me feel a bit better, it was that.

'Bonjour.' I greeted the seller and made my order in English because I hadn't spoken any French since school. As I watched him make my crepe with speed and skill, the smell made my stomach rumble. He handed it to me in a wrapping and I carried on walking beside the river, moaning as the first taste hit.

As I ate and strolled, I thought about how this trip had started in the worst possible way. I blamed Joe. How could he have just invited his friend here when I was the one who'd booked and paid for the apartment? Then again, I shouldn't have been surprised. Selfish was Joe's middle name. I sighed. I hated how he had made me feel so cynical about men and love. I never used to be. I had been hopeful before him.

Joe and I had met in June. It had been the start of summer in London and I had decided to write outside. I was in Hyde Park on a blanket with my notebook and a Marks & Spencer lunch when the guy on the blanket a few feet away cleared his throat.

'I'm sorry but I'm dying to know what you're writing in that notebook. I can offer a Mr Whippy in exchange for telling me?' he called over, nodding at the ice cream van nearby.

'I suppose if you add a flake...'

'It wouldn't be an ice cream without it.' And he bought me an ice cream, came to sit with me on my blanket, and after I told him I was writing a romance novel, Joe had declared, 'It won't be as good as the way we just met.' I had been putty in his hands. He was everything I had always fancied – tall, dark and handsome with smouldering eyes. He was an accountant and we'd joked how he was logical and I was creative, and that opposites attracted. We'd only been together six weeks when my landlord decided he wanted to sell the flat I was renting so Joe asked me to move into his. It was a whirlwind romance, and I fell hard.

Then at Christmas, I discovered he was, and had been the entire time we were together, cheating on me.

I felt like a fool still. I had been swept up in thinking I'd found my soulmate. But Joe hadn't felt the same. When I found out, I'd walked out of his flat and his life. And I'd been trying to put it behind me, but it wasn't easy. All I could think was thank God I had only been with him for six months, not six years, and found out what he was really like before we'd got married or something.

I hadn't heard from Joe since we had broken up. I had no idea if he ever thought about me or not. I didn't miss him. I missed what I thought we had. And most of all, I missed who I had been before we met.

But now he was invading this break that was supposed to help heal my heart after he had stomped on it. He was here in the shape of Ethan. It was so annoying.

I passed by a couple who sat by the edge of the river, talking softly, leaning against one another, and I looked away. I had always been inspired by moments like that but now, they made me feel stupid for thinking I'd found love.

I wondered if love was even real. Because when someone betrays you like that, how can you trust or believe in love again? And unfortunately for me, it wasn't only casting a shadow over my personal life. I was fine being single for a good long while now. But it was my career that I was worried about. I had dreamed of being an author since I was a little girl, a complete bookworm since birth pretty much, and now it was in jeopardy. Because of Joe. I was scared I'd never be able to write about people falling in love again.

And if I lost my writing career, it felt like I would lose myself as well.

My phone vibrated in my bag. I checked and saw I had a WhatsApp message from Carly.

> Bonjour! Are in you in Paris safe and sound? Send me a video of the apartment when you can. I'm dying to see it!

I knew she'd have kittens when I told her about Ethan being there.

> Yep, I'll call you soon and fill you in on everything.

I needed to decide what I was going to do before talking to her. This time, I wasn't going to let Carly or Luke persuade me to do something that would turn into more of a nightmare than it already was.

Then I noticed the light was dimming around me. It was approaching sunset. I looked up and let out a little gasp. Pretty pastel shades swirled in the sky above the Seine. Despite the chill in the air, the sight warmed me along with my crepe, and I thought that perhaps Paris would be able to inspire me.

But that was only if I was able to stay.

I finished my crepe and put the wrapper in the bin. It was getting too cold to carry on walking, so reluctantly I turned towards the apartment. I was about to find out if Ethan had found somewhere else to stay, otherwise one of us would have to leave. And I really didn't want it to be me.

The apartment came into view as the sun disappeared behind the building. The light was fading, promising a clear night, and I remembered that I really wanted to see the Eiffel Tower sparkle at night. I couldn't wait to see it. And the balcony would offer a great view. So, despite not wanting to talk to Ethan again, I headed inside and up to the second floor.

When I opened the apartment door, I was hit by a delicious smell. I walked in to find Ethan in the kitchen, cooking.

He looked up. 'You're back.'

I hovered awkwardly. 'Yeah, it was too cold to stay outside. And I'd love to see the Eiffel Tower lit up from the balcony.'

He nodded as he stirred something on the hob. 'We will have a great view. I know you don't like fancy food but I felt so bad about you coming here and finding me...' He looked at me again. 'I'm making French onion soup. Would you like some?'

I hesitated. I wasn't sure about trusting anyone connected to Joe but this looked like a peace offering. And smelled like a good one. 'I just had a crepe but I'm in Paris; there are no rules.' I took off my jacket and boots and dropped my bag on the sofa then I went to sit on the small dining table by the kitchen as Ethan carried over the food.

'Wine?'

'After today? Hell, yes.'

Ethan chuckled then handed me a bowl of soup with a side plate of crusty bread, and poured us both a glass of red wine.

My eyes narrowed. 'Are you trying to butter me up?' I enquired as he sat down opposite me.

'Kind of,' he admitted. 'I couldn't find any paid accommodation as everywhere is booked up for Fashion Week.'

I sighed. 'As soon as you mentioned it, I remembered. I only managed to get this place because someone dropped out at the last minute. I had forgotten... A lot on my mind, you could say.'

Understatement of the century.

Ethan nodded. 'I have friends who live in Paris but they've all gone away to Juliette's family's country estate. I was planning to stay with them for the rest of my course once this apartment is up. They'll be back soon. You can't get them to confirm anything,' he said with a fond shrug like this was a cute quirk of theirs. 'But as soon as they do, I can stay with one of them.'

As I mulled this over, I put my spoon into the bowl and tried the soup. 'Oh.' It was so good. He'd even topped it with cheese. 'Wow.'

Ethan smiled as he sipped his wine. 'It's okay?'

I nodded as I dipped in some of the crusty bread. 'Just what I needed.'

I glanced around the apartment. It really was beautiful. I didn't particularly want to go back to my tiny London flat that didn't feel quite feel like home just yet. Or face the music with my publisher. But what was the alternative with Ethan unable to stay anywhere else for now? 'I suppose I better book the next Eurostar train I can then.'

'But we might only have to be here together for a couple of days,' Ethan said. He saw my face. 'It's okay, I'll go home.'

'You said you were here for a cookery course?' I asked.

'Yeah. It's for two weeks with a renowned chef. It was an honour to get on it. My boss called in a favour. It's my chance to take on more responsibility at work. I'm currently the sous chef, I'm not sure if you know, and the restaurant is attempting to get a Michelin star, and if I could create the perfect sauce for my boss's venison then maybe, just maybe...' Ethan abruptly stopped. 'I'm talking too much.'

I couldn't help but smile. 'I don't mind; I'm always being told the same so it's refreshing for someone else to be doing it instead. This course sounds important.' I felt like I couldn't stand in the way of him doing this course. I sighed. 'I was going to work here too. I have a new novel to write and, well, let's just say the deadline is tight.'

'Well, then, you shouldn't go,' Ethan said firmly. 'As I said, I won't have to stay for your whole trip; we will be fine.'

My eyes met his across the table. 'We will?'

'Sure. I'm doing this course, you're writing, and it's Paris; we'll hardly see each other. We can share the apartment until my friends come home.' He gave me a hopeful smile.

'But...' I felt my cheeks heat up. 'There's only one bed.'

Ethan frowned for a moment. 'Oh, yeah, I forgot... I can take the sofa.' We both looked at it. It was small, a two-seater at best. Ethan was the same height as me but I could tell it wouldn't be comfortable. 'It's fine. You can have the bedroom. I'll move all my things out.'

'You'd really do that?' My head was spinning. He was being very accommodating to someone who was his best friend's ex.

'It's not a problem, Tessa. I can handle sleeping on a sofa for a couple of nights. This course is more than worth it. And then we both get to stay in Paris. And work.'

'Work,' I agreed, even though I had no idea if I'd be able to or not. 'I suppose we won't have to see each other much,' I said slowly. I knew based on what Joe had told me that Ethan would prefer me to stay out of his way, and I could do that. 'I mean, we definitely won't,' I added, more firmly. I wanted to make sure he knew I wouldn't be hanging around him.

'Oh yeah, of course,' Ethan said, his voice tight. 'I'll stay out of your way, I promise.'

'It would help me to be here,' I admitted. I didn't want to share that but the thought of going home was worse than staying here with him.

'Then it's sorted,' Ethan said. 'Yeah?'

This had the potential to be really awkward. Sharing a one-bedroom apartment with Ethan for who knew how long? But then I looked out of the window again and at the Parisian skyline, darkening and the stars beginning to shine. Things already felt more manageable being here away from London and its memories and the humiliation and the hurt, and the stress of my deadline. Yes, I was here with someone connected to my ex and who didn't want to be with me, but I really didn't want to let Joe win. I needed to write a book again. I needed to believe in love. I needed to love happy ever afters. And so, I needed Paris.

I could put up with Ethan being here too.

Plus the man could really cook.

'Okay,' I said.

Ethan's face relaxed in relief.

'I might need more of this,' I joked, gesturing to the soup.

'I'm glad you like it.'

I remembered then what he'd said when I had walked in. 'What did you mean before about me not liking fancy food?'

'Well,' Ethan began, shifting awkwardly in this chair, 'Joe did mention that the reason you both never came to my restaurant in London was because you didn't like the quote "pretentious" food we served there.'

My mouth fell open as Ethan's phone started to ring. He excused himself to answer it and I watched him go, wondering why my ex had said that because that was definitely not my view at all. It appeared Joe had lied about a lot of things while I was with him.

Before I could wonder why he'd tell Ethan such a thing, my phone beeped with a reminder and I hurriedly got up from the table because it was time to watch the Eiffel Tower sparkle for the first time. I rushed out onto the balcony and looked over to see the lights twinkling ahead. I smiled as it glittered. It seemed to say that even when things are dark, there will always be a light to guide the way.

And the tiniest tint of rose re-appeared on my imaginary glasses.

4

'It's something, huh?'

I turned in surprise to see Ethan leaning against the frame of the balcony doors. 'I've never been to Paris before so I've only seen it on social media,' I said, looking away from him and back at the sparkling tower. 'It's what I was most looking forward to coming here.' I didn't add that I'd been hoping Joe and I would be drinking wine on this very balcony watching it together, and enjoying the romance of it all.

'I'm glad you didn't leave before you got to see it,' he said.

The lights stopped so I faced Ethan again. 'Me too.'

'Sorry Joe didn't check with you before offering to let me stay here. Send me your details and I'll transfer you the money; I can't let you pay for all this.'

'I can't let you pay for it all either,' I countered. 'Especially if you're sleeping on the sofa and leaving... soon.'

Ethan tilted his head, that amusement in his eyes again. 'Half each then?' He saw me hesitate. 'I insist.'

Finally, I nodded. 'Thank you. I guess you're not all bad,' I added with a smile. I walked past him hoping he got my sense of humour, knowing not everyone did. Particularly my ex.

He chuckled. 'Sounds like your standards have been pretty low if that renews your hope in the male species.'

I turned and raised an eyebrow and we looked at one another. *Does he realise he's basically calling his best friend a low standard?*

'You're not wrong,' I replied. Ethan looked like he wanted to say something, but I shook my head. 'I'm tired. I think I'll head to bed.'

'Sure. I moved my things out so the bedroom is all yours. I... I hope you sleep well. And thanks again for letting me stay here for a bit.'

'Goodnight.' I headed off to the bedroom, wondering how much Ethan knew about what had happened between me and Joe. I was worried after hearing how Joe had told Ethan I hadn't wanted to eat at his restaurant. What else had he told Ethan about me? But I knew it didn't matter. It wasn't like I cared what Ethan thought about me, or that he would be at all part of my life after this trip. I just didn't like Joe having control of our story. It felt like our six months together had been a trick pulled off by a skilled magician and I no longer wanted any part of it.

I changed into pyjamas and slipped into the bathroom to brush my teeth. I heard Ethan on the phone and wondered who he was laughing with. Whether it was Joe or not. Joe had been so closed off about his friends and family, holding secrets close to his chest, making me believe he was mysterious and deep, when I now knew it was to keep me in the dark about his other woman.

With a heavy sigh, I closed the bedroom door and sunk into the large bed, snuggling into the crisp white sheets, feeling like I was lying on a cloud. Rolling onto my back, I listened to Ethan's low voice for a bit before it all went quiet and the apartment turned dark. It felt strangely intimate sleeping in the same small space as someone despite the fact a closed door was between us. I thought it might keep me awake as my brain loved to overthink, but weary from the stress of the past two months and travelling today, I slipped quickly into a deep sleep.

* * *

I awoke suddenly and groggily to my phone ringing on the bedside table. I rolled over in the bed, taking a moment to remember I wasn't in my London flat but a Parisian apartment. I had slept more soundly than I had in weeks, which was very strange but I was grateful for it. Everything always seemed worse when you added in lack of sleep to the equation. I grabbed my phone without looking at the screen. 'Hello?'

'Tessa, it's Stevie!'

I sat up immediately. I should have checked who it was before answering. I metaphorically kicked myself. 'Oh, hi,' I said trying to sound normal as my heart started to speed up. Stevie was my publicist at Turn the Pages.

'How are you?' Stevie asked me.

'Um, I'm okay. Actually, I'm in Paris.'

'Paris! I'm so jealous. A romantic trip with your boyfriend?'

I cringed. I hadn't told many people about what had happened with Joe and I hadn't spoken to Stevie since before Christmas. 'Actually, no, a solo trip. To do some writing.'

'Oh, what a great idea! I know Gita is dying to find out what you're writing. Well, we all are. You know what a fan of your books I am.'

Stevie was a sweetheart. She loved romance books and had spearheaded a whole new imprint at the publishing company for love stories, and had been a huge part of my last book becoming a bestseller.

Guilt washed over me. 'Thank you,' I managed to choke out.

'I wanted to speak to you about the book tour. I have arranged five stops all around the UK so far for publication week in the autumn,' she carried on merrily. She was arranging a book tour for a book I hadn't even started yet! I listened, my stomach tying itself in knots. 'So, does that sound okay with you?'

'Well, actually...'

'Oh, Gita wants a word, hang on. Enjoy Paris!'

Before I could stop her, Stevie faded away, there was a click and then my editor's voice came down the line. 'Tessa, are you avoiding me?' She laughed as if that couldn't be at all possible. Gita had taken me on for my debut novel at another publishers and when my contract was finished there, had poached me for Turn the Pages once the company started doing so well with romance books. They published my hero Deborah Day, and my last book had sold so well that it had looked like things were going to go from strength to strength.

Until I lost the ability to write.

'Of course not,' I said, my voice high-pitched.

'I know what you're writing will be brilliant but I do need just a small synopsis so we can make a start on the cover design, and get a pre order up for your fans, you know?' Gita said. 'Can you please email me something?'

'Sure,' I said, my stomach tightening. 'It's set in Paris,' I blurted out. 'I'm here on a research trip.'

'Oh, perfect! I love Paris, and books set there are always so romantic. I knew you were working on something special. I won't disturb you any more. I'm so excited to read it.'

I felt sick. 'Great,' I said, sounding so unenthusiastic I was sure she'd be able to tell.

'Right, I'll let you go and be inspired by Paris! Take care!'

Thankfully, Gita hung up. I threw my phone down onto the bed and shook my head. I had never had to bullshit my editor like that before. I usually handed in books early. But there were just three weeks to go until this was due, and she had no idea I hadn't written one word of it. Setting it in Paris wasn't a bad idea though. I *could* use this as a research trip. Maybe I could even write the expense off for tax. Only if I was able to come up with an idea while I was here though. Gita was expecting some sort of synopsis but my mind was a blank.

I reached for my phone to call Carly but she didn't answer. I hoped she'd call me back soon as I was desperately in need of best-friend guidance. I climbed out of bed, knowing I needed to start my day. I was determined, as well, to look somewhat more presentable than I had yesterday in case Ethan was going to report back on our time here to Joe.

Creeping out of the bedroom, I glanced into the living room. Ethan was fast asleep on the sofa, his limbs draped over it in a position that didn't look all that comfortable. It certainly wasn't a sofa made for sleeping on. Wincing, I headed softly into the bathroom, hoping he would give Joe hell for sticking us in this tiny apartment together.

After I came out from having a shower in my towel, Ethan was walking towards the bathroom, rubbing his eyes. We both froze. 'Uh, how did you sleep?' I asked, gripping the towel tightly around me. 'The bed is really comfy. I feel really bad that you had to have the sofa.' I kept talking through the awkward moment.

'It was fine, don't worry. Is it okay if I go in the bathroom? I need to get ready for the first day of my course.'

'Yes, yes, sure thing.' I went to move around him to get into the bedroom but he stepped the same way as me. So we both moved to the other side and almost collided.

'Hang on, you stay still.' Ethan walked around me and grinned. 'There we go.'

Ducking my head to hide my flustered cheeks, I hurried into the bedroom and slumped against the closed door.

Way to act like an adult who has everything together, Tessa.

I hurriedly got dressed to avoid any more half-naked encounters with Ethan. I pulled on a pair of jeans and my favourite branded hoodie. I was never one for loving dressing up and knew I'd need to be comfy and warm for wandering around Paris. Then I curled my hair so the fizziness was replaced by gentle waves. I added my usual minimum makeup of eyebrow pencil, concealer under my eyes, some natural blush, mascara and lip gloss. Glancing in the mirror, I was pleased that I looked a lot more presentable than I had done yesterday. I peeped out of the bedroom and heard that Ethan was in the shower, so I walked through the living room and into the kitchen to make a cup of tea.

My phone rang as I was making it and I was relieved to see it was Carly.

'Are you okay?' I asked as I picked up my mug of tea and walked towards the balcony.

'Yeah,' she said groggily. 'Sorry I missed you. I fell asleep early last night and really didn't want to get out of bed this morning. It's so cold here. Or maybe I'm coming down with something.' She yawned. 'But more importantly, how is Paris?'

I opened the door and stepped out onto the balcony. The day was crisp and clear again and I leaned against the railing and looked across at the Eiffel Tower. 'Well, it took an unexpected turn...'

'Oh my God – you met a Frenchman, didn't you?'

Rolling my eyes, I took a sip of tea before responding. 'When I said I was off all men, that includes ones that live in Paris. No, you won't believe this...'

I told Carly about walking in to find Ethan here.

'That is awful,' Carly squeaked when I had finished. 'Joe just gets worse! His best friend must be horrible. Can't you find somewhere else to stay? No, hang on, make him leave! You paid. Tell him to bugger off.'

'I did try but it's Fashion Week; the whole city is bursting at the seams. And he's here for a French cookery course with some famous chef; it's for work. He said he has some friends coming back to the city soon so it won't be for my whole trip. And I don't know, I feel bad. Joe lied to him. Made him think he'd paid for this place and told him it would be empty. Without checking with me. It's not Ethan's fault.'

'I suppose not, but then maybe you should just come home. You can't stay there with him,' Carly said firmly.

'I can't leave now though. Stevie and Gita just ambushed me with a double phone call and Gita wants a synopsis for the new book. So to give her something, I told her I was writing a book set in Paris and I'm here on a research trip.'

'Oh, Jesus.'

'Yup,' I agreed. 'Listen, maybe it'll be okay, Ethan will be out at this course, I will be around the city getting inspiration and he's sleeping on the sofa. I bet we'll hardly see each other and—'

'Hang on,' Carly interrupted me. 'There's only one bedroom? Tessa, are you sure you can handle this?'

'Handle what? Staying in a tiny apartment with my selfish, cheating, vile ex-boyfriend's best friend while desperately trying to come up with an idea for my next novel due in just three weeks, which I haven't written a word of? And I've already spent most of the advance thanks to said dickhead ex cheating on me and forcing me to move out alone into a ridiculously expensive flat at Christmas!'

Someone cleared their throat behind me.

I spun around, spilling my tea and just managing not to send my iPhone over the balcony. My phone case might claim to be drop-resistant, but I didn't think it could handle that.

'Uh, sorry,' Ethan said, stepping back awkwardly. 'I didn't realise you were on the phone until...' He trailed off, indicating he'd heard the last part of the conversation. The one where I'd slagged off his best mate and admitted my career was in trouble.

Why did things keep getting worse?

'I just came to say I'm heading off to my course,' he continued. He was a lot smarter today – wearing black trousers and a shirt and shiny shoes. His hair was still mussed up. It looked like it was similar to mine – always wanting to do its own thing.

I imagined my face was lobster red. I nodded tightly. 'Sure, okay.'

'I'll see you later then.' Ethan looked like he might say something else but then he turned and quickly left.

Once the apartment door had closed, I slumped against the balcony railing. 'Awesome. He heard all that and will probably be phoning Joe right now to tell him his crazy ex is here and falling apart!'

'Well, if he does then he's just as much of a douchebag as Joe. You're bloody entitled to be angry with someone who's cheated on you and then subjected you to sharing a one-bedroom apartment with his best friend.'

'You're right.' I sucked in a breath. 'I don't really care what Ethan thinks. I'm just stressing about this book, Carly. I need Paris to inspire me, and fast.'

'Get out into the city and I'm sure it will. And don't worry about Ethan or Joe. You won't have to even think about either of them ever again after these few days.'

'Good plan. And I'll stay out of Ethan's way. Because on top of our meeting yesterday and everything this morning, I can't bear any more embarrassing encounters with the bloke.'

'What happened when you met?'

'He walked out of the bathroom half-naked when I arrived, and I attacked him with my suitcase!'

She giggled.

'There's more; his towel slipped down, and I got a glimpse of... everything. Plus, I looked like utter shit.'

'Tessa!' She tried to stop laughing, then abruptly did. 'Wait, is he good-looking?'

'Hmmm, not really, not my type anyway,' I mused, although my mind did flit to what I had briefly seen under that towel. 'He's my height for starters,' I said. I liked a tall man. 'And blonde. He has a nice smile though. And his hair looks soft. And he's got amazing eyes. They are very blue. And he made me French onion soup last night. It was bloody delicious, so the man can cook.'

'That's quite a lot of good points,' Carly pointed out. 'But you definitely don't fancy him?'

'Right. And even if I did, he clearly doesn't have good taste in friends.'

'Definitely not. If he's friends with Joe, there must be something wrong with him,' Carly agreed.

'Okay, I better go. I need to get out of this apartment and find something to inspire a story idea.'

'Okay. Good luck. You've got this. Keep me updated. And Tessa...'

'Yeah?'

'Bring me back some croissants.'

I laughed. 'I will. Do some work, talk to you later.'

We hung up.

Carly worked from home too; she was a copy editor and proofreader. She was freelance working for different publishers, and sometimes we worked in cafés together but always ended up talking instead of working. While she could never write a book herself – or so she would say – she was brilliant at making them as good as possible and I loved bouncing ideas off her. I just wished right now my mind wasn't blank.

After finishing my tea, I threw my leather jacket and boots on, grabbed my cross-body bag and left the apartment.

The chilly air hit me when I went outside, immediately waking me up. I turned towards the Luxembourg gardens. When I researched Paris, this looked like a place I would enjoy so I thought I'd start there. It was a lovely morning. Crisp and sunny: the best combo. I put my hands in my coat pocket and strolled around the pond. Some people were sitting in the green chairs, others walked past me holding takeaway coffees, a family pointed out ducks on the water, and a group of tourists took photos of the stunning fountains. The city was alive as people headed for work or school or, like me, enjoyed the sights.

I took my phone out of my bag and snapped a picture as I stood by the water, watching the sunshine glistening on top of it. My social media accounts to promote my books had been neglected since my spilt with Joe so I posted the photo on all of them, announcing that I was on a research trip, although I felt like a fraud doing so. Excited comments flowed in from readers, keen to know what my next novel would be about.

You and me both, guys.

Finding an empty green chair by the lake, I sat down and took in the peace. I felt some of the tension roll out of my shoulders. This was really a beautiful place and I was happy I'd decided to come here.

Half an hour passed but nothing came to me. I still had no idea what I could write my next book about. Deciding that maybe brainstorming might help, I pulled out my notebook and pen.

Paris novel ideas:

My pen hovered above the page.

Main character meets a man who turns out to be like every other man and breaks her heart so she swears off love, moves to Paris and lives happily ever after with lots of cats.

'Paris already inspiring you?'

5

I yelped at the sudden voice, dropped my pen and looked up to see Ethan standing a couple of feet away. He looked amused again and bent down to pick the pen up. As he handed it back to me, I hastily closed my notebook so he couldn't see what I had written. 'What the hell? You scared me!'

'I seem to surprise you a lot,' Ethan replied with a shrug.

'The curse of being a daydreamer,' I said.

'I saw you as I was walking through the garden so thought I'd make a detour to say hi.'

I peered up at him. 'I thought you were at your course.'

'I was. We only had an hour's welcome meeting this morning then we're going back to the restaurant this afternoon to help the chef prepare for dinner service. It's mildly terrifying.'

'Only mildly terrifying?' I smiled. 'Just don't scare anyone if they are holding a knife.'

'The first rule of being a chef,' Ethan replied. 'This is my favourite spot in Paris,' he added, looking around. 'Thought I'd take a walk then take in some sights while I wait. I thought you might want the flat to yourself to write.'

'I'm still at the planning stages,' I said, waving my notebook. 'The very early planning stages. Basically, all I know is that the book will be set here in Paris. So it felt more productive to get out into the city.'

'I suppose Paris is like Disneyland for romance writers,' Ethan said with a smile. 'Are you hitting all the romantic spots so you can include them in the book?'

I hid my wince. 'I suppose I'll have to.'

'You're not keen?'

'Let's just say romance hasn't been a high priority the past couple of months,' I said, then decided I was telling him too much. 'Where are these romantic spots I need to visit then?'

Ethan shifted on his feet, still looking down at me in the chair. 'I could take you to one now. If you want? If it will help?'

'I was joking. Why would you know the romantic spots of Paris?' I asked, raising an eyebrow.

'That sounds like a challenge. Come on.' Ethan started walking without waiting for a response.

He can't be serious.

But Ethan was walking away, and he looked back, gesturing for me to follow. My curiosity was too piqued to resist so I jumped up, stuffed my notebook and pen back into my bag and hurried to catch up with him.

He started talking when I fell into step. 'I lived in Paris for a year before I got the job at Bon Appétit in London. I worked at a small family-run restaurant here. So I know the city pretty well. And I know just the place to inspire a romance writer.' He turned towards the nearest Metro station with purpose.

'It must have been amazing to live here,' I said, imagining that Paris must be inspirational for a chef. All the delicious food and great places to eat.

'It was. I try to come back as often as I can but the restaurant in London keeps me too busy most of the time, which is why I jumped at the chance to do this course. I'm planning to go back to where I used to work for a meal once my friends return to the city.'

'I'd love to see it,' I said, without thinking.

Ethan glanced across at me.

'Um, so, can you cook anything?' I cringed at the question, but at least it changed the subject.

'Probably. I love making pastries; it's my speciality, I suppose. But I also like good comfort food like my mum used to make.' I saw a flicker of sadness pass across his face. 'And I make a mean croque monsieur.'

We went down the steps then to the Metro, where Ethan got me a card that I could use while I was here, and soon we were on a train to Montmartre. The train was busy so we didn't talk much. My mind was very active though. I was confused how I'd ended up in Paris with Ethan.

I thought about the only two other times I had interacted with him before this trip. When Joe and I had been dating for a few weeks, I introduced him to Carly and Luke, and then I started asking about his friends. He hadn't been very enthusiastic about me meeting them, saying he 'didn't want to share me with anyone', but said that one Friday night, on our way out for a meal, we could pop by to a bar they liked to drink in. That was the first time I met Ethan, along with two other guys and two women. 'I know, I know, I've been MIA,' Joe had declared as we approached their table. 'I haven't been able to tear myself from this one's side,' he added, his arm around me, pulling me close. 'Don't blame Tessa though, it's all my fault.' I had instantly felt worried they had thought I'd been keeping him from them even though it had been Joe who had wanted to avoid them.

Before his friends could say anything, Joe had launched into the story he'd just been telling me about his boss embezzling funds and the drama it had caused at his work. I looked at the group and the two women smiled, and the men gave me formal nods. Ethan met my eyes for a moment but then looked away. Joe didn't properly introduce me to the group, and I felt awkward. He'd then decided we were in too much of a hurry to stay for a drink and, leaving, said we'd all hang out soon. I gave an awkward wave to his friends as he'd pulled me out of the bar, and as we left, I'd glanced back to see Ethan was watching us, and I wondered what he had been thinking.

The second time I'd seen Ethan was for Joe's birthday. Joe had hired an area in a bar and it was packed with people. He had told me to just come for an hour as he would mostly be work networking, booking me a car there and back so I didn't really have a choice. I asked for him to introduce me to his friends, but he'd only pointed out two. One was Ethan, and Joe told me, 'Don't be offended by him not wanting to meet you; he hardly likes anyone.' The other one was called Michelle; he had gestured for her to come over to us, saying she had read one of my books.

'Oh yes, I read it on the beach. My sister gave it to me as I'd finished the book I had bought. We have very different reading tastes,' she had said, before she was called away by someone else.

'Don't be offended, baby,' Joe said. 'She reads literary books, you know.'

I had slunk away into the car waiting to take me home feeling crap about myself and, suffice to say, I hadn't asked Joe to see his friends again. And when I tried to meet his work mates, it had resulted in us breaking up. So it was probably a good thing I hadn't tried harder to get to know his friends.

'We're here.' Ethan broke through my reminiscing and we got off the Metro and exited the station. Ethan led us into a small park, where we stood in front of a large tiled wall with writing all over it.

'This is *le mur des je t'aime*,' Ethan said quietly. He had a perfect French accent. 'Or "The Wall of Love".'

As I looked up at the blue titles made out of enamelled lava, Ethan explained it was created by two artists as a monument to love. The writing featured the words 'I love you' written in hundreds of languages.

'I have vaguely heard of it,' I said, gazing in awe at the white writing on top of the blue tiles. There were a few people around and I saw a couple taking a selfie with it behind them, leaning in to kiss. I looked away from them quickly to see Ethan was beside me. 'I can see why you thought to bring me here,' I said. 'It's beautiful. What are the red bits?' I asked, pointing to the irregular splotches of red paint dotted around the words.

'They are meant to represent pieces of a broken heart, and if you put them together, they would form a complete heart.'

'Like a puzzle.'

'Exactly. I think it's a reminder that we sometimes lose the importance of love in the world.'

Okay, Paris, I get the message.

I looked up at the wall. 'Can I tell you something?' I knew Ethan had heard what I'd said to Carly about how I was struggling to write because of what had happened with Joe. 'These past couple of months, I've wondered if I'd be able to write about love again. Because I realised so much of my writing was based on hope. Hope that true love is out there, that maybe one day I'd have it, but I don't know. Hope left me for a bit. It's here though.' I gestured to the wall. 'I can feel it here. And maybe that means it will come back for me. Does that sound really cheesy?'

Ethan smiled across at me. 'That's why I wanted to show you this wall. Love is always somewhere to be found.'

'Sounds like a greeting-card slogan.'

'Doesn't make it less true.'

He sounded completely sincere. I pulled out my phone to take a picture of the wall. 'I suppose a stunning French woman brought you here and you fell in love with her that year you lived here?'

'I wish,' he said ruefully. He checked his phone. 'I need to head back.'

'I might wander around Montmartre,' I said, putting my phone away. 'Make the most of being here.'

'You should,' he said. 'Tessa, don't let anyone take away what you believe in. You should still have that hope in love. Because I think it's out there for you. And for me,' he said so softly, I had to lean in to hear him. 'Even if I haven't found it yet, and even if you thought you had but you hadn't.'

He was alluding to Joe but not mentioning him by name. We looked at one another. Instinctively, I touched his arm. 'Thanks, Ethan. Honestly, I needed this,' I said, then dropped my hand and turned away because I could feel heat behind my eyes. I didn't want to cry in front of him.

I couldn't watch Ethan leave so instead I kept my eyes on the wall. This couldn't erase the hurt I'd felt after what Joe did, but it helped. Because I knew deep down that Ethan was right. I couldn't let Joe turn me into someone I wasn't.

It was like Carly said – I had always loved love. And I didn't want that to change.

I pulled out my notebook and pen and rested it on my arm as I quickly wrote.

As I stood in front of The Wall of Love, I realised that whenever you despaired that love was dead, something reminded you that it never would die. There would always be love somewhere. It might be big or small. You might not even always notice it. And right then, I certainly didn't welcome it. But it hadn't died or fled the earth or left me forever like I thought it had.

It was still here.
And so was I.

I looked at my words. The spark of an idea finally. Inspired by this wall. And a little bit by Ethan telling me that love was always somewhere to be found.

I imagined a woman who, like me, thought love had abandoned her, arriving in Paris and standing in front of this very wall, realising that it was her who had abandoned love, not the other way around. And maybe then she might be able to find her way back to it.

I hope I'll be able to one day as well.

6

Evening fell in Paris. I had walked around Montmartre for a couple of hours enjoying the cobbled streets, shops and artists in the square. I had then come back to the apartment, where I emailed Gita the paragraph I had written by The Wall of Love. It wasn't anywhere near a synopsis or even a blurb, but it was a fragment. And after the past two months of being completely stuck, it was very welcome.

Gita seemed to think I was being quirky too.

> Okay, I get it. You're keeping me in suspense! But OMG the idea of a woman who no longer believes in love going to Paris and healing her heart has me VERY excited! I can't wait to read it.

I was curled up on the sofa with my laptop, watching my favourite comfort show, when I read Gita's reply. She had taken the fragment I'd sent her and come up with a story. And I had to admit, considering how stuck I had been, it wasn't bad. What Gita didn't know though was it wasn't my character who no longer believed in love, but me. And how I was going to take someone on a journey to opening their heart again was anyone's guess.

The apartment door swung open, making me jump. I closed the laptop, pausing the episode of *Emily in Paris* I had been watching as Ethan walked in, holding a large paper bag.

'You're here,' he said, smiling. 'I wasn't sure if you'd still be out or not.'

'I was exhausted after walking around most of the day,' I said, sitting upright. My nose twitched. 'What's that?' I gestured towards the bag he placed on the kitchen counter. Something smelled really good inside it.

'I brought back some food from the restaurant for dinner; there's enough for two. Come on.'

As Ethan pulled out plates and cutlery, I climbed off the sofa and wandered over, watching him for a moment. As he pulled out takeaway containers from the bag, I crossed my arms over my chest. 'Why are you doing this?'

He looked at me. 'Doing what?'

'Being so nice to me.'

'It's not allowed?' There was that amused look again. He took off the lids of the containers and my stomach rumbled. It looked really good.

Then it hit me. 'You feel sorry for me.'

'No,' he replied, too quickly, as he started loading food onto two plates.

I snorted.

He shrugged. 'Okay, yeah, I do feel bad about Joe, and what happened between the two of you, and then me invading your solo holiday and everything. I just want to try to make things up to you.'

'Well, that's sweet but it's not really your job, is it?'

'I don't see it as a job; I like being nice.' Then he grimaced. 'That was cringey, wasn't it?'

I chuckled. 'Yeah, kind of. But I appreciate it. You're very thoughtful. Bringing this home,' I said, gesturing to the food.

'I like feeding people,' he replied. 'Take it over to the table, I'll bring the wine.'

'A girl could get used to this,' I muttered as I took the plates over. We were having beef bourguignon and fancy mash and vegetables, plus there were side plates of salad, and bread that seemed freshly baked. Ethan joined me, pouring us both a glass of red wine.

'This looks amazing,' I said. 'Did you help cook it?'

'Yep. Tuck in,' he said, nodding at me to start. 'I was on sauce duty so you'll have to tell me—' He stopped abruptly as I moaned. Then he cleared his throat. 'Um, good?'

'It's amazing. If this is what your food is like, I have to come to your restaurant as soon as we get back to London,' I said, nodding furiously, then I felt my face heat up. 'Um, only if you would be okay with that, obviously.'

'Why wouldn't I?' he asked, surprised. I decided it was best not to answer that. Ethan's phone rang then, saving me. 'Finally. I thought he was never going to call me back.' He swiped it up from the table to his ear. 'Joe, at last.'

My whole body went rigid as I watched Ethan get up and walk into the living room. I stuffed some more of the delicious meal into my mouth to stop myself from screaming out insults. I couldn't help but try to hear their conversation. Ethan paced back and forth as they spoke, at first quietly then his voice grew louder.

'You told me you paid for this place,' Ethan said. 'You didn't have the decency to check with Tessa whether it was okay for me to come here... Yeah, well, she surprised you then, didn't she? I'm going to give her half the money... No, I won't tell her that... I'm not sure whether to believe anything you've told me... To be honest, mate, I don't really care... I've got to go.'

I jumped as Ethan hung up on Joe and quickly marched back towards me. I hastily took a gulp of my wine to push the food down as I thought I might have forgotten to chew properly while I shamelessly eavesdropped.

'Joe said he forgot you had paid for this place and would never have expected you to come here alone. I think he was pretty taken aback to find out you did,' Ethan said as he sat back down.

'I bet,' I said dryly. 'Joe told me once that I didn't seem capable of much. Maybe I let him think that, I don't know. He was overwhelming sometimes. I think he made me feel that I needed to let him lead things. Maybe I didn't feel like I could quite be myself.'

'Hmm. You're right. He can be overwhelming. He can try to... take over. We met a long time ago. At school. You grow up and become different people but his family were really good to me. When I didn't have anyone else.'

There was a short silence. I wondered if this was Ethan trying to tell me that maybe they wouldn't be friends if they met now. I didn't know Ethan that well yet but he did appear to be a very different man to Joe.

'What did Joe say that you didn't want to pass on to me?' I asked eventually.

Ethan seemed to weigh up whether to answer or not. Finally, he did. 'He said he hopes you're well.'

'He hopes I'm well?' I repeated. No apology. No regrets. No admitting he was wrong. 'Why am I not surprised that was the message?'

There was another short silence. Then Ethan sighed. 'I need to say something. Joe told me, and some of our friends, a few things that I now wonder whether they were completely correct,' he said, slowly and carefully, as if trying to make sure he said the right thing. 'So I can't help but wonder if he did the same to you. About me.'

I leaned back in the chair. 'Huh. Maybe you're right.' I thought about Joe saying Ethan hadn't wanted to meet me. It seemed strange now that instead of avoiding me here like I had assumed he would, Ethan had taken me out to see a romantic location to help my book and now we were having dinner together. He seemed to really feel bad for what his mate had done to me.

Ethan continued. 'Joe has been a big part of my life, he still is part of it, so I don't want to sit here and slag him off, or get involved in what happened with you two, but I also don't want us to not get along because of him.'

'Me neither,' I agreed. 'So, what do we do? Act like we're meeting here now for the first time?' I joked.

'Why not?' Ethan replied seriously.

'I suppose we could try it,' I said. I was dying to know what Joe had said about me while we had been together, but I also knew that no good could come of asking. I was already furious with Joe and upset that I had given him my heart. Maybe it was better to just try to move on as best I could. And while I was with Ethan, put it to one side. We only had a short space of time together. After that, we'd go our separate ways. 'Okay, let's do that.'

Ethan smiled. 'Good. I'd like that too. So, I'm Ethan.' He held out his hand across the table.

I tittered but reached out and shook his hand. His skin was warm and his handshake firm. Our eyes met, and again, I felt an unfamiliar but very welcome ease settle over me. 'Nice to meet you. I'm Tessa.'

'Things you should know about me,' Ethan said when we let go of each other's hands. 'I am a sous chef, I am passionate about food and wine, and I have quite possibly the largest collection of cookbooks in London. I find them soothing to flick through. I love Paris, walking around cities, I'm addicted to coffee, the stronger the better, and I always have it black...' He grinned when I grimaced at that. 'I am a talker, am honest, so don't ask me something if you don't want to know the answer, I love cooking for people and will make you food whenever you want, and I'm very forgetful so I need lists, reminders, messages to remind me of everything, and I hate it when people are late. Or are rude to serving staff. That's a real bugbear.'

I nodded. 'With you on that one. Okay, I am an author, I love writing and books, and I also am addicted to Netflix and love to binge a series in a day. I hate coffee but have to have at least five cups of tea a day. I love hoodies, graphic tees, jeans and trainers and I hate wearing anything fancy. I am an overthinker, my brain is always on overdrive, I have a sarcastic sense of humour but it's never mean, I am an introvert and have to be pushed to leave my house because being cosy is everything, and I love playing board games.' I didn't add that was something Joe had been unimpressed by. 'I hate being lied to. Oh, and exercise. I really hate that too.'

'Anything other than walking around the city, it should be banned,' Ethan agreed. He smiled at me. 'I'm glad I know you better now.'

'Me too. Do you have your course tomorrow?' I asked, finally looking away from him because those blue eyes of his were kind of hypnotic.

'Yes, but not until the afternoon. We're making pastries so I might have some to bring home.'

'I'm happy to be your guinea pig,' I said, wondering why Ethan saying the word 'home' hadn't felt as strange as it should have. 'So, Paris tour guide, where should I go tomorrow for more inspiration?'

He propped a hand under his chin. 'I mean, it's meant to be raining so being inside sounds good. You're an author, you love books, where better than a bookshop in Paris? I know a really good café nearby for a hot drink afterwards.'

I looked at him in surprise. 'You want to come?'

'Can't have you lost on the streets of Paris in the rain.'

'I don't know, sounds kind of romantic.'

Ethan smiled. 'Spoken like someone who writes love stories.'

'Let's hope I still can.'

Ethan's phone beeped with a message. He picked it up. 'Oh, Juliette and Oscar are on their way back,' he said. He met my gaze. 'My friends who've been away in the country. They're coming back to the city tomorrow. So you might not have to put up with me for much longer.'

'Oh, right.' Suddenly, I wasn't quite so desperate for him to stay somewhere else. I was starting to get used to sharing this apartment with him. 'Great.'

'Great,' he echoed, but his eyes met mine and I wondered if he might have been getting used to being here with me too.

7

After dinner, we cleared up and poured out the remainder of the bottle of red wine into our glasses. It started to rain outside as Ethan had suggested it might do, so there was no view of the Eiffel Tower to look at. I supposed Ethan had nowhere to go without his friends and I was too cosy to bother even thinking about leaving the apartment on a rainy night. 'Maybe I'll watch a movie,' I said, hovering awkwardly as Ethan put away the last of our dinner things. 'I haven't been able to read much lately.'

'Too much on your mind?' he asked.

'I suppose so,' I said, feeling even more awkward. 'I'll take my laptop into the bedroom, leave you to relax.'

'Or...' Ethan walked over to the sideboard cupboard and opened it with a flourish. I peered inside and saw a stack of board games, cards and a chess set. 'You said you liked board games?'

'Ooh,' I said, my eyes lighting up. I went over and kneeled down beside him to look. 'You really want to play something?' I remembered telling Joe about my family's annual board-game tournament at Christmas and I could see his face fall, as if that would be the last thing he would want to do. We ended up breaking up before that moment arrived so I supposed he thought he'd had a lucky escape.

'I'm up for the challenge. What do you fancy?'

'Most of these are in French but there is a chessboard. Do you know how to play?' I asked.

'You're on.' Ethan grabbed the set and placed it on the coffee table. We sat opposite each other on the floor and arranged the pieces. 'I should confess I haven't played chess for about a year; when I stayed at Juliette's family home in the country, we played games most of the weekend.'

'I would say I'll take it easy on you but that would break my competitive heart.'

Ethan shook his head. 'I would never want you to take it easy on me.'

Our eyes met across the board and I wondered if he had meant that to sound flirty or not. Because it had.

'Ladies first,' he said quickly before I could respond.

'Okay.' I moved my first pawn. 'Who taught you to play?'

Ethan moved his first piece and glanced up at me. 'An ex-girlfriend. We used to play when we wanted to get out of studying for our chef diploma exams. You?'

I was immediately curious as to what this ex-girlfriend was like, what kind of woman Ethan had fallen for in the past. What he was like in relationships. I couldn't help but want to know more about him.

'My dad. I grew up playing games with my family.' I swiped one of his pawns. He tutted. 'I miss it now I live in London. They live up north so I don't get to see them as much as I'd like. How about you?'

'I don't really have any family,' he said. 'I used to spend holidays and a lot of time, uh, with Joe's family in the country. But I haven't seen them for about a year. I spent last Christmas with Juliette and Oscar and our other friends here in Paris.'

'I never went to his family's home,' I admitted quietly as I moved my knight to swipe another pawn from him. 'Maybe it was for the best; I'm not sure I would have fitted in with Joe's family.' I didn't add that I was surprised Ethan did.

'Their loss,' Ethan said. 'Is this your first trip to Paris? Oh crap,' he said as I took his rook.

I was grateful to stop talking about Joe and his family. 'Yes. I've always wanted to see the city so when Joe suggested it, I was excited... Anyway, my best friend Carly and her husband Luke encouraged me to come here on this trip alone. I've been really struggling to write romance. They thought maybe I could find my spark again here.'

Ethan swiped one of my pawns but I had planned for that as I had my eye on my queen getting into check position in a couple more moves. I sighed though so he wouldn't know.

'If there is anywhere that you can find romance again, it's Paris,' he said.

I looked at him. 'Have you left broken hearts all over the city?'

'Do I look like a heartbreaker?' He raised an eyebrow, clearly joking, but I thought that actually there would be a fair few women who would love to be romanced by him in Paris. Those eyes, his warm smile and the glimpse I'd had of his body... 'Don't answer that,' he said quickly. 'I did date while I worked here but never found that elusive connection, you know?'

I nodded even though I was surprised. Ethan very much gave 'take me home to meet your mother' vibes. Unlike Joe. Who I should have realised gave troublemaker vibes. With a capital T.

I had experienced heartbreak before, or what I thought was heartbreak, but once the hurt passed, I had realised it had been for the best, but something about Joe's betrayal had hit harder than any of my other relationships. I think it was because I had thought I'd felt that connection Ethan was talking about. That I'd finally found my person. I still hoped that it was out there but it was almost worse thinking you'd had it then realising you'd got it so wrong. I felt stupid for falling for Joe. And now I didn't think I'd ever be able to trust someone enough to give my heart away again.

'What are you up to?' Ethan asked suspiciously when I left my bishop open. He took it but eyed me across the board.

I moved my queen. 'Checkmate.'

'Huh?' Ethan looked at the board. 'I have been hustled, haven't I?'

I laughed as I swiped his king. 'I may be undefeated.'

Ethan chuckled. 'I can see why. I didn't even notice my king was open. I was too busy gloating about taking your bishop. Great game, Tessa. But next time, I will win.'

'I'd like to see you try.'

We smiled at one another.

'Well, I guess we better call it a night,' I said, although as I spoke, I realised I would have happily stayed up chatting and playing games with him. He somehow took my mind off worrying without trying. 'I'm sorry about you having to be on the sofa,' I said as I stood up.

'You have nothing to be sorry about,' he replied firmly. 'Mind if I use the bathroom first?'

'Sure.'

I watched him get up and walk off then I went into the bedroom. I pulled on my Disney pyjamas that I had brought with me, sure no one but me would see them, took off my makeup and put my hair into a ponytail as I did my skin care. When I heard the bathroom door open, I walked out and stopped as Ethan emerged in a towel again. 'Oh, sorry.' What was it with us stumbling on each other in towels? But Ethan's seemed particularly skimpy. I had to force my eyes to stay on his and not let them drift lower.

Get a grip.

Ethan ran a hand though his damp hair. 'It's fine, Tessa. Sweet dreams.' And the smile he gave me as he walked away made me desperate to know suddenly what he was going to be dreaming about.

'Goodnight,' I said, hurrying into the bathroom. I closed the door and sank against it. That was weird. Ethan was definitely not my type, like I'd told Carly, but there was something about the man when he came out of the shower in that damn towel that sent the blood rushing to my cheeks. And the way he smiled at me.

I went to the basin to brush my teeth and tried hard to not think about the fact he would be taking that towel off any second with only a thin wall between us.

* * *

When I woke up the following morning, the apartment was quiet. I crept out of the bedroom and was surprised to see the place was empty. Ethan wasn't there. I tried not to feel disappointed. He'd mentioned coming out with me before his course, but he must have found something better to do. I didn't want to be there when he got back, sitting around waiting for him, so I hurriedly had a shower and got dressed for the day.

It was really hard to not let that down feeling wash back over me. It had been such a crazy couple of months. After I'd found out Joe had cheated on

The Paris Chapter 43

me, and he admitted he'd been seeing Rachel the whole time we were together, I left his flat and stayed a couple of nights with Carly and Luke while I looked for a new place. I had been so angry but focused on sorting out practicalities that it wasn't until I was alone in my new flat that I let myself cry. And I hadn't stopped. It had been a couple of weeks before I'd been able to shake off that sadness. I felt a lot better now albeit still stressed about writing and my looming deadline, but I knew how easy it would be to fall back into that funk.

As I contemplated whether to go to the bookshop on my own, the apartment door opened and in walked Ethan with two takeaway drinks and a paper bag, wearing a puffer jacket. 'Okay, it's pouring with rain outside but we're still going to the bookshop, right? I bought you tea and a coffee for me, and two croissants. I thought we could have them on the way. If you'd be okay walking though? Do you have a raincoat?' He saw my face. 'Am I talking too much again?'

'No, I just thought... I guess I woke up and you'd gone.' I cringed inwardly, worried I sounded completely pathetic.

'I wouldn't just disappear when we had plans,' Ethan replied softly. He thought for a moment. 'You can trust me, Tessa. Come on, I can't wait for you to see the bookshop.'

Those words sank into my brain. *You can trust me.* Could I though? I really had no idea. But him following through with our plans meant something to me.

'Lead the way,' I said, smiling. When I'd hurriedly packed for Paris, I had thankfully stuffed my puffer jacket into my bag, so I threw that on over my jeans and followed Ethan out. I thought suddenly that he could become a good friend if I let him.

And if I make myself not think about him in that towel again.

8

I had heard of Shakespeare and Company. As Ethan and I walked side-by-side under the cover of two umbrellas towards the bookshop close to Notre Dame, I understood why it was such a draw to people in Paris. The quaint, small shop with its green frontage was a treasure trove. Books lined the walls everywhere I looked as I followed Ethan inside, my mouth falling open. It had that delicious old book smell. A member of staff actually climbed a ladder to reach the top shelf for a book like something out of *Beauty and the Beast*. There was even a quote painted on the wall, and I loved a motivational quote.

'You've gone very quiet,' Ethan said in a low voice. I realised then he'd been watching me as I spun around, taking in the shop.

'I kind of thought there would be no point coming to an English language bookshop while I was in Paris, but I would have missed out big time.'

Ethan smiled. 'I'm glad you like it. I love the history of the place,' he said as we walked deeper into the bookshop. 'How so many writers have visited, how they let writers sleep here, how they champion books... I don't know, it feels like you're walking where some really important literary figures have walked too.'

I looked at him in surprise. 'That's a very romantic sentiment.'

'Well, uh, I love books. And I admire anyone who can write one,' he said, ducking his head to avoid my gaze.

'I'm a hopeless cook so I admire what you can do,' I told him, my eyes searching the shelves for my place in the alphabet, like they always did in a bookshop. 'Oh.' I stepped forward and saw they had my last book, my biggest seller so far: *A Love Like Ours*. 'Look!' I picked it up and smiled as I flicked through it.

'Tessa,' Ethan said playfully.

I turned to see he was holding his phone up. I shook my head with a chuckle, but I held my book up as he took my picture. We drew the attention of a member of staff who came over and Ethan eagerly told her I was the author, and she asked me to sign the copy. It never got old signing one of my books. It was something I'd practised when I was younger and dreamed of being an author. Ethan took another photo as I signed it. We both then bought a couple of books and I picked up a branded sweatshirt. We left each holding a tote bag to stroll to the café Ethan had wanted to take me to.

'Let me send you these pictures so you can post them online,' Ethan said as we passed by stalls selling antique books and paintings of Paris, the Seine in the distance. The rain had created puddles everywhere and was still falling gently. 'What's your number?'

I gave him my number and he sent the pictures he'd taken.

We arrived at the small café tucked away down a side street. One that probably only locals knew about. It was warm and dry, welcome after being outside even for a few minutes, and Ethan insisted on getting us drinks, so I sat down at a table close to the large window. I watched people passing by with umbrellas and hoods up, then I put the tote bag on the table and ran my fingers across it. My book had been in a Parisian bookshop. I thought back to the first time I'd seen something I had written on a shelf. It had been surreal and wonderful. I had felt so proud of myself. I had made my dream come true.

And now I was worried it might slip away.

'You look deep in thought again.'

I jumped when Ethan sat down next to me. 'I was thinking about finding my book in Shakespeare and Company. I don't want to stop writing but what if I have to?'

Ethan passed me a cup of tea and wrapped his hands around the latte he'd got for himself.

'Thank you.'

'After I studied in London, I went for a job interview at a restaurant, and I had to make a dish for the chef. He was a pretty formidable character,' Ethan said. 'I was so intimidated. My hands shook as I cooked. I made one of their dishes and honestly, I fucked it up. I made a right hash of it and the presentation went terribly. I knew it wasn't good enough. But that chef actually ripped me to shreds. He told me I would never be good enough to work in any restaurant. I was useless. And I should just give up. I left that interview and went home and cried.'

'I don't blame you,' I said, shocked that someone could be that mean. 'You were just starting out; what did he expect?'

Ethan shrugged. 'I started applying for office jobs after that; I thought he was right – I wasn't cut out for it. Then one of my friends on my course invited me to come to Paris with him. He was dating a woman called Juliette.' Ethan paused to take a sip of his latte then he smiled as he reminisced. 'When she found out I wanted to be a chef, she dragged me into the kitchen at her family's restaurant and put me through my paces. I made her a pasta dish that I loved to cook and she thought it was delicious. She gave me a chance and I never looked back. But if I had listened to that chef, I'd never be where I am today. And you know what?' He raised an eyebrow as he looked across at me.

'What?' I asked, hanging on his every word.

'That chef came for a meal at the restaurant in London last month and sent his compliments to the chef. I'd made his dish.' Ethan raised an eyebrow. 'I have never felt so smug in my whole life.'

I burst out laughing and he smiled across at me, looking pleased.

'Did he know it was you?'

'I came out at the end of the meal and went to shake his hand. He said he remembered me and that he'd given me such a hard time because he knew I was better than what I'd shown him. He'd wanted to give me a push. Like chefs had done to him when he was first starting out. And if I could carry on after that, it meant I was in the right job.'

'Wow.' I took a sip of my tea. 'He thought he was helping. And in a funny way, he did. Look at you now. I remember the first time an editor told me I had promise. She rejected my book but it gave me the confidence to keep going, to show her that I could do it. I wrote another book and she loved it, and gave me a book deal. If I had given up because of her rejection...' I sucked in a breath. 'I don't want to give up now.'

'You still love writing?'

I nodded. 'Yes. And seeing my name on a book. Seeing that book on the shelf. Or when someone messages me to say they loved something I have written. That it helped them escape life for a little bit. That I can make someone smile after a bad day with my words.'

'It's the same for me. That feeling that someone loves something you've made. It's a special one.'

We smiled at one another. We had different professions but they were both creative. We both made things for people to hopefully enjoy, and we both took it seriously. We had passion for our work. It wasn't just a job. It was something special. I liked that we had it in common.

'You won't give it up,' Ethan said then. 'I saw the look on your face when you saw your book in the shop. You can't let that go.'

I looked at the photo he had sent me. I did look so happy. 'I don't want Joe to be like that chef was for you; I don't want him to stop me doing something I love. But walking into that party and seeing him kissing that woman, it just made me feel so stupid for believing in him and what we had, for thinking I'd found my happy ending after writing so many of them for my characters. It made me think that what I was writing was just one epic lie. Maybe no one ever gets a happy ever after in real life, so how I can bear to keep writing them in my books, you know?'

I saw Ethan's face, his mouth set in a hard line as he stared down at his coffee cup.

'Oh, sorry,' I said quickly. 'I know we said we wouldn't mention what happened between me and Joe... I don't want to put you in an awkward position; I know he is your best friend.'

Ethan took a second to respond, looking like he was weighing up what to say next. 'Tessa, I want you to know that I don't support anyone cheating, friend or not,' he said firmly. His phone on the table vibrated with a call then. 'Is it okay if I take this?' he asked me.

I nodded and took a sip of my tea, wishing I could know more about what he thought of what Joe had done.

'Bonjour, Juliette,' Ethan said enthusiastically. 'We were just talking about you.' He dropped me a wink and I smiled back. Then he started talking in rapid French. I listened in wonder, wishing I had learnt another language.

Then Ethan switched to English and looked at me as he held the phone to his ear. 'I don't know, Juliette,' Ethan said hesitantly. He glanced at me. 'I've already invaded her holiday enough. But... okay, okay, I'll ask her...' Ethan pulled the phone away from his ear. He looked nervous. 'So, no pressure to say yes at all, okay? But Juliette and my friends are back from her country place and they want to eat at her family's restaurant tonight. It's where I worked when I lived here. They would love you to come. They all want to meet you.'

'They do?' I asked.

'Of course,' he said, surprised by my reaction. 'It's not every day two people get stuck in a one-bedroom apartment together.' He looked kind of shy then. 'But I understand if it's too much. We are hanging out more than we thought...' He trailed off.

I hesitated. I had never loved meeting lots of new people, and my experience with Joe keeping me from his friends and family had sunk my confidence at doing so even further. 'You really want me to?' I asked uncertainly.

Ethan nodded. 'Of course. We're friends now, right?' I thought I caught hope in his expression.

It felt good knowing he wanted to keep hanging out with me. I breathed through my nerves and nodded. 'Okay, then.'

His face relaxed into a warm smile. 'Great!' He went back to Juliette and spoke again in French before saying, 'Okay, okay, bye,' and hanging up. 'Sorry for putting you on the spot like that. You'll find out that Juliette is very hard to say no to.' He was smiling fondly though. I wondered if they had dated. Or were dating. And my stomach clenched a little bit. 'They're coming round at seven. It will be fun. I'm glad you're going to meet them. They are really great people.' We looked at one another. It felt like Joe was on both of our minds. I hoped Ethan's French friends were nothing like him. 'You still want to?' he checked again. Maybe he wasn't as confident as I had assumed he was.

It felt like a key moment in this burgeoning friendship of ours. I could say no to hanging out with him and his friends and then he would leave to stay elsewhere. Ethan would go back to being someone I didn't know.

But that felt wrong. It didn't make sense that I wanted to spend more time with him, what with his connection to my ex, but I was enjoying the spots he was taking me to in Paris. He had a calmness about him that I was drawn to. Plus, I couldn't help but be intrigued about his friend Juliette. Ethan's whole face had lit up when he spoke to her. She had invited me out with them later. Which suggested Ethan had said something complimentary about me or enough to make her want to meet me.

I'd love you to come.

His words echoed in my ears. It was a very different sentiment to Joe. He had kept me from people he knew. I had started to feel he was ashamed of me. Now I knew it had been to make sure that no one could tell me about his other woman, but feeling that I wasn't good enough was hard to shake. So such an easy invite from Ethan did feel good. He told me I could trust him. I had no idea if I would ever be able to do that, but I wasn't ready to say goodbye to him forever either.

'I still want to come along,' I told him.

'Yeah?' He leaned back in his chair. 'Great. And I can maybe stay with Juliette afterwards, give you your space back,' he added quietly, avoiding my gaze.

'Oh, right,' I replied, thinking the apartment would feel kind of lonely without him there.

'Shit, look at the time,' Ethan said suddenly. 'I better head off to my course. Will you be okay?'

'Of course,' I assured him. 'I'll see you later, at the apartment? For seven?'

'See you there, Tessa.' He drained the rest of his coffee and got up and, with a wave, disappeared into the Paris rain.

I let out a sigh. I had just agreed to a night out with his French friends. What was Paris doing to me? I pulled up the picture Ethan had taken of me then I opened up Instagram. I searched for his name and saw he had an account on there. His photos were mostly, unsurprisingly, of food and a few of his friends. There wasn't one of Joe that I could see. Which was a relief. I pressed the follow button.

Then I went to my account and posted the photo Ethan had taken of me in Shakespeare and Company. I tagged him and thanked him for taking me to such a wonderful bookshop and said how happy I had been to find one of my books in there. I looked at my smile in the picture. I seemed more relaxed than I had been for a while. Was that just because of Paris – or Ethan too?

Then I put my phone down and panic hit me. I wondered how sophisticated Ethan's friends were. I had nothing nice to wear. I had no idea what one even wore to a Parisian restaurant. I was a jeans-and-a-t-shirt woman. I liked to be comfortable. I didn't enjoy dressing up. I didn't really own many dresses or skirts. I didn't feel like myself if I wore them. And heels felt like torture devices to me.

Why can't you wear a dress for once?

Joe's words echoed through my mind. He had given me a sneer looking at me one evening before we went out for a meal. I had on jeans, a t-shirt and my leather jacket and trainers. I had felt so shit when he'd said that to me. I hated that he had made me feel like I should change if I wanted him to be happy with me. If I wanted him to love me. I had been so worried he would leave me. I wish I had known what kind of man he was and walked away before he was able to hurt me like he had done.

Ugh!

Getting up, I left the café and checked on my phone for shops nearby. I had heard of the department store Galeries Lafayette Paris Haussmann. The rain had started to ease so I decided to walk there.

I didn't want to keep replaying conversations with Joe over and over in my mind forever. It was like one of my books except I couldn't change the ending or throw in a plot twist. Real life never went the way you wanted it to. I couldn't control it like I could my stories. I fantasised about all the things I could have said or done while I was with Joe. But would the outcome have changed even if I could go back and do it differently? And did I even want to any more?

If I was honest, Joe had made me unsure whether anyone could love me for who I was. And I hated that. I didn't want to think that way. Joe had been a liar and a cheat. He was in the wrong. So why did I still feel like what happened was somehow my fault?

Fuck him for making me feel like this.

I found the department store after a long but pleasant walk. It was stunning inside, similar to Harrods in London, and I walked around in awe. I had felt pressure to dress more like Joe wanted me to even though I felt uncomfortable. But I didn't want him to be in my head about my style any more. I wanted to be myself. To dress how I wanted to. I didn't want to feel like I had to change for someone again.

Wandering around the clothes section, I had to stop myself thinking about what Ethan's friends would be dressing like and focus on what I wanted to wear. Ethan had only seen me in jeans and he had still invited me tonight. Still wanted me to come. No mention of what I needed to wear. I hoped that meant he didn't care. I wanted to wear something that made me feel good, not something that I thought I should put on to fit in then feel miserable all night. Like I had so many times while I was with Joe. I couldn't get that time, those nights, back, but I could make sure I didn't fall into the same trap again.

I spotted one of my favourite brands then. It was pricey but they did some really chic streetwear and even though I knew I probably shouldn't spend too much money in case I couldn't write this book, there was something about being on holiday that made it easier to throw caution to the wind. To worry less about my looming deadline. To try to just enjoy myself.

I saw a grey faded T-shirt with a phoenix on it. I snapped a photo and sent it to Carly.

> Too on the nose?

She replied quickly as always.

> We love a not-so subtle dig.

She added a thumbs-up emoji.

I headed to pay for the top and sent another message to Carly as I waited in the queue.

> Are you feeling any better?

> Not really, think it might be the flu or something. Luckily, I don't have much on for the next couple of days so going to rest. That tee for anything special?

> I'm going out to a restaurant tonight, with Ethan and some of his Parisian friends.

> You're hanging out with Ethan now?!!!

I smiled at the exclamation marks.

> He's actually a nice guy. He took me to a bookshop today! I have no idea why he's friends with Joe, they are so different. It's nice having him around. I've been stressing less about the book.

After paying for the t-shirt, I added it to the bookshop tote bag then decided to take a slow stroll back to the apartment as the rain had finally ceased. Carly replied as I walked along the river.

> Anything that makes you stress less is good IMHO.

> Aw thanks. Make sure Luke takes cares of you!

I put my phone away. Carly, Luke and London felt very far away right now. It was a novelty to feel less stress after having so many weeks of feeling weighted down by it. Even my muscles felt less tense. My shoulders weren't raised up to my ears. There was still a long way to go for me to feel ready to write again, but I was starting to miss it. And that could only be a good sign.

I opened up Instagram and saw that Ethan had followed me back and liked the picture of me in the bookshop. I smiled all the way home.

9

The front door burst open at 7 p.m., excited voices shattering the peace of the apartment. I looked up from where I sat on the sofa with my laptop as Ethan walked in followed by a woman and a man.

'Hi, Tessa,' Ethan said as they noticed me and abruptly stopped talking. 'Are you writing?'

'Uh, no, just watching *Emily in Paris*,' I said, nervous that his friends might not be impressed by that.

'Love her outfits,' the woman said brightly, her French accent strong and beautiful. 'And your t-shirt. I adore that brand.'

Some of my nerves slid away with relief that she had complimented me. I smiled, pleased she liked it. 'Thank you,' I said, taking her in. She was beautiful and immaculately styled in a black dress and cropped jacket, her blonde bob sharp and straight and her lips a bright red.

'This is Juliette, and this is Oscar,' Ethan said. 'This is Tessa. Tessa is a romance author here on a research trip.'

'And I used to be Ethan's... how do you say it – bossy?' Juliette said as I got up and she walked over to give me a kiss on both cheeks.

'I couldn't have put it better myself,' Ethan said with a laugh.

'You mean boss,' Oscar told her, also kissing me. He was tall and lean with dark curls and a well-trimmed bread.

Juliette waved her hand dismissively. 'Whatever. Tessa, you are gorgeous. I love your hair, and what is that perfume? I must have it.'

Smiling, I thanked her and told her it was La Vie Est Belle. 'I couldn't bring anything else to Paris, could I?'

Juliette laughed. She had a loud, husky laugh. 'The British humour. I'm so happy you're coming out with us.'

'Thank you for inviting me,' I replied. Juliette was instantly putting me at ease. Relief washed over me that this wasn't as awkward as I had been fearing since earlier.

'I have to show you my restaurant and then Oscar's bar. You will love them, and we need to practise our English; Ethan always wants to talk in French,' she said, throwing him an adoring look. I wondered again if they had dated or not. She was stunning.

'You have to try my new cocktail,' Oscar added, throwing an arm around Ethan's shoulders. 'Tell her, Ethan.'

'I don't think you have any choice,' Ethan said, laughing at his friends.

His good humour was infectious. 'It sounds great. I'll just get my jacket.' I went into the bedroom and pulled on my leather jacket and trainers and then slung my grey bag across my body. I fluffed up my curls and touched up my lip gloss before returning to them.

When we headed out of the apartment together, the night was cool but dry and the lights of Paris glowed around us.

Juliette slipped an arm through mine and Ethan and Oscar trailed after us. I was taken aback by their warmth and couldn't help but contrast the feeling to how I'd felt walking into that London bar with Joe to meet his friends for the first time. I'd felt like an outsider that night. Awkward and uncomfortable. But not tonight. Juliette didn't give me a chance to feel that way. I wondered how Ethan was friends with such different groups of people. They didn't seem to connect in any way.

'You need to teach me all the ways you chat up men in London for when I come over in the summer,' Juliette said as we walked through the Paris streets.

'I never chat up anyone,' I told her, loving how the British phrase sounded in her accent. 'That sounds hideous. And I have to warn you, men in London are generally twats.'

She laughed heartily at that then looked back at Ethan. 'She's hilarious, pretending she doesn't attract all the men to her; I bet they are all over her! How do you say it? Honey pot and bees?'

'Like honey to bees,' Ethan told her.

I raised an eyebrow. Was he joking or not? 'I can assure you that is not the case,' I said. 'My ex told me once that if we'd met in a bar, he would never have approached me as I wouldn't have been wearing heels and a dress, and that's what men like.'

Juliette made a choking sound. '*Putain!*'

I didn't know what it meant exactly but I recognised it was a swear word. I couldn't help but glance at Ethan. He was quiet, looking at the ground. I felt bad for slagging off his mate again. But I wasn't saying anything that wasn't true.

I shrugged. 'So *you* need to teach *me*.'

'French men will love you,' Juliette declared. 'Right, Oscar?'

'If I wasn't in love with Louis...' Oscar said, throwing me a wink.

'I'm off all men,' I joked to him. 'But I'd make an exception for you.'

Oscar chuckled. 'She's a delight. Where have you been hiding her, Ethan?'

'I'm wondering the same thing myself,' Ethan replied.

I looked over at him curiously but he didn't meet my gaze. We arrived at the restaurant owned by Juliette's family then. 'Cinq?' I said, looking up at the red sign.

'It means five in French because they offer a five-course meal,' Ethan explained as he opened the door, letting me pass through ahead of him.

Inside was as red as the sign. There were red booths and cushions on the smaller tables, red drapes across the window, and hanging on the walls, all the prints and paintings were different shades of red. It was very eye-catching. The lights were low and the background music funky. There was a bar that took up one wall. The whole place was packed and lively. It looked like one of the city's hotspots.

'You like?' Juliette said, smiling at the awed look on my face. 'Wait until you try the food! Maman, I made a new friend!'

Juliette's parents came over and greeted me warmly, then we were shown to a booth in the corner. I scooted across and Ethan sat next to me, the other two opposite us.

'There is no menu; they change the five courses weekly and everyone gets the same,' Ethan explained as a waiter appeared and poured red wine for us all. Oscar and Juliette were talking across the room to people they knew at the next table.

'So this was where you used to work?' I asked, looking around and trying to imagine him here.

'Talk about a learning curve. It was fast-paced and challenging and I loved every minute of it,' Ethan said, smiling at the memory. 'They gave me such great experience. I only had a twelve-month contract as someone was working abroad and they returned; I would have stayed otherwise.'

'It must have been hard to leave Juliette.' I tasted the wine. It was glorious.

'Hard?' Ethan looked across at me.

'I thought that maybe you two...' I trailed off awkwardly.

'Oh, no, we were never together. Juliette is a free spirit.'

Juliette heard this comment and smiled at us. 'What Ethan means is, I'm not a, how do you say, a relationship person.'

'Juliette has broken a lot of hearts in Paris,' Oscar said, giving her a fond look.

She shrugged. 'I don't want to be shackled by anyone,' she said. 'But Ethan likes relationships. What do you think of relationships, Tessa?'

I looked at Ethan, who was blushing furiously. I tried but failed not to find it sweet. 'I don't know. I used to be like Ethan, but now I wonder if we shouldn't all be like you, Juliette.'

'Ah, a man hurt you,' she said, nodding wisely. 'He was a fool? Is that right?'

'That's right,' Ethan said. I wasn't sure if he was confirming her English or the sentiment. Or both.

'Yeah, he did, and now I'm wondering if I even believe in love any more,' I said, wondering if the wine was loosening my tongue too much. 'Which isn't great for a romance writer. Ethan has been trying to help – he took me to the love wall. And to a bookshop today.'

'That was very nice of him.' Oscar raised an eyebrow at Ethan.

'He's just trying to make up for the fact he gate-crashed my holiday,' I joked.

Ethan shook his head. 'No, I want to help you, Tessa.'

'That's very sweet,' Juliette said as she and Oscar looked at one another.

'Oh, good, the first course,' Ethan said loudly then.

I took a long gulp of wine because Ethan's words had made me feel much better than I knew they should have.

We had a lively meal. Juliette loved telling stories and she asked me to correct her English, but honestly, it was pretty fluent. And when Oscar and Ethan chatted in French, I heard again how Ethan's French was brilliant. It made me wish I could join in. It was such a beautiful language. Everything sounded sexier in French somehow. It might have been the red wine though. More kept appearing as if by magic.

When the men went to talk to a mutual friend, Juliette came to sit beside me. We'd just had the final course, a glorious chocolate tart, and I was full and pretty drunk.

'While we are alone,' she said, signalling something to our waiter, 'tell me what happened with your ex.'

I hesitated for a second, embarrassed to tell my sorry tale, but Juliette was looking at me with full attention like she really wanted to know. I took a breath. 'Well, he cheated on me,' I said in a rush. 'It was with someone he worked with. He'd been with her the whole time we were a couple. I found out when I went to one of their work parties and saw them together,' I confessed.

'I can't believe he did that to you,' Juliette said, shaking her head. 'You were heartbroken?'

'I was. I suppose I've always been a romantic and I thought that I had found "The One",' I said, doing air-quotes around the word. 'Now I don't know how I'll ever trust anyone again.'

Juliette sighed. 'I wish he hadn't made you feel that way. Is that why you're in Paris? To try to get over him?'

'Well, we were supposed to be here together. I thought this was going to be such a romantic trip. Then I found out about his other woman. My friends persuaded me to come here anyway. I'm here alone.'

Juliette shook her head. 'Not alone. You have us. And you have Ethan.'

'He's Joe best friend though. My ex.'

Ethan and Oscar returned then and sat down opposite us.

Juliette turned to face Ethan. 'You!'

'What did I do?' he asked in surprise at the venom in her voice.

'Joe was the one who hurt Tessa?'

'Ah.' Ethan sighed. 'Yeah, he did.'

'That bastard! I've told you before – how can you still be friends with him?' Juliette pointed at me. 'And now you tell me your friend hurt my friend.'

I couldn't help but smile at her calling me that.

'I hate what he did to Tessa,' Ethan said quietly.

I felt bad for Ethan being torn between the two of us.

'Let's not talk about it,' I insisted. 'I don't want Joe ruining tonight. This has been so much fun.'

'We drink to that,' Oscar declared. 'At my bar!'

We left the restaurant and walked the short distance to Oscar's bar. It was down a long staircase and had a low ceiling, was dimly lit, with a polished wood bar. It was achingly cool. Somewhere I would never have gone by myself. Everyone greeted us like old friends and we soon had one of Oscar's signature cocktails in our hands.

As we sat down at a round table, a band started playing on the small stage. A jazz band with a female singer who had a beautiful voice. The music was slow and sexy and I leaned back to listen and sipped my cocktail, thinking that I would never have expected to be spending the night like this. I was enjoying myself so much though.

As we applauded the first song, I leaned over to Ethan. 'Thank you for tonight; this has cheered me up so much.'

Ethan smiled. 'Good. No one can be miserable around Juliette.'

'All of you are fun,' I said.

Ethan had surprised me too tonight. He was quieter than his friends, like me, but he was easy to talk to and he was funny too. He'd had us in stitches doing an impression of the head chef at his work. He always seemed so relaxed and it had helped to relax me. That and the booze.

'I really am grateful you included me. You didn't have to.'

'I wanted to,' he insisted. His blue eyes pierced mine as we looked across at one another. He moved his leg and it brushed against mine. I wondered if he felt it too.

It suddenly felt a lot warmer in the bar. I opened my mouth to answer but the band started up again and the music swallowed my words. I tore my gaze from Ethan and looked back at the singer, but I could feel that he was still watching me. And I wasn't sure why his gaze made me feel uncomfortable. It felt like he was really seeing me, and I had a sudden feeling that no other man had paid me that much attention before. Which didn't make any sense, but the warm feeling in my body remained the whole time I sat next to him.

10

We didn't stumble out of Oscar's bar until 1 a.m. I was decidedly tipsy.

'Oops,' I giggled as I seemed to trip on nothing but Paris air.

Ethan placed my hand on his arm. 'Hang on to me, let's go home.'

There was that word again. Home. I liked it.

I looked at him. 'But aren't you leaving?' I nodded to Juliette, who was walking ahead, singing with Oscar, arm-in-arm, as they weaved past glistening puddles on the pavement. The thought of him staying with her and not at our apartment was disappointing.

'Do you want me to leave tonight?' Ethan asked.

'No,' I said, so quickly we both looked surprised. 'I mean, you didn't pack anything.'

'True,' he said, giving me that amused look again. 'And I really shouldn't leave you this drunk alone. What if you need me?'

'A very good point,' I said, happiness pooling in the pit of my stomach that he wasn't rushing off to stay with Juliette. He wanted to look after me. I stumbled and Ethan wrapped an arm around my waist. I steadied myself against him. He was stronger than I had thought he would be. 'I blame those cocktails. But they were bloody good. And I needed fun.'

'You had fun then?' He smiled.

I nodded furiously. 'I had a great time. I'm glad you're staying with me.'

'Yeah?'

Juliette stopped and looked back at us, pulling Oscar to a stop beside her too. 'We go this way, you go that way,' she declared, dramatically pointing. We walked up to them. She grabbed me and pulled me from Ethan into her arms. 'Tessa,' she said, squishing me against her. 'We see you lots while you here, yes?' She leaned into my ear. 'And maybe I tell Ethan that there is no room at my flat so he has to keep staying with you the whole time, yes?' She pulled back and laughed, letting me go. 'Goodnight, my darlings!'

'Goodnight, Juliette.' Ethan gave her a kiss and hugged Oscar, who had just kissed me.

Waving madly, Juliette and Oscar disappeared into the night. I watched them go, still stunned by what Juliette had said and how I wondered whether I did want to ask her to not let Ethan stay with her so he could keep on staying with me.

What is wrong with me?

'Did she say something to upset you?' Ethan was looking at me curiously.

I shook my head. 'Of course not. Come on, we go this way!' I pointed and he laughed, hurrying after me. When I stumbled a little, his arm held me steady again. I wrapped an arm around his waist too so we were pressed together. I told myself this was because he wanted to make sure I didn't fall over, but his strong, warm body against mine made my stomach somersault anyway.

We walked to our building and inside and up the stairs. We had to separate for Ethan to unlock the apartment, then we went in. Ethan pulled his phone and wallet out to put them down on the kitchen counter.

'Juliette has tagged me in something,' he said, looking at his phone. 'Oh my God, look at what she's posted.' He passed me his phone and I saw Juliette had shared a series of photos from the night on her Instagram, tagging us. I smiled at one of me and her, our arms wrapped around each other like we were best friends, and one of the four of us. I was squashed up with Ethan, my elbow propped on his shoulder, and he was looking at me with a huge smile on his face.

'I love them,' I said quietly. I would have to ask Juliette for her to send them to me. I wanted to be able to remember this night.

We looked at each other in the dark kitchen for a moment. I was not feeling quite as tipsy as I had in the bar. Now that it was just the two of us alone in the apartment, that realisation seemed to dampen my alcohol high. I watched as Ethan went over to the fridge and pulled out a bottle of water. I shrugged off my jacket and dumped it with my bag in the counter, then I flopped down onto the sofa, kicking off my trainers.

'Here.' Ethan held out a bottle of water. 'Drink some.'

I sipped on it as he sat on the opposite sofa and drunk some water himself.

'I really like Juliette and Oscar,' I said, leaning back against the cushions.

'Good. They really liked you,' he replied. 'Juliette wants to adopt you, I think.'

'You really have never slept with her?'

Ethan spluttered on his water. He eyed me across the room. 'Why, would it make you happy or sad if I had?'

I looked back at him, unsure how to respond.

He took pity on me. 'No, never. We are better as friends. I think we knew that as soon as we met. Sometimes, you just know.'

'Sometimes, you make the wrong decision,' I pointed out. I put the water down on the table and curled my legs up on the sofa. Ethan watched my every move. 'So, if Juliette isn't your type – what is?'

'I don't have a type; if I connect with someone then that's all I'm looking for.'

'God, that's a good answer.'

'I guess Joe was your type though?' Ethan asked quietly.

I suddenly wished I was sober for this discussion because Ethan seemed to be waiting for my answer and I didn't want to get it wrong. There was something in the air tonight, wasn't there? Maybe that connection Ethan was talking about. Even though that was a crazy thought. I couldn't connect with my ex's best mate. Besides, love was off the table for me. For good. 'Yeah, I guess Joe was my type, or the type I've always thought I should be with...'

Ethan's eyes slid away from me as he nodded. 'He's everyone's type,' he muttered.

I hated that Joe was good looking. That he had attracted me to him so much. 'But what you said just then, about connection, I'm not sure we ever had it. I never felt like I could be myself with him.'

Ethan looked at me again. 'I'm sorry to hear that. You should always be yourself, Tessa. Yourself is pretty great.'

'You're too nice to me,' I said, pleased though.

'You don't deserve nice?'

The question hung in the air and I wasn't sure what to say.

'Maybe you should go to bed,' Ethan said then.

'I'm not tired,' I replied truthfully. 'I like talking to you.'

'Yeah? I like talking to you too.' Ethan was quiet for a moment and I thought maybe he did want me to go to bed when he suddenly leaned forward. 'Will you tell me what happened between you and Joe? Just once. I don't know if I heard the' – he seemed to consider the words – 'right story.'

It was interesting he had said 'right' and not the 'full' story. I wondered if he sensed Joe had told him something that wasn't quite the truth. I didn't know why Joe would lie to his friend but then again, he'd pretended to have paid for our trip to Paris so maybe it wasn't only me who he liked to lie to.

'How much do you know?' I asked curiously.

'Joe told me he had met someone and didn't know what to do. But he didn't say much more. When he brought you to that bar, I was surprised to see you. He confessed after that night he had seen you a few times. I couldn't get much more out of him than that,' Ethan replied.

I sighed as I realised Joe had lied to everyone. 'It was more than he told you then,' I said. 'We met in Hyde Park and things moved quickly. He was so keen. I had to move out of my flat after just a few weeks of us seeing each other. Then he asked me to move in. So for pretty much the six months we were together, I lived at his flat.'

'He didn't tell me that,' Ethan said quietly.

'It makes sense now how he kept me away from people he knew and didn't really want to hang around my friends either. He only met my best friend and her husband once. And you know I only met his friends twice, if you can even say we properly met. Joe said he preferred to have me to himself. But now I know, he just didn't want to get caught out.' I was angry how him trying to cover his tracks had made me feel bad about myself. 'He made me feel like he was embarrassed to be seen with me...' I trailed off, the sting of his rejection still fresh. 'Anyway, he had a couple of work events while we were together but he never asked me to go along, and then I heard him talking about his work Christmas party on the phone with a colleague, and it was clear his colleague was bringing his wife. So afterwards I asked him why he hadn't invited me to go too. He said, "I thought about it but I know you hate parties; you'd just sit by yourself in the corner, and that would be so awkward for me."'

Ethan sucked in a breath but didn't say anything, so I continued. I looked away as I spoke, not wanting to meet Ethan's eyes.

'I felt awful. I thought Joe believed I was too quiet, too shy, that when we were out, I didn't make enough of an effort with people and so he didn't want me to come anywhere. I know I'm not a huge extrovert, that I don't really love parties, I can be a bit shy when I first meet people. I really felt like it was all my fault so that night when he left to go to that work party without me, I thought I better do something to stop him leaving me.'

I sighed. 'So I put on a dress and heels, which as you might have guessed from what I've worn here in Paris, I really hate doing, and I went to this fancy London hotel to find him and go to his bloody work do because I thought he wanted someone like that and I didn't want him to break up with me.' I shook my head, hating how I had been so desperate for his approval and affection, I tried to become someone different. 'I walked in and I saw him, his arms around a woman there, chatting and laughing. I stopped and watched as he leaned in to whisper to her, then she wrapped herself around him and they kissed. I have never felt so stunned. I asked someone if they were together, and they looked surprised and said they had been a couple for years. Years! But not only that – Joe lived with Rachel at her flat. So all the travelling he'd said his work was making him do was a lie. He had been splitting his time between the two of us for the six months we were together.' I cringed at how easily I had believed everything he had told me while we were a couple. Never once suspecting he had another girlfriend. I opened my mouth to finish the story. 'So I went over and threw a glass of wine over him and walked out of the party.'

11

'You threw a glass of wine at Joe?' Ethan repeated in shock.

I looked across at him and grimaced. 'I've never done anything like that before in my life. I'm always the person who comes home and thinks about a conversation for a week, telling myself things I should have said or not said, and generally beating myself up about it.'

'He deserved it,' Ethan said.

'Yeah?'

'Yeah,' he replied decisively.

That made me feel better.

'What happened between you then?'

'Well, I went back to our flat. If I can even still call it that,' I said. 'I called my best friend Carly, and she and her husband told me to start packing up my things and they would come and help. I could stay at theirs. Joe came back while I was packing and I asked if it was true he'd been seeing Rachel for the whole six months we were together and he said it was, and he hadn't meant to hurt me. They had been a couple on and off for a long time. She wanted commitment but he hadn't been sure and had kept on seeing me. When Carly and Luke arrived, they made him leave. We packed my things and I haven't seen or heard from him since.' I said the last bit all in a rush to get it out, then my chest sagged.

Ethan was quiet for a moment. 'I'm sorry, Tessa. Joe feels like he has a lot to prove to his family, and I think that affects how he treats people. His father is a demanding man. Joe feels he has to be successful. And that's why he shows off. His money, his clothes, his looks... He learnt to look down on others from his family. I've always thought he's an unhappy man.'

'Maybe, but that doesn't excuse him cheating.'

'No, of course not! I didn't mean that. But I think he thinks more about who he should be with than who he really wants to be with. He should have been happy to have found someone he loved but instead, he's chosen someone his family knows.'

'Oh?' I hadn't known that. Joe hadn't told me anything. He'd just let me leave.

'Yeah, Rachel is an old family friend, the daughter of someone his dad plays golf with. Tessa, please don't think it was because of anything you did. Joe has been pushed towards Rachel for most of his life. I don't think he loves her. She's successful, rich, from the same world that he is. That's important to him.'

'But if she's always been in the background, why did he even ask me out in the first place?'

'Maybe he just couldn't not ask you out,' Ethan said, looking away. 'Even though he knew he shouldn't.'

'He hurt me, Ethan. Whatever pressure his family might have put on him, he didn't need to do that. He could have been honest with me instead of stringing us both along. Instead of making me feel like I wasn't good enough. That I just wasn't enough.'

'I wish you hadn't felt like that,' Ethan said softly. 'But I get it. He can make people feel that way.' I could see in his eyes that Ethan had felt that way at some point too.

It really sucked that Joe had that power over people.

'I need to go to bed now.' I jumped up and the room swam for a second, but I stumbled out and into the bedroom. I sank down onto the bed, my head a complete mess. I had been humiliated by Joe. He had made me feel worthless. Blaming me for everything when it was him who had been playing games and lying and not being true to himself. I would never understand that.

But finding out that maybe Joe would have done what he had done to any woman because he cared more about who his family wanted him to be with than who he actually wanted helped a little bit.

Maybe it wasn't my fault after all.

Talking with Ethan hadn't reduced my anger towards Joe or the fact I'd wasted time and my heart on such a man, but it did stop me feeling as ashamed as I had done. I thought I'd pushed him to cheat because I wasn't enough. But maybe I just wasn't enough for *him*. Because I didn't have a fancy upbringing, I didn't have a typical job, I wasn't from a wealthy family. But if that's what he really cared about then him doing what he had done was a good thing. I certainly didn't want to be with a man like that.

'Are you okay?'

I looked up to see Ethan in the doorway. I nodded. 'I feel like I'm starting to wonder if we just weren't meant to be. That maybe it wasn't because I'm not good enough... He just couldn't let himself love me. You know that cliché, maybe it was him and not me after all?'

'I think you're right about that,' Ethan said. 'Of course you're good enough. You're more than good enough for... anyone.'

'So are you,' I said firmly.

'I don't know about that,' Ethan said.

'You'll find someone incredible. Never let Joe make you feel less than because you don't have his money or family or whatever. You're twice the man he will ever be.'

We looked at one another. Was I imagining a sudden heat in the air?

Ethan stepped into the room. And my pulse sped up. We were quiet for a moment, then Ethan shook his head like he needed to break the tension. 'Joe is a lot taller than me though,' he said, his lips twitching.

I smiled, relieved that he was joking after such a serious chat. 'Yeah, he does win there.'

'Hey!' Ethan walked up to the bed and grabbed a pillow, tossing it towards me but so gently, I caught it easily. 'He does always like to bring my height up.'

'Hmm, I can imagine he does. God, what a tosspot.'

'Tosspot?' His eyes twinkled.

'It's a valid diss word,' I replied. I got up onto my knees and moved back so I could flop on the pile of pillows. 'Sit with me?' I asked. 'It's comfier than the sofa.'

'I think most things are.' Ethan climbed onto the bed and sat next to me, leaning back against the headboard. 'Oh, man, I shouldn't have given up this bed so easily. The sofa has wrecked my back already. This bed is paradise in comparison.'

I nodded. 'So good, isn't it? I've slept so well here.' I felt Ethan turn to me with a glare, so I moved my head so I could meet his eyes, and I chuckled. 'Sorry, that was rubbing it in.'

'It was.' He gave me a crooked smile. 'But I really don't mind.'

We lapsed into silence until I turned onto my side. Ethan copied me so we faced one another. We were closer than we had ever been. I noticed the brightness of his blue eyes. And the softness of his fair hair. And the faint line of stubble on his chin that was at odds with his youthful face – in a good way. Like maybe there was an edge to him that you'd only find out if you really knew him. The thought lit a spark inside me that was unexpected.

I want to know him.

I felt my gaze drop to his lips. I wondered how he would kiss. Gently? Sweetly? But then it would turn hungry...

'Tessa,' Ethan said in a low voice. I quickly lifted my eyes back to his. 'Um...' He shook his head. 'I think I better go. You need to sleep. And this... I should go.'

'What if you didn't?' I whispered. I liked this. Lying next to him. My heart started to pound. I had no idea what I was doing, but the thought of him getting up and going to sleep on the sofa made me ache.

'We've both been drinking,' he said with a sigh. 'It's not that I don't want to stay and talk to you but I'm worried that I might...' He trailed off. I wasn't sure what he was about to say but it made me wonder whether he could feel the same spark in the air. I was scared of it too much to ask him though.

'Why don't you stay and sleep here? Just sleep,' I said. 'It's nice.'

Ethan smiled. 'Yeah, it is nice.'

'We can stay in our clothes,' I added. It would be safer that way.

He shook his head. 'I don't think I should.' His gaze flicked to my lips then. 'You're so close,' he whispered.

My heart leapt at the thought he might be thinking about what kissing me would be like too. But it was coupled with a twist inside my stomach because the thought of closing the small space between us was too hard to contemplate. Letting someone in again was something I wasn't ready for. Ethan was making me want to though. There were so many emotions coursing through me. I wondered if he could tell or not.

'I'm sorry, I just... want you to stay,' I whispered back.

He watched for me a moment then nodded. 'It's okay,' he said. Then he reached out and brushed back a hair from my face. A shiver ran down my back. I wondered if he noticed. 'I'll stay.'

'You promise?' I whispered back. I wasn't exactly sure what I was asking, but it felt like I needed to ask him that.

'I promise,' he replied as if he understood.

Maybe he did. Maybe he was thinking some of the things I was. All I knew was there was something comforting about Ethan being beside me, and I wanted to hold on to that. He was calming even though the pull I felt towards him was terrifying.

My eyes closed and side-by-side, facing each other, we fell asleep like it was the most natural thing in the world.

12

When I opened my eyes the next morning, I was startled for a moment to see Ethan sleeping beside me.

Then the night before came back in snapshot like Polaroid pictures, faded and dream-like but beautiful memories.

I'd had so much fun with Ethan and his friends. And then afterwards, I'd felt closer to him than I had with anyone new for a long time. I could tell Carly and Luke anything, and my parents were always there if I needed them, but new friendships or relationships never seemed to scratch the surface.

I stared at Ethan sleeping, hoping it wasn't creepy, and I couldn't help but compare last night with my six months with Joe. I don't think I'd ever felt as comfortable with another man as I had last night with Ethan. The thought was scary but somehow, Ethan also felt safe.

'I can feel you,' Ethan murmured then. He opened one eye, then the other, and smiled sleepily, pushing his ruffled hair back off his face. His eyes were really a beautiful blue. A crack of morning light streamed in through the blinds, lighting them up.

'I love your eyes,' I said, before I could stop myself.

'Yeah?' He smiled and reached out to gently touch my lip. 'I love your smile.'

My heart started to hammer as we stared at one another. He slowly withdrew his hand. I wanted it back. 'I'm sorry I begged you to stay,' I said softly, wondering if I should feel embarrassed. I kind of did, but I couldn't lie – I was enjoying waking up beside Ethan.

'I'm not,' he replied. *Tu es belle.*'

'Speaking French is pretty sexy,' I admitted, trying to remember enough French to translate his words. *Belle* was beautiful, I was sure of that. My heart beat even faster. I had been so sure that I wanted to stay the hell away from men, but now this guy was right beside me in bed telling me lovely things in French. I wasn't sure when I'd realised Ethan was extremely cute. But now I had, I couldn't un-see it.

'Good. I need all the help I can get.' Ethan smiled but I sensed there was something underneath that casual sentence. He seemed as nervous, as unsure, as me.

'I don't believe that,' I said.

'If we met out one night, I would never have the guts to chat you up. Even if I really wanted to,' Ethan admitted.

I suddenly longed to meet him out as strangers, no complications between us. 'Would you have wanted to?' I asked him nervously.

'Of course I would. Are you fishing for compliments?' He smiled and I bit my lip because if I was honest, I really wanted to hear him say nice things. 'You're gorgeous. We already established though, I'm not your type.' He said it casually but as someone who also lacked confidence, I could feel his nerves. My heart stuttered at him calling me gorgeous. I loved how honest he was with me. It was refreshing after Joe. And it helped me feel like one day, I could trust Ethan.

'If you said something sexy in French, I think you'd be anyone's type,' I blurted out then.

'Including yours?'

We looked at one another. I wanted to be as honest as he had been. 'You sound very sexy when you speak French,' I admitted, my cheeks heating up.

'Hmm. Looks like I need to speak in French more often around you then,' he said, smiling.

'How do you say "kiss me" in French?' I blurted out.

Ethan sucked in a breath and shifted in the bed.

'God, I'm sorry.' I winced at my lame flirting and went to roll over, desperate to get out of the bed. And find somewhere to hide for the rest of my life.

Ethan touched my shoulder and I froze. I couldn't look at him though.

'I would say *embrasse-moi*.'

'Huh. Appropriate,' I said, glancing back at him to see if he was taking the piss.

Ethan was giving me a fond look. 'Come back. Please. Don't go unless you want to...'

I rolled back and we locked eyes again. 'It's really "*embrasse-moi*"?'

'I promise,' he whispered, his gaze dropping to my lips. I smiled and he reached out to touch my lip again. 'Tessa, seriously, I would love to kiss you, but I don't know if that's what you really want?'

My indecision was clearly screamingly obvious to us both. My body was drawn to him. The bed was soft and cosy and made me want to close the small space and tumble into his safe, warm arms. To be held, touched, kissed... I ached for it. But everything had changed in such a short space of time between us. From thinking he would rather be anywhere else than with me to being on the bed together talking about us kissing. I needed to catch up to it all.

'I don't know,' I admitted. I was terrified of being hurt again. I didn't think Ethan would ever intentionally hurt me, but how could I be sure? And this attraction was confusing. Ethan wasn't like anyone else I'd been with. It was unexpected.

Ethan nodded. 'Then we wait until you're really sure. I won't kiss you unless you ask me to, Tessa.' Ethan's eyes seemed to blaze then. He leaned in towards my ear and whispered, 'Maybe until you beg me.'

My breath hitched.

Ethan pulled back and looked at me. I had a feeling my eyes were just as dark as his. I bit my lip. And his curled into a smile. 'Hmm, I have a feeling you quite like that idea.'

My breathing had definitely turned ragged. 'You'll have to wait and see, won't you?' I murmured.

'Yeah, I guess I will. Well, I know what I'll be thinking about all day...' He sat up and climbed off the bed, glancing at me over his shoulder. His clothes were crumpled but the effect worked on him. 'You begging me and me doing exactly what you want me to.'

My mouth fell open and he chuckled.

'I need to get ready for my course; it's an early start today.' I watched him walk to the bedroom door. 'How about dinner when I get back?'

I could only nod, stunned by what he'd said about begging him. And how much I wanted to.

God, that was... hot. Ethan could be sexy? I found Ethan sexy? Well, fuck.

I felt light-headed and a little bit dizzy, like I'd just stepped off a roller-coaster.

I flopped back on the pillows when he left and exhaled loudly and slowly.

My phone buzzed on the bedside table. It was a message from Juliette.

> Brunch? I only take yes as the answer.

Smiling at the way she'd written it, I replied to agree to the plan, my stomach rumbling in anticipation. Brunch and girl talk after last night and this morning sounded perfect to me.

* * *

I met Juliette at a small bistro close to the Louvre. The rain had cleared and there was a hint of sunshine between the clouds as I walked there from the apartment. I scrolled through the photos on Instagram from last night and saw that I looked the happiest I had in a very long time.

As I approached the bistro, I noticed that Carly had liked the one Juliette had taken of me and Ethan holding our drinks up at the camera, cheesy smiles on our faces.

I opened up WhatsApp and messaged her.

> Okay, you were right.

> I always am but what about specifically this time?

> Paris being a good idea!

> You looked like you were having fun last night.

Then she added five winking emojis.

> It was a really good night. How are you? Feeling better I hope?

> It's weird, it feels like I'm about to get the flu but nothing is appearing, very odd. Just taking it easy working from home on the sofa. I miss you!

> I miss you too. Not long until I'm back in London, don't worry.

As I put my phone away, I felt a bit sad at the thought of returning home. The change of scenery and company had been more healing than I thought it would be. I still hadn't put pen to paper so to speak, or more literally, fingertips to laptop keys, but the prospect of writing a story about a woman going through something similar to me wasn't quite as daunting as it had been when I arrived in Paris. Whether I could actually write the story was another matter, but one step at a time.

As I opened the door to the bistro, soft French music floated out to greet me. It was cosy with a polished wooden floor, velvet chairs and funky lights hanging from the ceiling. Juliette waved to me from a corner table, and I went over. She got up and kissed me, then we sat down and I slipped off my coat.

'It's unfair how good you look after last night,' I told her as I looked across and was struck again by her flawless skin and hair. I was sure I was the colour of stone.

Juliette shook her head. 'You're too sweet. I didn't even bother with makeup today. I need all the coffee this morning. You?'

'I can't drink coffee,' I admitted.

She looked outraged.

'I'm sorry, I just need tea.'

Juliette called the waiter over and ordered the basket of croissants and pastries, a coffee for her and tea for me. 'So,' she said when we were alone, propping her elbows on the table opposite me. 'We need to gossip about men. Have you fucked Ethan yet?'

I coughed. 'What?!' I mean, Carly was always honest with me, but that was direct and a half.

She smiled and shrugged. 'Sorry, I sensed that there might be something between you two. And you're in a one-bedroom apartment.'

'Um, well, no, we didn't really know each other until Paris, and it's complicated with me recently breaking up with his best friend after all.'

'Joe is not a nice man, is he? I met him once and I didn't like him.'

'Where were you six months ago?' I sighed. 'The more I get to know Ethan, the more I can't believe they are best friends, to be honest.'

'Ah. I know why,' she said. The waiter came back with our order, so we paused to take a sip of our drinks and a bite of freshly warmed croissants. 'You are ready for the story?'

I nodded eagerly. 'Yes, please. Because they are so different.'

'Hmm. Well, they met at boarding school. Ethan got in on a scholarship; he's really clever. Joe was there because he's from a rich family.' I smiled, liking how matter-of-fact she was. 'Ethan lost his mother young. He never knew his father. Joe and his family almost unofficially adopted him, I think that's what you say? They had him at their big country house every holiday, bought him things he could never afford on his own and when it was clear he wanted to be a chef, Joe's father paid for him to study.'

'Wow. So, they are more like brothers.' I understood their relationship much more now. 'I guess Ethan maybe feels a debt towards Joe then.'

Juliette waved her hand in the air. 'Debt? Yes! This is why he won't open a restaurant with me.'

'I had no idea you wanted to do that.'

'Well, you know I work in my family's restaurant?'

I nodded as I chewed my pastry, hanging on her every word.

'I would love my own place and when I met Ethan, we had the same dream. To open a place mixing French with English, but he won't do it until he pays Joe and his family back.'

'Because they paid for him to study?'

Juliette nodded. 'He is very... What's the word?'

'Proud?'

'Yes. His pride means he feels he has to do that before we can have a restaurant, and he won't let me pay for it myself; he wants us to be partners.' Juliette shrugged. 'So, we are stuck for now. And that's why they are friends, because of how much they have helped him.'

I admired Ethan for wanting to pay back his debt, as he saw it. And for being loyal to Joe, who I was certain hadn't done much to deserve it.

'But I know that he hates what Joe did to you,' Juliette added.

'We did talk a bit about that last night,' I said.

'I wish he would ditch Joe. Joe is mean to him,' Juliette said.

'He is? Ethan did say he makes comments about his height...'

'Joe likes to make people feel bad about themselves.'

I nodded. 'You're right. He does. I felt pretty shit about myself the whole time I was with him, and afterwards. I'm only just starting to feel like it wasn't all my fault. Meeting Ethan has helped with that.'

'Joe never introduced you two?'

'To hide his cheating, Joe kept me away from his friends. I only met Ethan twice really briefly. That's why it's been so strange getting to know him so much this week.'

'But you like getting to know him?' She smiled as I blushed. 'Hmm. Well, I heard Joe putting him down, making jokes about him, and it pissed me off. Is Joe a good man? No. He has looks and a fancy city job. Joe said being a chef is not a manly job.' She scoffed. 'Joe isn't manly to me. I think Ethan can be jealous of Joe, but I also believe that Joe is jealous of Ethan.'

I thought about that. 'Ethan said Joe can't do what he really wants because of his family; he probably envies Ethan's freedom. And he must see Ethan as a better man than he ever will be. Sorry if I sound bitter but he really made me think he loved me and all the time, he was with another woman.'

Juliette tutted. 'Bastard.'

I nodded in agreement. 'Yes. It's kind of put me off men, relationships, all of it. I'm finding it hard to write my next book because I don't know if love is really just all bullshit.'

She grinned. 'Bullshit, yes, but it makes the world go around. And you must see Ethan is nothing like Joe. And the way he was looking at you last night, Ethan thinks you're incredible. And you deserve a man who thinks like that.'

My cheeks were now bright pink. 'Well, that's sweet. I don't know. Ethan's becoming a good friend. I don't want to ruin that by...'

'Fucking him?'

'Exactly. But...' I took a sip of tea. 'This morning, I thought about it. Fucking him, I mean. Well, just kissing, actually; I'm British after all.'

Juliette burst out laughing. 'I love you, Tessa, and I can see why Ethan is hooked.'

'A man has never been hooked on me, I can promise you that. I need to be more like you, Juliette, and keep my heart to myself.'

'No,' she said, so quickly and firmly I was taken aback. 'You know why I am the way I am? Because I've never found anyone I'm willing to risk my heart on. But if I did find it, if you found it, then we must risk it. Don't you think?'

'That, Juliette, is the million-dollar question.'

'I don't understand.'

I laughed. 'It probably doesn't translate. The thing is, I've been burnt once. I'm not sure I can ever risk it again.'

'You will when it feels right. The same about your writing. When you're ready, it will come back.'

She sounded so certain, I envied her. I wasn't sure I was certain about anything any more. But maybe that was okay.

Maybe you have to become lost so you can find exactly what you're looking for.

13

The sun came out in the afternoon so I took a mug of tea and my laptop out onto the balcony to enjoy it at the small table out there. I opened up the document I had titled 'Book Three' at Christmas. It had remained a blank space since then. Writing used to not only feel easy, it was also a need. When working my last novel, I'd stayed up all night to write the ending – I was so inspired, so desperate to get the words floating around in my head onto my laptop. My fingers tapped away at the keys so furiously, I worried the neighbours might complain. But now, my laptop was like an object I didn't know how to use.

I took a deep breath and typed out the two words that used to fill me with excitement. *Chapter One.*

At least it's no longer a blank page!

I picked up my phone and took a picture of my set up on the balcony. It looked like a writer's dream. Even though I hadn't actually written anything, I posted it on Instagram with the caption:

#amwriting

Stevie from Turn the Pages commented on it instantly.

I can't wait to read this!

My editor Gita liked it. Then Carly responded.

I'm coming on the next research trip!

The likes flew in rapidly. Then one name caught my eye.

'What?' I almost spilled my tea everywhere. Hastily, I moved my mug away from my laptop and stared at my phone. Yep, there it was. The last name I wanted to see in my Instagram notifications.

JoeHarrison10 liked this

I had unfollowed my ex on Instagram but I knew he hadn't unfollowed me. I debated blocking him but I didn't want him to think I cared. So, he was not only still looking at my posts but was now interacting with them.

What the fuck?

Any hope I had of coming up with some words for the first chapter disappeared in a puff of smoke. I closed the laptop and put my head in my hands.

In my existential crisis, I missed the apartment door opening, so when a voice spoke in the balcony entrance, I jumped.

'Uh oh, what happened?'

I lifted my head to see Ethan leaning against the doorframe, looking down at me with concern.

'Just opened my laptop to try to write something, then shut it right back up again. I'm a failure.'

'You need to be kind to yourself,' he said, shaking his head. 'You've been through a lot. Creativity doesn't come when we want it to at the best of times; when you're not feeling yourself, you're not going to be inspired. That's what this trip is for, right? A chance to get yourself back. The words will come when you feel that.'

I stared at him. 'You're a wise man, Ethan Taylor.'

He grinned. 'Always easier to give advice to other people.' He saw my phone on the table lighting up. 'You're popular today.'

'Oh, yeah, well, everyone thinks a balcony in Paris is inspiring,' I said, gesturing around us. 'And it is beautiful. It's just not helping.'

'*Yet*. Not helping *yet*,' Ethan corrected. 'There's still time. If you want to take your mind off it, I do have an invite for tonight.'

'Oh yeah?'

'It's Juliette's brother's birthday. Juliette is having people over to her apartment. I know you don't like parties but we could show our faces, have a drink then escape?'

The word 'we' hung in the air.

I like it more than I know I should.

I nodded. 'Okay,' I said, wishing that word hadn't enveloped me in warmth like a hug. I got up from the table and followed Ethan back inside, carrying my laptop in and putting it on the coffee table. I shoved my phone in my pocket, not wanting to see Joe's name on my screen again. I thought about telling Ethan but that felt like it would be giving Joe even more power. I didn't want him to know seeing his like on my post had even registered in my brain.

'How about pasta to fuel us?' Ethan said then, wandering to the kitchen.

'You might be the best roommate,' I replied.

'Ah, now I see why you've let me stay: it's not for my company, it's for my food.' He began taking ingredients out of a bag on the counter. He looked up at me and grinned.

I smiled back. Ethan somehow made everything feel better. 'You caught me.'

His smile faltered a little bit. 'I just thought I should check: I know last night you asked me to stay, but...' He started to chop vegetables. 'Are you sure? I mean, if we're going to Juliette's then I could stay there tonight if you want...' He trailed off again. I could feel his awkwardness. I kind of liked it that he was as unsure as me about all of this. It made a change. Usually I was the one overthinking in relationships. I wondered now if it showed I had cared more than the other person every time. Or they had made me feel unsure. I wanted someone to let me feel sure.

'I still want you to stay. If you do too,' I said, braving the honesty again. Ethan made me want to be honest. Made me want to say things I usually just said in my own head.

He glanced up at me. 'Great,' he said.

I cleared my throat. 'So, how was your course today?' I asked, climbing up on one of the bar stools to watch him cook, hiding how wide my smile was to hear him say he wanted to stay as well.

Ethan tutted. 'Not great. A customer complained about their meal and the chef went out into the restaurant and told him they had no taste and to get out.'

'I can't believe the chef acted like that! Is he not worried people will stop coming to his restaurant?'

'I think he kind of leans in to that stereotypical, aggressive-chef persona. Thinks it's part of his brand now. And to be fair, that dish was perfect and the customer seemed to be trying it on, hoping to get it for free. People were filming. It's blowing up on social media so you probably won't be able to get a table there for months now. His food is exquisite, otherwise I would have fled by now,' Ethan said as he chopped basil. I watched his dexterity with the knife in awe. I would slice my fingers off if I attempted to chop like that.

'What's your favourite French saying?' I asked after a moment.

Ethan considered the question. '*La vie est trop courte pour boire du mauvais vin.* Life is too short to drink bad wine.'

I chuckled. 'Amen to that. Shall I get us some?'

'After today? Hell, yes.'

I poured us both a glass of French red wine. I raised my glass and he clinked his against mine. 'I think you're right about what you said just now – about being kind to myself. I've been beating myself up these past few weeks about not being able to write. And I know that's making this block worse. My friends persuaded me to come on this trip so I could take inspiration from the City of Love, but maybe it's more about taking time for myself. Hanging out with you and Juliette, it's been really fun; it's meant I haven't been constantly worrying like I was at home. Don't get me wrong, I'm terrified about this deadline and having to write a romantic story,' I said, grimacing at the word *romantic*. I watched as Ethan tipped the vegetables into a pan on the hob. 'But trying to make myself do it isn't working. I need to try to chill.'

'I get the impression chilling isn't very you?' Ethan smiled over his shoulder at me.

'My default is worry and anxiety, but you are inspiring me. You are very chill.'

'Not always. I have worries. I worry about the future, and people I care about, but I know that worrying won't stop bad things happening. I'd rather try to take things as they come, as much as I can.'

'God, I want to be like that.'

'You shouldn't try to be anyone but who you are, Tessa.'

I stared at his back, surprised at the very sudden prickling feeling behind my eyes. If I was honest, my six months with Joe had made me feel that I was lacking in some way. That I needed to change if I was going to find someone to love me. That a man like Joe needed more than me. But maybe it was actually the other way round and I needed more than Joe. Maybe I was okay after all. Maybe I could just be myself.

I eyed Ethan. 'Can I say something?'

'Hmm,' he said, arching an eyebrow.

'You and Joe are so different,' I blurted out. 'I can't picture how you even became friends. Juliette mentioned you've been friends since you were really young though?' I wanted to hear Ethan tell me their story.

He glanced back at me again. 'Yeah, we met at boarding school. I got a scholarship and a lot of that was due to my love of cricket. They took it very seriously. Joe was a great player on the team, and that bonded us. My dad was never around and my mum worked a lot so Joe invited me to stay one holiday, and that was it. It became tradition. We'd play cricket, he taught me to ride, their cook let me in the kitchen, and I don't know, his family became like mine. Especially when my mum died. And my dad disappeared from my life for good.'

'I'm so sorry, Ethan.'

He nodded. 'I was fifteen. It was a shit time. Joe and his family were there for me. Brothers don't always get on or aren't always alike, are they? But they are still brothers. I guess that's how it's always been with us, but...' He ran a hand through his hair. 'As we got older, we realised we are different. I don't always agree with him and he knows it. I suppose we stay friends because our past bonds us. But I don't know what will happen in the future. Listen, Tessa, I don't agree with how he strung you and Rachel along at all. And he knows that. That's why he didn't want us hanging out.'

I nodded. 'I should have realised something was up with how Joe kept me away from the people in his life. I didn't even meet his family, not once. I was really blind.'

'It's his fault, not yours,' Ethan said simply.

I wish I could see it as that black and white.

'So, you know all about my ex – what about yours?' I asked curiously. 'There hasn't been anyone you've wanted to settle down with?'

'I had a girlfriend for about three years. We met when we were both studying to be chefs,' he said. 'But we were both really focused on our careers. I got the offer to live and work in Paris and I took it. She didn't want to come and I understood. I suppose it came down to us not seeing our future together. My career is really important to me like yours is, but for the right woman, I would want to settle down, yeah. Get married, but I don't really see myself having a family though.'

'I know what you mean,' I said, nodding. 'Is it because of your father?'

'This is getting very deep,' he replied.

'You don't have to—'

'I told you, I like talking to you,' he cut in. 'I don't want to be like him and if there is the slightest chance, I don't want to take the risk. What about you?'

'My parents are still together, we get on well, but I don't know. I like life in the city, writing when I want to. Like you say, it's always been important to me. Which is why I feel so lost right now. I always pictured myself getting married but not necessarily having a family. I suppose it depends on who I end up with and what we envision for our life together.'

'Listening to you, I can't picture you two together. Joe is all about the family life. I know he pictures his wife at the family country estate popping out, like, four kids.'

'He never told me that.' I frowned. 'We didn't talk about the future much, which should have been a red flag I now realise. He didn't see his future with me.'

'But you saw it with him?'

'I did at one point. I thought he might even propose on this trip here,' I said, gesturing around the apartment. 'God, I feel stupid for thinking that. Rachel was the one he wanted to marry, not me.'

'I'm not sure it's as straightforward as that,' he said carefully.

'Well,' I said with a shrug, 'like you say, maybe we were never the right fit. I think I was swept up in our romantic meeting, thinking I'd met a hero right out of one of my novels. You know what he's like.'

'Oh, yeah, he always got the girls,' Ethan said. 'As he never fails to remind me,' he added dryly.

'But does he ever keep them?' I asked.

Ethan turned and met my eyes and shook his head. 'No, and definitely not the ones worth keeping.'

I tried not to get carried away thinking I might fit into that category, but as we held each other's gaze, something passed between us. A thread of connection that I hadn't seen coming. But a thread that I didn't want to break yet. I took a gulp of wine to help steady myself because I was suddenly filled with want. Want to kiss the man who had just told me to be myself. Something I had longed for Joe to do but he had never done.

'Thank you,' I choked out. 'You're so sweet, Ethan.'

He turned away and poured pasta into boiling water. For a minute, I wasn't sure he'd heard me but then I saw his shoulders slump. 'That's what they tell me,' he muttered as if it wasn't quite meant for my ears.

14

Ethan was quiet while we ate our pasta, then we split up to get ready for Juliette's brother's party. When I came out of the bedroom, Ethan was on the sofa with another glass of wine, scrolling on his phone. He looked up and did a double take. 'You're stunning,' he said. Then he coughed like he'd been too honest. 'I mean, you look nice... great... I, uh, like the outfit.'

I smiled, trying not to feel too pleased, but it was hard not to. I was wearing a faded t-shirt tucked into leather trousers with my ankle boots, and slung over my shoulders was my black blazer. I'd curled my hair and done my eyes smoky for the occasion. Ethan seemed taken aback by both how I looked and how he'd complimented it.

'Thank you. I like your shirt,' I said, noticing that he'd put on a dark shirt and trousers. They suited him. 'Oh, it's sparkling.' I moved towards the balcony to look at the Eiffel Tower. 'The perfect start to the night,' I said, smiling at the lights. 'How is this city so magical somehow?'

'I love seeing it through your eyes,' Ethan said quietly, standing up and coming over to stand beside me. 'I kind of stopped looking at it.' He nodded at the Tower. 'But it's beautiful.'

'We forget to look at beautiful things and appreciate them, don't we? I'm the same when I suddenly remember to look up at sunrise or sunset. It's always worth it.'

'You're right.' Ethan smiled across at me. 'So, shall we go to the party? And I meant what I said about not having to stay long. Although I think Juliette has everyone eager to meet her new English friend who writes romance.'

'Oh God, I hope the birthday boy takes the attention away from me,' I said, biting my lip. There was nothing I hated more than being the focus of a group of people.

'I wouldn't count on it,' Ethan murmured. His hand grazed the small of my back as I stepped off the balcony in front of him. I was surprised that it didn't feel strange. It felt familiar. I grabbed my handbag as he closed the doors to the balcony, and he picked up a gift bag from the kitchen counter as we left the apartment. 'I got Seb his favourite bottle of whisky,' he said when I raised my eyebrow at it.

We walked out of the building and Ethan led the way around the corner to another apartment building.

'Juliette's place,' he said when we reached the main doors. 'She and Seb are always at the family restaurant so they said they wanted to have the party here instead.'

Juliette's apartment building was more modern than the one we were staying in and when we reached her floor, we saw the door was open. French music with heavy bass was playing loudly.

'Her neighbours must be a relaxed bunch,' I said as we headed inside.

'I suspect, knowing Juliette and how she makes friends so easily, they are all here.'

I looked around. The apartment was packed with people. There was a long table set up with drinks and canapés, and hanging from the ceiling were LED candles, making the place look magical.

'Tessa! Ethan!' Juliette appeared out of nowhere, kissing us both on the cheeks, a cloud of Chanel No.5 perfume floating around her. She was wearing bright-red lipstick that imprinted on our cheeks and a skin-tight black dress, making her figure look even more stunning. 'Ethan, you handsome man!' she shouted over the music. 'And Tessa, *trés jolie*. That blazer, I must have it.'

'*Merci beaucoup*,' I said back loudly. 'I know some French,' I added to

Ethan, who was grinning at my bad accent. 'You look gorgeous, Juliette. Thanks for inviting me.'

'You're part of us now,' she replied with a wave of her hand. Her words warmed me from the inside out. She pointed though the crowd. 'Seb is over there with that detestable man Alain,' she said with a grimace. 'Oh, Celine, there you are!' She disappeared again and Ethan and I exchanged a smile.

'Let me introduce you,' Ethan said. He held out his hand and I took it, letting him weave me through the people in the living room towards the kitchen. I could tell who Seb was instantly; he looked so similar to Juliette and wore all black like she did. Ethan hugged Seb and gave him the whisky, wishing him a happy birthday and then leaned back. 'This is Tessa,' he said.

Seb grinned. '*Enchantée.* My sister hasn't stopped talking about you,' he said, kissing me on both cheeks.

'I can see why,' the man with him declared. Alain was introduced as Seb's friend from university. He was tall and dark and very much my type. 'Excuse my English but I will die if you're not single.'

'Ignore him, he knows exactly what he's saying,' Seb said as I blushed.

'Shut up, Seb,' Alain snapped. He leaned in so close, I took a step back. 'You really are a pretty little thing, aren't you? I could show you a good time if you let me, darling.'

I understood why Juliette had called him detestable. He was sleazy with a capital S. Very much not my type after all.

'No thanks,' I said firmly. I looked at Ethan, who was staring at us. 'Can we get a drink, please?'

'Hell, yes. Excuse us.' Ethan took my hand again and led me firmly away from Alain and into the kitchen. 'What a twat,' he said angrily, shaking his head.

I shrugged. 'He's good looking, probably thinks he can get away with it.'

'I can't see the attraction personally,' Ethan said. 'Wine?' I nodded and he poured us both a glass. 'I hate it when people think someone must find them attractive. I mean, does that give you the right to treat people like a piece of meat?'

'Preaching to the choir here,' I said, raising my wine glass. I took a long gulp. 'I'm avoiding all tall, dark and handsome men from now on.'

'Should I be offended or pleased I'm not classed as one of them?' Ethan said. He smiled but it didn't quite reach his eyes.

It was funny. Ethan wasn't like anyone I'd fancied before. I doubted I would have noticed him at this party if we hadn't come to it together, but he had an energy about him. It was the calmness. I felt drawn to it, as someone opposite to that calm, I supposed. He felt like a safe port even though I didn't know him all that well still. I remembered telling Carly when were younger that I never wanted to be with a man who wasn't taller than me, but that felt spectacularly shallow now. Ethan being my height meant I could easily look into those blue eyes of his and find them gazing back at me. A warm feeling ran through my body from his attention.

'Neither of us are tall or dark,' I said, leaning in so he could hear me. 'But of course, you're handsome.' I'd had a couple of glasses of wine, which meant that was easier to say without wanting to melt into my shoes from embarrassment. I wasn't lying. Those eyes but also his warm smile, his soft hair, his cosy jumpers, his voice when he spoke in French, it was all attractive. And maybe more so because you had to really look at him to see it. And I had been looking at him a lot the past couple of days.

'And sweet?' Ethan was looking at me with an expression I couldn't read.

'Sweet is good,' I insisted.

He shook his head. 'So, want to meet more people or see my favourite part of Juliette's apartment?'

'You already know the answer.'

* * *

I followed Ethan down a few steps until we were in a small, cosy room. A whole wall was made up of shelves with vinyl records stacked in rows, and there was a sofa and two beanbags plus a fur rug and a record player in the corner. The party suddenly seemed very far away.

'This is so cool,' I said, going over to look at the records. 'Juliette has a huge collection.'

'She loves music. She can sing beautifully. I think one time she wanted to be a singer, but then it's hard when you have a family business, you know?'

'Juliette told me at brunch that she wants to open her own restaurant,' I said, walking across the wall to look at all the record spines. 'With you.'

Ethan turned to me. 'She told you? Yeah, that is the dream.'

'It would be amazing. I'd be first in line.'

'Yeah?'

'Now you know I like fancy food.' I nudged him playfully.

Ethan went to put a record on the player. 'It's a long way off.'

'Because of Joe?'

Ethan's hand stilled. 'I don't want to talk about Joe right now.'

'I get it. But I understand why you feel like you have to pay him back. He has a way of making you feel like, I don't know, you owe him something.' I sighed. I remembered when Joe bought me a necklace for my birthday. He made such a big deal about how expensive it was, it made me feel uneasy to wear it. I had left it at the flat we shared when I moved out. I had felt relieved not having it any more.

'And yet you moved in with him,' Ethan said as a dreamy French song started playing. The singer was full of emotion so even though I couldn't understand what she was singing about, goosebumps pricked up along my arms. We looked across at one another. 'You'd never describe Joe as sweet.'

Was that why he was upset – because I called him sweet? I crossed the room quickly to stand in front of him. 'No, I wouldn't, but surely you don't want to be anything like him?'

Ethan sighed. 'No.' He looked at me. 'Are you still in love with him?'

I shook my head. 'No. I'm not sure I ever was, to be honest. Because I didn't know him; he didn't let me in. It was all superficial. Yeah, he's good looking, he's generous, he was fun and he was great company, but we never really talked. About our feelings, what he wanted from life, what we thought about... I don't know...' I trailed off and thought back to looking at the sparkling Eiffel Tower with Ethan. 'About noticing the beauty of the world. He never told me to be myself. I never told him how much I worry about things.' I stepped closer. Ethan's eyes were warm but uncertain as he looked back at me. 'I don't think it was ever real. That's what hurt the most. That I wasted six months thinking I'd found something that I hadn't.'

'You wish it had worked out though?'

'Because I want to believe in happy endings again, not because I want one with Joe.'

'Dance with me.'

'Huh?'

Ethan had wrong footed me. His arm came around my waist.

'Please?'

'Okay.' I wrapped my arms around his neck as he pulled me closer and we moved in slow circles to the beautiful song he had put on. I could count on one hand the number of times in my life I'd slow danced with a man. I had a scene in one of my novels where the main characters dance and readers always said that moment melted their hearts. This was really tugging at my romance-author heartstrings. I felt myself melt into him.

I leaned against Ethan's shoulder and his hands tightened on my waist. He felt strong and steady. My heart started to thump inside my chest at his closeness and how much I was enjoying it.

'I want you to know that I noticed you, Tessa,' Ethan said then, leaning close to my ear. 'That night Joe brought you to meet us. I know it was really brief but... I thought you were beautiful.'

I pulled back to look into his eyes. 'You didn't notice me that night,' I said, my voice barely above a whisper.

'I noticed you, Tessa.'

I couldn't lie. I hadn't noticed Ethan. I'd been so nervous, so desperate to make Joe's friends like me, so eager for his approval, to make him happy, all I'd paid attention to was him. Then I'd felt so confused that he'd swept me in and out of that bar so fast, not introducing me to anyone, worried he was ashamed of me – I'd felt like a failure of a girlfriend. I hated how he had manipulated the situation to make me feel bad to cover up his cheating.

'I wish I had noticed you too,' I said honestly. 'But we are here now, aren't we?'

Ethan started to say something, but voices in the doorway broke us apart.

Juliette appeared, Oscar and Seb behind her, a bottle of tequila in her hand. 'Shots, everyone?' She saw us step back from one another. 'Shit, are we interrupting?'

'No,' Ethan said, too quickly. I glanced at him. 'Shots sound perfect to me.' He avoided my eyes. Seb handed around shot glasses and Oscar poured out the tequila. I gripped my glass, my heart still beating faster than normal.

Ethan noticed me. He thought I was beautiful before Paris.

My mind was whirring.

'Perfect, let's raise a toast, yes? To my baby brother, I cannot believe you are twenty-six. To all your dreams coming true!' Juliette said, raising her shot glass in the air.

We joined in the toast then all poured the tequila down our throats. I shuddered at the burn. Oscar immediately poured another and this time, he toasted Seb, then it was Ethan's turn.

'You are like the brother I never had,' Ethan said. His toast was so simple, but Seb looked really emotional at his words and clapped him on the back.

Then a final round was poured out and they all looked at me expectantly.

'Oh.' I shifted on my feet, nervous. I was feeling very light-headed from the shots. 'Happy birthday, Seb. I hope you have a wonderful year. How do I say "Cheers" in French?'

'*Santé!*' they all chorused, and we drank our final shot.

Oscar pulled out his phone. 'A picture for Instagram.' They all crouched down around me. Juliette slung an arm over my shoulders and Oscar snapped a few pictures of us. 'I'll tag you all!' he said, typing into his phone.

I pulled my phoned out and looked at the photos Oscar had shared. Ethan was next to me in the picture, barely touching me, but I had felt that touch everywhere.

15

I walked around Juliette's apartment, trying to find Ethan. After we'd had shots, we'd all gone back up to the party and he'd faded into the crowd. I wanted to talk to him. To carry on that conversation. To have him look at me again the way he'd been looking at me. I couldn't get his words out of my head. I wanted to hear more. I couldn't help it. It was like I was hooked on Ethan talking to me.

As I walked through a group of people, I finally spotted him.

And my heart sunk.

Ethan stood in a corner talking to a woman I hadn't seen before. She was smaller than him, leaning against the wall as he stood close to her, talking into her ear. She was smiling up at him, a definite flirtatious look in her eyes. I stopped walking and watched. Ethan ran a hand through his hair and smiled back. That cute smile that he used when he talked to me. I was annoyed he was using it to talk to her. I wanted him to be talking to me. But I knew I hadn't earned that right at all.

'Go over there.'

I jumped when Juliette was suddenly beside me. 'I don't want to interrupt.'

'Yes, yes, you do,' she said.

'That would be selfish. I'm not ready for...' I looked at her. 'Joe hurt me so much; I wouldn't want to ever hurt someone else like that. What if I hurt Ethan?'

'I will kill you.' She saw my face and she took my hand and squeezed it. 'Ethan gets a say, Tessa. You haven't told him you like him, so tell him and see what he says.'

'It's come out of nowhere.'

'Has it?' She tipped her head.

I bit my lip. I remembered Ethan that first day in the apartment walking out of the bathroom in just his towel. I could have turned around and gone straight back home. But I hadn't. I told myself it was because of my career, that I needed to try to get inspiration from Paris, but maybe part of me had been intrigued to be in the space with Ethan. To share the apartment with him.

Maybe I wanted to get to know him.

'When I came back,' Juliette continued, 'Ethan asked if he could stay with me. I said of course but did he really want to, and he said if you wanted him to go, he would, but he hasn't turned up at my door with his suitcase, has he?'

I swallowed. 'No. I didn't ask him to go. I don't want him to go.'

Juliette nodded. 'And he doesn't want to go either.'

I turned back to see Ethan looking over at us. I smiled at him.

Juliette kissed my cheek. 'Go home, Tessa. I'll call you tomorrow.' She disappeared back into the crowd.

Taking a fortifying breath, I walked over. 'I want to go home,' I said to Ethan over the music. I could feel the woman he was with looking at me curiously. 'Will you come with me?'

If he was surprised, he didn't show it. 'Meet me outside,' he said before turning back to her. I nodded and set off, trying to hold back the nerves that suddenly fluttered through my body. There was a reason neither of us had run from sharing the apartment together. It thrilled and terrified me.

As I stepped outside the party, my phone buzzed in my bag. I looked at the screen. My stomach somersaulted. It was Joe.

Joe was calling me.

What the hell?

'Tessa?' Ethan was beside me then, noticing my stunned expression. I held up the screen so he could see. 'Oh. Do you want to take it?' he asked slowly.

I wavered. On one hand, I never wanted to speak to Joe again after how much he hurt me. But there was curiosity too. Why was he calling me now, after two months of no contact? I looked up into Ethan's eyes. 'No.' I cancelled the call and put my phone away. 'No, I want to walk home with you.'

Ethan didn't say anything, but he held out his hand and I took it. We walked out of Juliette's building together. Ethan's fingers threaded through mine were warm, and they felt like they belonged in mine. It was comfortable, familiar, like we always walked holding hands. But they made me nervous too. Especially after that call from Joe. I had once imagined I belonged with him.

I stole glances at Ethan as we strolled in silence to our apartment. He smiled across at me. Relaxed, easy. Like this was nothing to be worried about. I felt calmer instantly. Being with Ethan was like putting drops of Rescue Remedy on your tongue.

'Are you okay?' he asked me. 'About Joe calling you?'

'I don't understand why he was,' I said. 'I wish he hadn't. Especially tonight.' I wished I could stop myself from wondering what he was going to say to me. But it was there. I tried to focus on Ethan again. I knew that was the best thing for me.

'This is complicated,' Ethan said, shaking his head, but he kept hold of my hand as we reached our building. We walked up to our apartment and Ethan held the door open for me. He followed me inside and turned on a light. We took off our jackets and tossed them aside. And then we faced each other.

'I don't want him to come between us,' I blurted out.

'He's already there though, isn't he? I only first saw you because he brought you into that bar. I'm only here with you because of him...' Ethan paused and walked to the sofa and sank down into it. 'I wish we had met in a bar without him and that I'd been brave enough to walk up to you and tell you that you are beautiful, say sexy things in French to you, take you home and...' He trailed off and my imagination went wild instantly.

What would he have done? What would I have wanted him to do?

I swallowed hard. 'You were chatting up someone tonight.'

Ethan shook his head. 'No. She came up to me. I have no idea why.'

'Ethan, you know why. She was clearly flirting with you.'

'I don't think so...'

There it was. The same insecurities as me. I wanted him to know he didn't need to feel that way even if I found it hard not to myself. 'Don't act like you don't know you're cute as hell.'

He raised an eyebrow. 'I didn't realise I was. Or that that's what you thought.'

'Do you like that I think that?'

'Tessa,' he groaned, like I was causing him pain.

'We're not here together because of Joe,' I said firmly. 'Juliette made me see. When I walked in and saw you here, I could have run back home. Or you could have.' I went over and sat down next to him. 'But we didn't, did we?'

'I liked the idea of getting to know you,' Ethan said. 'I wanted to help you. I still do. I don't want you to ever be hurt again.' He reached out and squeezed my hand. 'And yeah, I like hearing that you think I'm cute. That you like my eyes and find it sexy when I speak in French. But I also know that you're not looking for anything right now. And I don't want to get hurt. And I sure as hell don't want to hurt you. Maybe I should go and stay with Juliette. Maybe staying here, you and me, just isn't a good idea.'

'But I thought you wanted to kiss me too,' I said, confused.

'God, I do. There just seems to be a hell of a lot of reasons why we shouldn't.'

Despite the situation, I giggled.

He smiled.

'The thing is, you saying we shouldn't kind of makes me want to do it more.'

Ethan cocked an eyebrow. 'I knew you had a naughty side.'

'Says the man who told me I needed to beg him to kiss me.' Heat in my body was fast replacing nerves.

'Hmm, but then you told me I was sweet.'

'Sweet is good!' I cried. Then the tequila shots mingled with my need to get closer to him made me feel fearless for a moment. I moved to sit astride his lap on the sofa. His breath hitched. 'You are sweet and kind, and you have looked after me. I feel safe with you. And they are good things. And I know you think that means I don't find you sexy, that I see you only as a friend, but that's what I want right now. In fact, it's probably what I should have been looking for all along,' I said urgently, looking into his eyes.

His hands came up to hold my waist as I placed mine on his chest. I could feel his heartbeat as fast and hard as my own.

Ethan reached up to touch my lip. 'I want you to want me. I want you to find me sexy. I want you to want me like I want you.'

It was my turn for my breath to hitch. I leaned forward to brush my lips against his.

He stilled.

'I want you to kiss me.'

Ethan smiled slowly and I caught a naughty twinkle in his own eyes then. 'I thought we already discussed this?'

I shook my head, but I smiled. 'Shameless. Fine.' I leaned forward and brushed my lips against his ear. Ethan's hands returned to my waist, holding me tighter. 'Ethan, will you please kiss me? I want you to. I need you to.' I pulled back to look into his darkened eyes.

'Tessa, with you on my lap looking at me like that, asking me to kiss you, I feel like the sexiest man alive,' he said huskily. He reached up to brush my hair back softly, a smile playing on his lips. He put one of his hands under my chin and drew me back in. When his lips touched mine, I shivered. Ethan wrapped his arms around me and I hooked mine around his shoulders as my mouth melted into his. He kissed me slowly and deeply, murmuring as he pulled me closer, his tongue caressing mine. His hands moved up to my back, stroking me through my T-shirt.

I shifted myself forward on his lap and Ethan groaned into my mouth. I could feel him through my jeans and couldn't resist rocking against him to help ease my own growing ache.

Ethan then broke away from my lips and dropped frantic kisses down my neck, making me shiver again. 'We're taking our time,' he said softly, between kisses. 'I'm not rushing this; I'm not messing this up.'

'Hmmm,' I said as his mouth came back onto mine. This time, the kiss was hungrier. I had wondered what Ethan's kisses would feel like. And they felt like he was kissing a part of me that had never been touched before. Like deep in my soul. I could feel his kiss right down to the tips of my toes. I wanted to be closer to him. To connect with him like I never had with a man before.

I trembled as he pulled away from my mouth to kiss me softly on my cheeks, then my forehead, then my nose, then across my jaw. 'It would feel good to speed it up a little bit though? Like your hands could be under my shirt right now,' I whispered between his kisses. 'Or you could just take it off.'

Ethan suddenly stood up. I clung with my legs around his waist. 'I'm taking you to bed,' he said.

'That works for me,' I replied, pulling him back for a kiss, but he just kissed me once then pulled away and carried me wrapped around him into the bedroom.

Ethan leaned down and slid me gently off him onto the bed. 'Goodnight, Tessa,' he said, looking down at me with longing in his eyes.

'Goodnight? What do you mean?'

'I should go,' he said.

I looked up at him standing by the bed, straining against his jeans. I was breathless from his kisses. I was hot and horny. 'Are you serious?' I choked out.

'Slowly,' he said. 'You need this to move slowly. We both do. I can't... this can't be a one-night thing for me.'

'Oh.' I couldn't help it; I felt the sting of rejection.

It flooded back. How rejected I had felt when I realised Joe had been cheating on me. That he had taken *her* to that party. That when I said I was leaving him, he didn't try to stop me. That he had chosen Rachel, not me. And here I was again. Ethan was turning me down too.

He must have seen the hurt look in my eyes because he climbed onto the bed beside me and took my hands in his, forcing me to look at him. 'You felt how much I want you. But you've been so heartbroken, you can't face writing about love any more. You just had a phone call from your ex. Who I've known since we were kids. It is complicated, even if we try to ignore that. That kiss was incredible. You are incredible. I don't want to fuck this up.'

'It's not fair,' I whispered then. 'You're only making me want you more saying that.'

He chuckled and I smiled. 'You have no idea how much I want this. But I'm going to let you sleep now.'

I squeezed his hands to stop him letting go. 'Will you stay? Just sleep with me again. Please. I really liked it.'

'I did too,' he said. 'Okay, we can do that.' He climbed off the bed. He took off his jeans and then pulled back the covers, climbing under in his T-shirt and pants. He looked at me. 'Just sleep,' he said, smiling at the look I was giving him. Because Ethan's body was extremely appealing.

I sighed. 'I promise. Just sleeping.' I couldn't help wanting to torture him a little bit though, like he had done to me. I got off the bed and stood by the side of it and pulled off my T-shirt. Glancing up, I saw that he was watching me. I unbuttoned my jeans and slid them off, so I was standing there just in my bra and underwear. I turned around, hearing him groan, and smiled to myself as I unclipped my bra and slipped it off, tossing it onto the floor. I walked to the chest of drawers to pull out a pair of pyjamas. Then I turned around.

'Jesus, Tessa,' Ethan said as I stood in front of him in only my thong.

'What? I'm getting ready for bed.'

'Come here. Please come here,' he begged me. Then shook his head. 'No, no, put the pjs on. I'm turning away.' But he didn't. He watched me as I slowly put the top on, buttoned it then pulled the bottoms on and up. When I'd finished, he exhaled loudly. He looked up at the ceiling. 'I get how many points for that?'

I laughed as I climbed into the bed. 'You're definitely going to heaven.'

'I might already be there,' he replied as I laid down beside him. He held up an arm and I scooted closer, snuggling up to his chest. His arm wrapped around me as if it had always belonged there. 'You, though, are definitely going to hell.'

I burst into laughter and he chuckled. I was having such a good time with him.

'I love hearing you laugh,' he said into my hair as he held me against him.

'I love that you make me laugh,' I murmured back, already feeling sleepy.

This thing between us, whatever it would turn out to be, felt like a breath of fresh air.

16

I woke up still snuggled up against Ethan. I opened my eyes, last night drifting back to me like the remnants of a really good dream. I looked at him sleeping, those bright-blue eyes of his closed, his chest rising with his steady breaths. I remembered the feel of his lips on mine and I smiled.

Kissing Ethan had felt as easy as breathing but sweeter than any kiss I'd had before. I ached to get closer to him. But at the same time, I understood why he had stepped on the brakes. This had been a whirlwind. I had no idea how to feel, especially after that call from Joe. He hadn't left a message or sent a text so I was in the dark as to why he had tried to contact me. I wanted to forget about him completely, but it was so hard.

My phone buzzed on the bedside table. I rolled over, wondering if it was Joe again, but it was Carly requesting to FaceTime. I grabbed my phone and as quietly as I could, I climbed out of bed and tiptoed out of the bedroom so I wouldn't wake Ethan up.

'Hi,' I said in a low voice, making my way into the kitchen to make a cup of tea.

'Why are you whispering?' Carly asked, frowning. 'Oh, you're in your pjs. I'm sorry, did I wake you up?'

'No, I had just woken up anyway,' I said, switching on the kettle as I was in desperate need of tea. 'We went to a party last night. It was eventful so I slept a long time. Are you feeling any better?'

'Your hair is a mess.'

'Gee, thanks,' I said as I leaned against the kitchen counter while I waited for the kettle to boil.

Carly peered at me suspiciously. 'I mean, it's very tousled.'

'Christ, are you a detective or something?' I looked at the doorway and lowered my voice. 'I maybe kissed Ethan a little bit.'

She shrieked. 'Tessa! You're supposed to be swearing off all men and focusing on writing!'

'I know. But you wanted me to be inspired in the City of Love, right?' I saw her look of concern. 'It's okay. It was just a kiss. I promise.'

'What was the kiss like?'

'It was really good. And, God, I want more.'

She sighed. 'I saw the Instagram picture you were tagged in; you and Ethan looked very cosy together. But you'll be careful though, won't you?' she asked me.

I shifted my feet, uncomfortable with her scrutiny. I decided to change the subject. 'Are you in the bathroom?'

'Yes. I'm taking a pregnancy test.'

I just caught my phone before I dropped it on the floor. 'What? You're what?'

'Well, you know I've been tired and feeling like I had the flu coming? Well, I realised I'm late. So, yeah...'

'You let me talk about Ethan!' I cried, forgetting to be quiet.

'I was trying to distract myself.'

'So, hang on, you're FaceTiming me while you take a pregnancy test?' I propped the phone up on the counter against the fruit bowl while I made my tea, shaking my head. 'Only you.'

'We promised when we were sixteen, we said we would always take them together,' she hissed.

I nodded. We had a friend who'd had a scare and we agreed we would never want to be alone if we had to do one. 'You couldn't wait until I come home?'

'You know Luke will be wondering why I'm not PMS-ing soon.'

'Luke is too good at buying chocolate for that,' I agreed. He knew her too well for her to hide it from him. I made my tea and took a sip. 'How do you feel?'

'I don't know. We've always said that we would have a family, but before now it felt so long off. I thought in my thirties... Then I reminded myself, I only have a couple more years until I am thirty. How did that happen?'

I nodded. 'I know. I still think of us as teenagers.'

She twirled a strand of her hair: a nervous habit. 'It's scary. I'm scared. But I have good butterflies too.'

'You guys will make the best parents,' I told her sincerely. 'And I'm godmother and aunt, okay?'

Her phone alarm buzzed. 'Oh God, it's time to look. No, Tessa, I can't do it. I don't know what I want the answer to be! Help!'

'You'll only know when you see it,' I said.

'Can you look for me?' she asked, a hopeful expression on her face.

'Seriously?' We stared at one another. Years of friendship flashed before my eyes. I'd been there for everything. So had she. This was just another chapter. 'Okay.' I took a breath and put my mug down. 'Hold it up to the screen.'

She carefully picked up the test and then slowly turned it to face the iPhone camera.

'Can you see it?' she asked. 'Tell me. But only if you think I can handle it. If you think it's good news. Will I like the answer? Tessa? Tessa?'

To my side, I could feel Ethan walking into the kitchen, but I kept my eyes on Carly. I beckoned him closer with my finger. 'Yes to it all. You're pregnant, Carly.'

'What?' She went very still.

'You're pregnant!' I cried. 'God's sake, turn the test around so you can see for yourself!'

'Oh, yeah, good idea.' She turned it slowly and her mouth fell open. 'Oh my God. Oh my God.' She stumbled backwards and hit the bath and screamed. She fell back against the basin just as the bathroom door opened.

'Are you okay? Carly? Tessa, is that you?' Luke walked in, looking confused and worried.

Carly hopped about, swearing in pain.

I bit my lip because this was just them to a T. 'Guys, you're having a baby!' I shouted, clapping my hands.

'We're what?' Luke cried.

Carly managed to hop towards him with the test.

'Are you joking?'

'We're deadly serious,' I said as Carly fell into his arms. 'Congrats, guys, I'm going to let you—'

'You're the best!' Carly cried over her shoulder. 'We love you, Auntie Tessa!'

'I can't believe you two took the test together,' Luke said, laughing as he and Carly started jumping up and down excitedly. 'Actually, I'd expect nothing else!'

'I really stubbed my toe,' Carly cried then.

'I'll speak to you later,' I called out as they leaned in to kiss, before ending the call with a grin on my face. I looked up at Ethan, who was now the other side of the kitchen counter. 'My best friend is pregnant.'

'So I gathered.' He smiled. 'They sound hilarious. That was the weirdest and most wonderful call to listen to. I'm sorry, I didn't know you were on the phone. I woke up and you'd gone and...' He trailed off uncertainly.

'Waking up with you made me happy,' I assured him. I stepped closer. 'I don't know if it made you happy but I wanted you to know that.'

'Of course it made me happy. When I saw you'd gone, I was worried in case you regretted it.' I was so close now that Ethan lifted his arms and touched my waist lightly. 'I really didn't want you to regret kissing me.'

'I don't. I think the tequila made me a bit too bold though. I can't quite believe I climbed onto your lap or that I took all my clothes off in front of you.'

His mouth twitched. 'That was the best part of the night. So, was it just for last night or can I kiss you again?'

'I'd like more,' I confessed. I reached up and wrapped my arms around his neck, stepping fully into his embrace.

Ethan leaned forward and brushed his lips against mine. I scooted closer and he kissed me again. He took his time, pulling me closer and dropping soft touches against my lips before parting them and caressing my tongue with his. I murmured and leaned against him, enjoying the strength in his arms, the warmth of his chest against mine, the way he kissed me like I was something to savour.

He then broke away from my lips and dropped soft kisses on my cheeks and along my jaw and down my neck before looking at me with a smile. 'I could kiss you all day.'

'Just kiss?' I was both impressed and frustrated with his restraint.

'I thought you'd want to take it slowly too,' he said, looking at me seriously.

I leaned back against the counter so I wasn't pressed together with him any more. I sighed. 'I know we should. You're right.' I didn't want to admit that I fancied him more than I expected I could. That I longed for him to erase the past six months. But I knew he couldn't. And I shouldn't have expected him to. I was still hurt and still scared to trust someone else. Even though deep down my heart was telling me that Ethan was a man I could trust. That I was desperate to open my heart again and trust him. 'It's just taking it slowly is even more scary than if we'd slept together last night.'

'We did sleep together,' he said softly.

I rolled my eyes. 'You know what I mean.'

Ethan reached up to stroke one of my arms. 'Why is it scary?'

'Because the longer we wait, the more feelings there will be.' I blurted out my fear even though I was embarrassed. But Ethan's honesty was addictive. I wanted to be open with him in a way I'd never been open with a man before. I didn't want to go back to who I was when I was with Joe – afraid to say what I was thinking or feeling in case he didn't like it or didn't feel the same way.

'I know,' he said. 'I'm scared too,' he added, his eyes bluer in the morning light than I'd ever seen them. I didn't know how I'd missed how gorgeous they were. 'I've never felt this way before.'

I sucked in a breath. 'I want to believe you but it's hard...' I had believed Joe loved me once and I had been burnt by that.

'I know what you mean,' Ethan said. 'I'm so different to who you were with before...'

There they were again. Our insecurities.

'These past few days with you have been unexpected for us both,' Ethan continued. 'It's complicated. I know how much you loved Joe...' He swallowed hard. 'I want to believe that you could love me one day.'

I really wanted to tell him that I could, but I wasn't sure.

'I don't want this to stop,' I said. That I *was* certain about.

He leaned in to give me another soft kiss. Then he let go of me. 'It's your last day in Paris. Do you want to spend it together?'

'Yes, please,' I said eagerly.

'I have to go to my course this morning but I'll let you know when I'll be ready to meet up and we can do something.'

'Okay,' I agreed.

I wished it wasn't going to be our last day here. I wanted to believe we would have many more days together. But I didn't want to get my hopes up and face being disappointed again either.

17

When Ethan left for his course, I took my time getting ready for the day. I had another cup of tea on the balcony to enjoy the morning view for the last time. I looked out at the Parisian architecture and skyline and took photos of it, and made a mental note of how it felt so I could write about it in my novel, hopefully soon.

I had a bubble bath and as I got ready, Juliette messaged me to see if I fancied having lunch and then to go shopping with her as she didn't have to work until tonight and wanted to hang out while Ethan was at the restaurant. I thought it sounded like a perfect way to start my final day in Paris, so I finished getting ready quickly, pulling on jeans and a jacket and leaving my hair loose.

As I walked to meet Juliette, I tried to breathe in the Paris air and calm my nerves. But it wasn't easy. I didn't want this trip to come to an end for a few reasons. I would have to face the music at home regarding my next book. I wasn't sure if I was ready to start writing it, and the deadline was getting closer by the hour. I had no idea if I could pull off a first draft when Gita was expecting it, and that would mean I'd have to confess just how behind I was. And that thought, and her reaction and the fear my publishers might be so angry they'd drop me, really made me not want to do that. I was also worried about what was going to happen with Ethan once we left Paris and our apartment. We'd spent so much time together over the past few days and now we'd be going back to our normal lives. I didn't know how we'd fit in with each other. I had no idea what was going to happen between us. Or really what I wanted after everything I'd been through with Joe. And my shaky relationship with love in general right now. I just knew I didn't want to say goodbye to him.

I'd miss Juliette and Ethan's friends too, I realised as I spotted her sat at a table outside a bistro, giving me a wave when she saw me walking towards her. She wore a trench coat with black trousers and ballet flats, her hair in a chic bun. 'I wish I was as stylish as you,' I said after we had exchanged hellos.

She stood up to kiss both my cheeks.

'You're too lovely,' she said. 'I love your style, it's very streetwear London edgy. Sit, sit.'

I joined her and looked around. We were planted on the street at a small, round table, watching people walking on by. It wasn't warm but it was dry and, in my jacket, it was enjoyable to feel the fresh breeze on my face. The waiter came and Juliette pressed me to join her in having a glass of wine. We both ordered a croque monsieur and then leaned back in our chairs.

I let out a sigh.

'What's wrong?' Juliette asked me, raising an eyebrow.

'Just kind of sucks that this is my final day in Paris,' I told her. 'And everything is up in the air!'

'I think you need to translate that...'

'Well, I was hoping Paris would inspire me to be able to write my next novel. I kind of have an idea and I've told my publisher that it will be set in Paris, but I haven't been able to start it,' I admitted. 'And there is everything with Ethan too.'

Juliette's face lit up. 'Something has happened between you, *oui*?'

'Yeah, kind of...' I found myself starting to smile just thinking about it. 'We kissed.'

'Oh, finally,' she said, leaning forward. 'It was, how you say, fireworks?'

'It was. It was one of the best kisses of my life.' Our wine arrived and Juliette clinked her glass against mine. I took a sip. The wine here was phenomenal. 'This whole trip has been unexpected.'

'That is good, *oui*?'

'Yeah, I think so. Honestly, I don't think I would have really considered Ethan if I hadn't got to know him first. Is that bad?'

'No. You have learnt that connection is the most important thing.'

'Hmmm.' I rested my hand on the wine glass. 'That's a good way of putting it.'

'I had the best sex of my life with an older man.'

I choked. 'What?' Juliette never failed to surprise me.

She shrugged. 'He is fifty, and it was hot. He made me laugh. That got me into bed.'

'Wow.' Twenty years between them, but it hadn't mattered. Did that mean the way I met Ethan didn't really matter? 'I guess you're right. We have connected. But what happens when I go back to London?'

Juliette was thoughtful for a moment. 'Do you have to?'

'What do you mean?'

'Well, if you're here for inspiration, to write your book, and you are enjoying being with Ethan and us...' She paused and looked at me. I nodded firmly. 'So, why not stay for a bit longer?'

'Huh.' It wasn't a completely crazy idea. The thought of facing my publishers in London without having written any of my book was terrifying. If I could write something before confessing I was well behind on my deadline, that would be much better. And Ethan was here for another week for his course so we wouldn't have to say goodbye yet. 'I'm not sure I could justify the money though...' I said, biting my lip. The Airbnb, if it was even available for another week, was expensive and my income depended on me writing, which I currently couldn't seem to do.

'Stay with me!' Juliette cried. 'Ethan was going to but he can easily stay with Oscar and you can have my spare room,' she beamed. 'It's perfect!'

'Oh, I couldn't possibly...'

Juliette held up her hand to stop me talking. 'We are friends, yes?' she demanded.

'Of course, yes, we are...'

'*Exactement.* So you will stay with me for however long you want to stay in Paris. Okay?'

I remembered Ethan saying that Juliette was impossible to say no to and now I knew he was completely right. I found myself nodding along. '*Oui, merci.*'

My phone beeped and I couldn't help but smile when Ethan's name appeared on the screen.

> I think I'll be ready in two hours. I'll meet you at the apartment and we can go out somewhere. xx

'Ethan wants to meet in a couple of hours,' I told Juliette.

'Lots of time to go shopping then,' she replied happily.

'What do you think Ethan will say about me staying here longer?'

'He will be happy,' she said with a smile.

'Really?'

'Of course.'

Our food arrived then and we paused our conversation. Juliette's optimism was catching. Despite so many things being up in the air, I did feel better in Paris. So maybe it did make sense to stay and see what else this city could do for me.

'I'm going to text the older man and see him tonight,' Juliette suddenly said once the waiter had left us.

I started laughing and she joined in.

After our lunch, Juliette took me to an area of Paris where there were a few vintage shops. She told me that I'd love the quirky style in them and then we'd go to a designer shop so she could find a sexy dress for her date. Juliette's appetite for life was infectious. I knew that no one was carefree all day every day, but she seemed to try hard to be. And that seemed like a great way to live.

'My best friend in London is pregnant,' I said as we looked through a rail of clothes side-by-side.

'I don't want children but I'm happy for those who do,' Juliette said. 'She is happy?'

'Yeah. She's been with her husband since we were all at school. I guess I've always wanted what they have together. But I've realised that everyone has their own relationship. And trying to find what someone else has will never work. It's like what you said about finding someone you connect with.

Not someone who seems to tick all the boxes you dreamed of when you were growing up. Joe seemed like a Disney prince to me.'

Juliette giggled. 'I can see that. But no one is perfect like that. Ethan is good for you. You smile more than when you did when you first got here.' She pulled out a stunning dress and held it up for my approval. It was something I'd never wear and for a second, I felt less than again. It was the kind of dress that Joe kept telling me he wanted to see me in. I knew Juliette would look amazing in it so I nodded for her to get it. 'Are you okay?' she asked, noticing I had gone quiet.

'Do you ever find it hard being yourself?' I blurted out.

Juliette frowned. 'Why would you want to be anyone else?'

She went to buy the dress and left me watching her go. The question hung in the air, and I knew I would be thinking about it for a long time.

* * *

When Ethan came back to the apartment, I was making a cup of tea in the kitchen and scrolling on my phone. 'How was it today?' I asked, looking up and smiling as he walked in. He was carrying something under his arm.

'It was fine although the chef was particularly demanding.' Ethan sighed. 'Honestly, I'm kind of wishing it wasn't a two-week course at this point. But I know it will be helpful if I have my own restaurant one day.' He looked unsure about it.

'You can do it,' I told him.

'Confident about my work but not your own?' Ethan smiled at me.

'Good point. Actually, I have some news on that front...' I leaned against the kitchen counter and he stepped closer.

'Oh, yeah?'

I nodded. 'Juliette had an interesting idea today. We had brunch and went shopping. I told her how I felt like it was a shame to be leaving Paris when I'm just starting to feel inspired again and she suggested I come and stay with her so I could work on my book here,' I said a little nervously in case he wasn't excited by the idea.

But Ethan instantly wrapped his arms around my waist. 'Are you going to do it?' he asked eagerly.

'I think I might...'

He leaned in and gave me a soft kiss on my lips. 'I would love you to stay longer. Obviously for selfish reasons. I want to get to know you better and do more of this...' He kissed me again. 'But also, if it will help you write again, you have to do it. Where better to write a book set in Paris than Paris itself?'

I smiled, happy he was keen for me to stay longer. 'Exactly. I have just over two weeks until my deadline and I need to get something down on the page, and soon. I haven't told my publisher how stuck I am, but they are excited for a book set in Paris so I think this could be a good plan. Juliette said I could stay with her and you could stay with Oscar once we have to leave here. What do you think?'

'Let's do it,' Ethan said. 'So...' He ran a hand through his hair. 'I got you something.' He let go of me, reached behind him and handed me a bag. 'I walked past this stall selling prints and, I don't know, this one reminded me of you.'

Curiously, I opened up the bag and pulled out the print. It was of a woman sitting in an armchair holding a book, a cup of tea beside her, and behind her was a window showing the skyline of Paris including the Eiffel Tower. To my intense embarrassment, I felt my eyes prick.

'God, what did I do?' Ethan asked, searching my eyes anxiously with his.

'No, I...' I wiped away a tear that had rolled down my cheek. 'I'm being silly. It's just I feel like you see me.' I thought about what Juliette had said about being myself. Did this gift mean Ethan was happy with who I was?

Ethan took the print and put it out of the way, then he cupped my face with his hands. 'That's not silly.'

'After I left Joe's place,' I said in a quiet voice, 'I found a flat in Putney to rent and just kind of threw my things in there and didn't bother with making it my own. This will be the first piece in there that I love.'

Ethan touched my damp cheek. 'You've had a tough time, Tessa. Be kind to yourself. You'll make the flat your home. And when we go back to London, we'll be neighbours.'

'Huh?'

'I live in Putney too and the restaurant I work in is around the corner.'

'Oh.' We looked at one another. I let myself hope that we could see each other back in London. 'That's crazy.'

'I love being able to see the river; it reminds me of looking out at the Seine here. It feels like you're in London but also very far away.'

I nodded. 'I know exactly what you mean. It's been the best part of the last two months, getting to know the area. I would love to try your restaurant.'

'A table at Bon Appétit is yours anytime,' Ethan replied. 'I didn't only get that print while I was out...' He trailed off, looking embarrassed. He showed me the other item in the bag. It was a copy of my last novel, *A Love Like Ours*. 'I want to read something that you've written. If that's okay with you?'

'Of course it is. I...' My words caught in my throat again. A man I had been with had never voluntarily read one of my novels before. 'I hope you like it,' I said shyly.

'Why wouldn't I? You wrote it, and I think it's pretty clear that I like you.' Ethan reached out and wiped another tear away from my cheek. 'Are you really okay?'

I nodded.

'So, do you want to go out somewhere? I'll take you anywhere in Paris you want to go.'

I thought about all the places I'd seen over the past five days and all the places I had yet to see in this incredible city. But then I looked around the apartment that we had shared, and would soon need to leave.

'I'd rather stay in here with you,' I admitted.

'You would?'

'It's our last afternoon in this apartment,' I said. 'It just feels...' I trailed off.

'Right,' Ethan supplied.

'*Exactement*,' I replied, copying what Juliette had said earlier.

He smiled. 'We'll make you fluent one day.'

I liked the idea that Ethan could be around for that 'one day'.

18

We ended up sat on the bed side-by-side with my laptop perched on the ottoman at the end, a hot drink each and an array of snacks scattered around the bed. We both wore a pair of jogging bottoms and a T-shirt.

As soon as I had suggested we could stay in, it started to rain, making us both happy to curl up and get cosy together. I glanced across at Ethan when *Ratatouille* started on my laptop. I had laughed when he suggested watching it – it seemed perfect to me, a film about cooking set in Paris. And I'd seen it before so I didn't need to concentrate on it. I could just relax here with Ethan. And this man was very relaxing. Without even trying, he seemed to make me feel calmer.

'I can feel you looking at me,' Ethan said then.

I jumped. 'Oh, sorry,' I said, shifting my eyes back to the screen.

'I didn't say I didn't like it.' Ethan turned to me on the bed. 'What's up?'

'I didn't think we'd end up sharing this bed.'

'No.' His mouth twitched. 'You were really pissed when you found me in this apartment.'

'More pissed at Joe than you,' I reminded him. 'I was worried it would be so awkward staying in this place together. But it wasn't. I think you could make any situation chill.'

The Paris Chapter

'You should see me at work, I'm not as unruffled there. Here with you, it's easy to be.'

'I'd love to see you at work,' I said.

'Yeah? Well, you can come to the restaurant in London anytime.'

'I wish I knew how things will be when I go home. What if staying here longer doesn't help with my book like I hope it will?' I leaned back against the pillows with a sigh. 'I still don't know if I can write again.'

'I think you can,' he said. He climbed across the bed and paused the film before kneeling beside me. 'Let me ask you something – when you wrote your first romance novel, were you in a relationship with your soulmate?'

'Hell, no. I had just been dumped by my boyfriend of almost four years over the phone. And I thought, *Fuck this, I'm going to write a novel*, because what did I have to lose?'

Ethan's mouth twitched. 'I hope you dedicated it to him.'

'He emailed me when it came out and told me he regretted dumping me.' I shrugged. 'As much as I love reliving my terrible love life, your point is?'

'My point is you wrote a happy ending then even though you'd been dumped. You still loved love.'

'I was younger and more hopeful then,' I said. 'I think it's because I thought Joe was it, you know?' I saw a flicker of hurt in his eyes. I sat up on my knees. 'Of course he isn't now, I realise it was all an illusion and he's not who I want, but what if I never get it right? What if I never meet The One?'

'Maybe there isn't a one. Maybe we just have to hold on to love for as long as we have it and keep opening ourselves up to it even after we've been hurt. I honestly don't think I really have been in love though. Not the kind of love in your books.' He saw my raised eyebrow. 'Yeah, I started reading your book on the way back from my course. You're talented, Tessa; don't let Joe ruin what you're good at, what you enjoy. And think about the readers who love your books. Some of them have found their soulmates, others haven't, some are in love, some are heartbroken, some are going through a tough time, but your books are an escape for them all. Something to brighten up their days. Whatever they are going through. Reading has always been that for me.'

I nodded. 'Me too.' I thought about readers who had reached out and told me the same thing. I was so proud when someone told me one of my books had made them smile. 'Damn, you're right. I don't write for people like Joe. I write for people like us.'

'The hopeless?'

'The hopeful.' I leaned in and kissed him. When our lips met, I felt it.

Hope.

Ethan pulled me closer, his hands touching my hips and sending heat through them. I wrapped my arms around his neck and the squishy bed coupled with us both on our knees didn't really work out. Ethan tipped backwards and pulled me down onto the bed with him. We laughed and I looked down into his blue eyes. 'You know, it would be kind of a shame not to make use of the one bed in this apartment. Just once.'

Ethan reached up and brushed my hair from my face. His eyes turned hungry as his lips met mine again. This time, he kissed me harder, and his hands on my back slid down to my bum and he squeezed it. When he moved to kiss my neck, I let out a little gasp. 'God, that sound,' he groaned.

I shifted and sat astride his lap again. I ran a hand through his hair then leaned down to kiss him. When his tongue touched mine, I whimpered and Ethan pulled me closer. He slid his hands up from my waist to cup my breast through my T-shirt as he moved his lips to below my ear, kissing me there and moving down to my collarbone. 'Is this okay?' he said, looking up at me.

'Yes,' I breathed.

His lips found mine again as he stroked my breasts and I needed to be closer. I moved higher on his lap and squeezed my legs tighter around him, feeling him as aroused as me through our jogging bottoms.

He grunted when I created friction and his mouth pressed harder against mine, kissing me desperately.

I moved against him again. 'Should we get naked?' I gasped out.

'We both need to take this slow,' Ethan said softly as he broke our kiss to look at me, the words coming out as breathless as I felt. He rocked against me and I whimpered. 'We should keep our clothes on but that won't stop me making you come.'

His words sent a delicious thrill through me. I moaned and moved against him harder as his mouth returned to mine. Ethan's hands held my waist as I moved on top of him, and he thrusted against me. I could feel how hard he was and I wondered if he could feel how wet I was. It was like I was a teenager again, and there was something about us having to keep our clothes on that drove me crazy. I moaned when Ethan went back to caressing my breasts, running his fingertips over the fabric, my nipples hardening underneath instantly. Then he moved and hit the spot I needed him to most. I clung to him and cried out in pleasure.

'What are you doing to me?' I gasped as we moved harder and faster together.

'You feel so good,' he said, looking at me in wonder. 'Like this. I can't even imagine what it will feel like to be inside you.'

'Oh, God.' I moaned at the thought. I ached to feel him. There was something about this man that made me want to do things I'd only written about before. I was usually shy and tentative in bed, especially at first, but Ethan made me feel so comfortable, it was easy to let go.

'Is this okay?' he gasped then, reaching up to smooth my hair back off my face.

'Faster,' I gasped back. I gripped his shoulders and his hands clung to my waist. 'Yes.' I rolled my hips and this time, Ethan trembled beneath me. 'You like that?'

'Fuck yeah,' he said, so I did it again and let out a moan. 'I can't stop thinking about what this will be like when I'm actually inside you. You'll be so wet... so tight...'

Usually, dirty talk was something I avoided like the plague, with my overthinking about most things that came out of my mouth, but Ethan's frantic murmurings just made me moan louder. It was like his honesty just carried on into the bedroom, and knowing he was thinking about being inside me while I was thinking the same thing made it incredibly hot. 'You're going to fill me up, you're so big...' I murmured back. Ethan pulled me closer down on him and when I rolled my hips again, I cried out as pleasure surged through my body, travelling out from the throbbing between my legs down to my toes. I shuddered against him as he rocked with me twice more before crying out too.

'Jesus, Tessa,' he cried, holding me tightly against him as he shuddered along with me. 'If you can make me come as hard as that with my clothes on...' He pulled back to look at me, eyebrow raised. 'Your moans, fuck.'

I came back to earth and looked away. 'I'm sorry.' I started to slide off him, but Ethan gripped my hips and kept me in place.

'What the hell are you sorry for?' He was searching my face but I was avoiding his eyes. He took hold of my chin gently in his fingers and tilted my face so I had to meet his eyes.

'Being so loud,' I said, embarrassed at being so into it now the moment had passed.

'Are you being serious?' He shook his head. 'Do you know how hard I was trying not to come before you? Your moans drove me crazy. Fucking crazy.' He cupped my face and drew my lips to his, kissing me tenderly. He pulled back and met my eyes again. 'I have dreamed about making you moan like that.'

When I saw he was being serious, my chest sagged with relief. I smiled through my blush. 'Okay, good. I honestly don't know what you did to me back there.'

'I want to do it again,' he said huskily. 'Over and over. Do you?'

I nodded. 'I think I may have made that clear.' But then I giggled, the high I had felt coming back from his reassurance.

Ethan leaned back and smiled, reaching up to touch my lips. 'God, I love making you smile. You look even more gorgeous when you smile. I want to make you smile like this every day.'

'I was thinking you make me feel like a teenager again,' I said.

'Good. You should feel that carefree and fearless.'

I'd turned as serious as he had. 'This is new for me,' I admitted. I shifted again and this time, his hands slid away and I climbed off his lap and sat back to look at him. 'I don't usually feel like this.'

'How do you usually feel?' he asked, watching me intently.

'Worried,' I admitted. I didn't want to compare Ethan to Joe but it was hard not to. When I first started seeing Joe, I overthought everything, and now I knew part of the problem was he wasn't fully in it like I thought he was. I was always worried I wasn't what he wanted. With Ethan, it was different. He made me feel like I might be exactly what he wanted. That was a crazy feeling so soon though.

Isn't it?

Ethan mulled my words over and nodded. 'I get that. I've felt that way too. It's hard when you take a leap with someone but you don't really know if they have taken that same leap. So, let's be honest with each other, yeah? Tell each other how we are feeling, what we want... and don't rush. Wait until we're both ready. Until we both know what we want.'

I smiled. I knew that was the right thing to do but I also knew after what had just happened, it wouldn't be easy. Ethan was making me feel things I had always wanted to feel. And it had come when I was at my lowest point. My mind was having trouble keeping up with the sudden turn my heart was making. That Ethan was encouraging it to make. 'Okay. But just as you know, I want more.' I flopped down on the pillow beside him, contentment flowing through my body.

Ethan looked across at me, his eyes dark. 'Good. So do I.'

A thrill of anticipation ran through me at the thought of what would happen between us if we let ourselves take our clothes off. It was like I'd been asleep but Ethan was waking me up. And I didn't want to have to close my eyes again.

19

The rain continued as dusk fell and Ethan and I both agreed we wanted to stay in the cosy apartment for our last evening here. Ethan said he would go out for provisions. I went into the bedroom to put my things back in my suitcase ready to move in with Juliette tomorrow.

> How soon can I see you when you come back to London?

Carly messaged me as I was packing. I felt bad for not having told her my new plans. London and my best friend suddenly felt very far away. I phoned her and she answered instantly.

After we said our hellos, I explained what was going on. 'I thought I might stay in Paris a bit longer...'

There was a short silence. 'Because of Ethan?'

'Um...' I hesitated because her tone sounded annoyed. 'Well, no, not exactly... I told Gita that my book will be set in Paris and I think being here will help me start to write it.'

'Have you started?'

'Not yet,' I admitted.

'Because you've been spending so much time with Ethan?'

'No, you know I've been stuck. He's helped – taking me to romantic spots and showing me the city. I have an idea, I just need to start writing now.'

'And will you, if you're still with him?'

'He's doing a cookery course; I'll have lots of writing time. And being here is inspiring me. And, okay, kissing Ethan has been nice and maybe I don't want to have to stop doing that,' I said, touching my lips, which still tingled from our kisses earlier.

Carly sighed. 'I'm worried, Tessa. You sound invested in this guy already. But you need to be careful. Joe really hurt you and you only split up two months ago...'

I sank down onto the bed, the packing forgotten as I was reminded of his betrayal. 'I know that. It's not like I'm rushing into a relationship. We are just getting to know each other.' I blushed thinking about our activities on this very bed. It had felt so good.

Am I lying to Carly? Am I lying to myself?

'And like I said, I'm not staying for Ethan,' I added, feeling defensive. 'I really need to try writing this book before I tell Gita I won't make the deadline. I need something to show her. Ethan is just an added bonus.'

'Tessa, you know I love you and I was all for you going on the Paris trip to get some distance from all the shit you've been through. I hoped it would give you inspiration for your book, but you can be impulsive when it comes to men. You sometimes equate them with your worth as a person. Like Joe. You moved in with him after only six weeks! And you told me that sometimes you didn't feel good about yourself while you were together. What if that happens all over again?'

'Wow,' I said, her words penetrating my skin like a bee sting. 'I didn't realise that's what you thought of me. So, because I moved too quickly and fell in love with him, what Joe did to me was all my fault?'

'Of course not! But you maybe didn't know him well enough when you moved in. And I hated how he made you feel bad about yourself. I don't want that to happen with Ethan. And, I mean, he's Joe's best friend. You don't know him very well yet.' Carly sighed. 'You're not doing it so Joe will find out, are you?'

The question startled me. 'What do you mean?'

'Are you trying to make Joe jealous?'

I was taken aback. Joe, of course, knew we'd turned up at this apartment together and had no doubt seen the photos on social media of us hanging out with Ethan's Parisian friends. But Joe didn't know we'd kissed or what we'd got up to today. 'He wouldn't care anyway; he cheated on me. He's with Rachel.' I wasn't sure if I wanted Joe to know about us. Part of me would enjoy him knowing that another man wanted me when he hadn't. But I was worried what he might say about me to Ethan. If Joe thought I wasn't good enough for him, would he feel the same way about his friend?

'But it's kind of weird, isn't it? To be with his best mate. It keeps you in his orbit.'

'Joe isn't in Paris,' I said, relieved about that for sure. 'I'm here with Ethan, not him.'

'That's my point though. It's only been two months since you were with Joe. It feels like things are moving kind of fast with you and Ethan. You've only known him five days but now you are staying in Paris to be with him?'

'No, to work on my book!' I cried. 'Look, Carly, whatever you think, Paris has been good for me so far, and I don't want to give that up just yet. I'm staying with Ethan's friend Juliette for a few more days and I am going to try to write.'

'I hope so, Tessa,' she said. 'You know that I'm just trying to look out for you.'

'Ethan is nothing like Joe,' I said, but uncertainty had crept in. Being with Ethan this afternoon had been so amazing, but Carly did have a point when she said that I didn't know him all that well. And reminding me how quickly I'd moved in with Joe. Not knowing him well turned out to be an understatement.

I heard the apartment door open and close then. 'I'm going to go and have dinner now,' I said quickly to Carly, not wanting Ethan to hear any part of this conversation. 'I'll talk to you soon. Bye!' I hung up before she could stop me and took a breath before I left the bedroom.

The problem was, I did understand my best friend's concern. I had sworn off love so hard I hadn't been able to write about it, but this afternoon, I had been swept up in Ethan's kisses and touch. It had been easy to picture more with him. I *wanted* more. And that was terrifying based on my last relationship experience.

Was I being too impulsive? What if I got hurt all over again?

Ethan was in the kitchen unpacking food from a brown paper bag when I walked in. 'Hi there,' he said, smiling warmly when he saw me. 'I thought we could have picky bits maybe over a game of chess. What do you think?'

Seeing him helped. Our eyes met and sparks flew, but it was hard to ignore the seed of doubt that had settled in my chest. I trusted Carly and she was worried about this. 'Sounds good,' I said, forcing on a smile. 'I'll get some wine and set up the game,' I offered as Ethan started to arrange a fancy board of cheese, bread, olives, and cold meats. I poured two glasses of red wine and took them over to the sofa area, finding the chessboard and setting it up on the coffee table as I knelt on the carpet.

Then my phone beeped with a message. I assumed it was Carly wanting to talk again, so when I saw Joe's name on my phone screen, I did a double take. I had started to think his phone call the other night was just a mistake. A bum dial even. But now he had sent me a text.

I looked over at Ethan in the kitchen, but he was humming as he sorted out the food, so I opened up Joe's message to read it.

> When do you get back from Paris? Could we talk?

It felt like my phone was on fire. I put it down onto the coffee table as if I had been burnt. I stared at his words on the screen in shock. My pulse sped up at the thought of seeing him again. I wasn't sure if it was from fear or hope.

'Something wrong, Tessa?'

I jumped as Ethan was suddenly close by me, holding the wooden board of food, looking down at me on the floor with concern. I thought about lying but I was never very good at that.

'Joe just texted me. He wants to talk when I go home.'

Ethan put the food down on the coffee table next to the chessboard. A shadow crossed his face as he sank into the sofa. 'I see. Do you want to?'

'No,' I said quickly, but I bit my lip. 'I'm not sure. I wonder what he wants to say to me.'

Ethan reached for the glass of wine I had poured and took a long gulp from it before replying. 'I guess you need to ask yourself if you want to hear it or not,' he replied. His voice sounded strained.

'I mean, you know how much he hurt me but...' I trailed off, feeling that sting of rejection all over again.

'You're curious?' Ethan asked me.

'Maybe a little bit. Is that crazy?' The feelings Joe's message had stirred up were confusing and irritating. I wanted to forget the six months I was with him, but looking across at his best friend was a stark reminder that I was unlikely to be able to do that anytime soon.

'You'll only know what Joe wants to say if you meet up with him,' he said.

'So, you think I should?' I asked, worried that if he said yes, it meant that he didn't care about me like it felt earlier he might do.

'Maybe I shouldn't be involved in this.' Ethan shifted uncomfortably on the sofa.

I was embarrassed. 'God, of course, he's your friend and we... Well, I'm not sure what we are.' I coughed nervously and wished I had lied when he'd asked me what was wrong. There was sudden tension between us, and I hated that Joe had caused it. And my conversation with Carly too. We had been happy just an hour ago, I had thought. I wanted that back. Even if it was just for the rest of the night.

'Anyway,' I said brightly. 'I'm staying in Paris so there is no need to decide anything.' I had meant Joe but I supposed the same was true for me and Ethan too. I needed to stop myself from doing what Carly said and rushing ahead of myself. 'I'll just tell him I'm not sure when I'll be coming home.' I was relieved I could put off deciding whether to talk to him or not.

After I sent a message back, I put my phone face down on the coffee table so I wouldn't see if Joe replied, I looked at Ethan. He was quiet, looking anywhere but at me. I longed to know what he was thinking. 'I don't want our evening ruined,' I said quietly. 'Joe has done enough damage.'

Ethan's eyes came back to me finally. 'He has,' he agreed.

I looked at the food, desperate to change the subject and get away from the shadow cast by my ex and his best friend. 'This looks great,' I told Ethan as I reached for some cheese and bread. 'All my favourite foods together.'

Ethan was watching me closely but after a beat, he leaned forward and picked up a piece of cheese too. 'I'm glad you like it. I was thinking as I was putting it all out what you said about your flat in Putney not feeling like home... There is a street in Paris with homeware and antique shops; we could check it out if you like?'

I nodded eagerly, relieved he had followed my lead and moved the subject on. 'I'd love some things from Paris, to remember this trip.'

'We could go after my course finishes tomorrow, if you like?'

'Sounds good to me.'

We both smiled at one another. I realised we had spent the past five days in forced proximity in this apartment but now we'd be staying apart, we were choosing to spend time together. Carly's words and the message from Joe faded away a little bit.

'So, are you ready for me to beat you again?' I asked, gesturing to the chessboard.

'Fighting talk, Tessa?'

'Always when it comes to board games,' I replied with a smile.

'Where does this competitive streak come from?' He raised an eyebrow.

I considered that as he gestured for me to make the first move. I moved a pawn. 'I've always played games with my family and I think they helped my overthinking. I can just concentrate on what I'm playing; my brain focuses on that and not on other things. Like right now, you're watching me but I have tunnel vision for the game.'

Ethan moved a pawn too. 'Oh, so I will never be able to distract you?'

I glanced up with a smile. 'You can try.' I quickly looked back at the board and took one of his pawns.

'So, not even talking about what we did earlier could distract you?' Ethan asked as he took his turn.

'What happened earlier?' I teased him as I moved my knight and took another pawn from him. I had a sip of my wine and glanced at him.

Ethan was frowning at the chessboard, and at my question, he looked up. 'You can't fool me. You want more.'

I hesitated as he made the move I was expecting. I tried not to show that. 'Do you want more?' I asked nervously.

'How could I not?' he asked with surprise.

His answer did take me away from the game for a moment. I was confused by how quickly he had reassured me. I wasn't used to that. It made me feel good. I tried not to think about what Carly had said about linking my worth to men. I wanted to just enjoy tonight.

Ethan moved his queen and I tried not to react as he made the move I had been hoping for. I moved my queen into the perfect position. And then I smiled. 'Checkmate.'

'What?' he asked, startled. He leaned closer and looked. Then groaned.

'I'm sorry.'

'No, you're not,' he replied.

'Not even a little bit.'

Ethan sighed. 'I will beat you one day, Elliot.'

'I look forward to it, Taylor.'

'Seriously, how are you beating me so easily?'

'Your moves are easy to anticipate, Ethan,' I replied with a shrug.

'They are? Shit. I need to work on that then, don't I?' Ethan got up then and left the sofa to join me on the floor, startling me. I looked into those blue eyes of his and felt like I was in trouble.

'What move are you anticipating now, Tessa?'

20

'Surprise me,' I said boldly.

Ethan looked taken aback for a fleeting moment but then he grinned and leaned in, putting a hand up to touch the back of my hair and draw me towards him.

I expected Ethan's lips to meet mine hungrily but he kissed me gently, moving slowly and softly, planting small kisses on my lips with his. I let out a whimper.

'God, that sound,' Ethan said, breaking away to look at me, his eyes darkening. 'I really like kissing you.'

'Same,' I said, pleased. Every compliment, every sign that he wanted me, thrilled me. I couldn't help it.

'Want to stop at kissing?' Ethan asked me then.

'No,' I said softly.

'Let's get more comfortable.' Ethan stood up and held a hand out to me. I took it and he pulled me off the floor with him and we both collapsed on the sofa together. His hands moved around my back to pull me closer, still kissing me softly. I whimpered again and he reached down to the edge of my T-shirt. 'Can I touch you?' he whispered, his fingertips sliding under the fabric to touch my skin, which was covered in goosebumps from his kisses.

'Yes,' I breathed.

'Are you sure? We can keep our clothes on again?'

'Nope.' I grabbed the T-shirt from him and lifted it off me.

Ethan chuckled softly as his eyes dropped to my bra. 'Hmm. I prefer this, I have to say,' he said. His eyes moved back up to mine. I looked back at him hungrily. I was sure he could tell how hard I was breathing right now. 'I want to know: what move are you anticipating now, sweetheart?'

It took an incredible amount of restraint not to lose all control when he called me that. I moved one hand into his hair and stroked it. 'I think you're going to...'

He leaned in and kissed my collarbone, rendering me speechless. He trailed kisses down my chest then my breasts, pulling my bra down and drawing my hard nipples into his mouth with relish. I held on tightly around his neck, rocking my hips against his jogging bottoms. He grunted and sucked on my nipple in response.

Then Ethan pulled back. 'Want to stop?'

'No, definitely not,' I said. What he had said had aroused me just as much as his touches. I leaned in to kiss him deeply. His tongue finally found mine and I wriggled closer on his lap, making him murmur contentedly. I leaned back and raised an eyebrow, wondering what his next move was.

Ethan grinned and suddenly he flipped me so I was on my back on the sofa. 'I'd love to make you come again, but only if you want me to.'

'At this point, I'm halfway there,' I gasped. I didn't know how this man could turn me on so much barely touching me but I was sinking into the sofa like I had turned into putty. 'Ethan, you're driving me crazy.'

'Good.' He reached for my jogging bottoms then slipped them off me. I lifted my bum to help, then I was in my underwear. 'I finally get to touch you like this,' he said, sliding his hand down the centre of my chest, skimming my bra, to my stomach then to trace the edge of my underwear. 'I thought about it the night you took all your clothes off and I stupidly stayed in bed.'

I giggled as I thought back to that. 'Oops. You were very restrained that night.'

'Just hiding my raging erection and very improper thoughts.'

My giggling got worse. 'Ethan!'

Ethan smiled at my reaction. 'I really wanted to touch you. Have you wanted me to touch you, Tessa?'

'Yes. Please,' I whimpered.

'When?' he asked, his voice low and urgent. 'I need to know.'

We looked at each other. I recognised the insecurity in his tone and the expression on his face. I was just as insecure. I wondered if hearing from Joe had made it worse for both of us. We now needed reassurance from each other. 'I wanted you to touch me that night too. And earlier when we kept our clothes on... or maybe when I saw you coming out of the bathroom in that skimpy white towel.'

Ethan's eyes widened. 'We could have been doing this for five days?' His hand began to stroke me over my underwear. 'All I want to do is hear you moan again,' Ethan said, leaning down to pull at my underwear. I lifted my bum again and he slid them off and crouched down beside me. I was throbbing with want now and when he dropped kisses along the inside of my legs as I lifted them up and parted them for him, they began to tremble. He put his hands on them. 'It's okay, sweetheart,' he whispered between kisses, calming me. 'I want to taste you, to make you come with my tongue. Can I?'

'Fuck, yes,' I said, my hand coming down into his hair and clutching hold of it.

He grunted in response, then finally his kisses travelled up to where I craved him. When his tongue found me, I shivered with relief.

God, this feels so good.

I moaned as Ethan licked me. His hand joined his tongue and he alternated between stroking me with his fingertips and his tongue, slowly and deliciously. He took his time with me like he did with everything and I was a shaky mess above him, groaning at his every touch. When he started to move faster and when he applied more pressure, I thought I might die. 'Ethan, I don't know what you are doing but don't stop,' I begged him. I grabbed hold of the sofa as I began to writhe, Ethan not lifting off me for a second.

'Right there,' I gasped when his tongue hit a spot that sent pleasure shooting through me. Ethan slipped two fingers inside me then, his mouth staying where it was, and when he sucked on me, I lost complete control. 'Bloody hell,' I cried as my whole body shook. Pleasure rolled through me like a wave and I wanted to ride it forever. I shuddered, my legs turning to jelly, heat shooting through my body as I slowly came back down to earth.

'That was... incredible,' I breathed as Ethan lifted off me. My legs flopped down onto the sofa, as did my head.

'That was so hot, Tessa, my God,' he replied, reaching down to take his bottoms off. He pulled himself out of his boxers and began stroking. He was so big and hard, my eyes widened, thinking about how he would feel inside me.

'Want me to touch you?' I asked, struggling to sit up.

'Please,' he murmured.

'You better come here.' I giggled, unable to move. I scooted over and then lay down beside him. He moved his hand away and gasped at my touch. 'You sure this is all you want?' I asked as our eyes locked.

'It's all I need, I'm so close,' he said, leaning in to kiss me. I stroked him harder and faster and he gasped into my mouth. 'Just like that,' he said, pulling back to look at me. 'You know exactly what I need.'

'So do you,' I said, still in wonder at how good that had been.

'Oh, God, yes,' Ethan cried out, his own release joining mine.

I moved my hand and he leaned in to kiss me hard on the lips. I felt him shudder against me like I had done and I finally knew what it was like to really let go with a man, realising that before now, I hadn't ever done that. It had never been as good as that before.

This is scary.

I had brushed off Carly's concerns on the phone but fear trickled through my veins. This had felt so intimate considering how little time I had known Ethan.

Are we moving too fast?

'Are you okay?' Ethan asked, noticing me go quiet.

I nodded. 'Yes. A little bit overwhelmed maybe...' I admitted, stuttering over the words.

'I get that. I feel that too,' Ethan said. He looked worried. 'We said we'd go slow; was that too much?'

'I wanted it badly,' I said, but I felt as worried.

'It was so good. It feels good with you.'

'It does for me too,' I agreed. 'But it has only been two months since Joe and we have only been here a few days...'

'I know.' Ethan moved and I wanted to protest, but I sensed our moment of getting carried away was over. 'It's late. Shall we go to bed?'

'Together?' I asked hopefully.

'Together,' he agreed, holding out a hand to help me off the sofa.

Our last night in this one-bed bubble. I was half upset, half relieved. Because what happened on the sofa had been really intense. And although I wanted more, I was also worried about getting even more carried away next time.

21

Morning arrived too soon. I woke up in bed with Ethan breathing deeply beside me. We had fallen asleep quickly after last night's activities. And in the cold light of the day, I was shocked at myself. I had let go with Ethan more than I had ever before. And looking at him now asleep, I felt so close to him. But then I remembered sleeping beside Joe for months. Could I ever trust my heart again?

I slipped out of bed, nervous in case Ethan woke up and we would need to discuss yesterday. I of course knew Ethan fancied me. There was no faking the chemistry between us. What we had done together had been hot. So hot. But I didn't know if his feelings ran any deeper, or whether this had any chance once we left Paris. I didn't want to make another mistake. It was best to put off any talk of what we were to each other. I couldn't face being rejected again.

I used the bathroom and got ready for the day, checking I had packed everything ready to move to Juliette's apartment.

When I went into the kitchen to make a cup of tea, Ethan emerged from the bedroom, also dressed. We eyed each other.

'Tea? Coffee?' I asked.

'I'll make a coffee,' Ethan said, walking over. 'How did you sleep?'

'Fine, thanks. You?'

God, this is awkward.

'I did too,' Ethan said as he started to make coffee.

I finished making my tea and took a sip for something to do, wincing because it was far too hot. 'It's kind of sad leaving this place,' I said, looking around. 'It's a lovely apartment.'

'I'll have good memories of it,' Ethan said, stirring his coffee.

'Yeah?'

He looked over and smiled. 'Of course. I hope you will too.'

I nodded. 'Definitely,' I said, smiling back. I was relieved that he didn't regret yesterday. I realised I had been worried that he did. I hated not knowing what he was thinking.

'So, after my course, want to still go home shopping?' Ethan asked, leaning against the kitchen counter to take a sip of his coffee.

'I would really like that.'

'Great. I'll come and get you from Juliette's. I need to pack up my things so I can lock up this place before I go to my course.'

'And I'm going to try to start writing,' I said, taking a deep breath. My phone call with Carly had scared me. She was right that I couldn't stay in Paris just for Ethan. I had to try with this book or my career would be over. There was no way I'd make my deadline, but if I could make good headway then I could speak to Gita about an extension.

'I have no doubt you will do it, Tessa.'

When he said things like that, I felt deep down in my heart that he was very different to Joe. Joe never seemed to care about my writing. If anything, it felt like he saw it as a hobby and not a real job. I just wished I wasn't so scared that my judgement was screwed up, and that I was wrong about Ethan like I had been about his best friend.

Ethan stepped over to me. 'When I woke up alone in bed again, I was scared you'd changed your mind about staying in Paris.'

'No. I want to stay,' I assured him.

'It just feels a bit like a dream, this thing between us. It's hard for me to trust it,' he said haltingly.

'Me too.'

'So, we don't need to rush anything, right? Let's keep spending time together here. And see what happens. Can I kiss you?'

'Yes, please.'

Ethan closed the gap between us, wrapping his arms around me. He gave me a lingering kiss then held me close. I sank against his strong chest and hated that things were complicated between us.

'I wish we had met first,' I admitted.

'Me too. Is there... is there a chance for us, do you think?' Ethan asked hesitantly as he held me close.

'I hope so,' I answered him. I hadn't felt hope when it came to love since I broke up with Joe, so my heart was beginning to heal.

And maybe these next few days in Paris could help it to heal completely.

* * *

Juliette welcomed me to her apartment with a big hug and a glass of wine for us both despite it only just being midday. She showed me into her guest room and I gasped. It was a small but beautiful room decorated in rich creams with a wooden floor, ornate bed and narrow window that had a view across the rooftops of Paris. In the corner was a small writing desk and chair. 'I found this in Montmartre. It will be nice to see it finally be used for writing,' Juliette said, gesturing to it.

'There is no way I can't be inspired here,' I said, running my fingers across it. 'I'd love something like this in my London flat. Ethan is going to take me shopping later to see if I can find any French home décor as my flat is very empty.'

'French furniture is the best,' Juliette declared. 'Get settled. Drink your wine and write. And help yourself to anything. This is your home now. I need to go to the restaurant. You and Ethan come for dinner there, yes?'

'Sure,' I readily agreed. 'I can't thank you enough for this, Juliette.'

'You know it is my pleasure. Bon courage!' After wishing me good luck, and giving me a kiss on both of my cheeks, Juliette swept out and left me alone.

I quickly unpacked then took my wine and laptop to the writing desk. I picked up my phone and snapped a picture of the set-up, the window behind the desk and the sun shining through it. Then I opened up Instagram.

Staying with my lovely friend Juliette in Paris now. Look at this view I have while I write. I'll never want to leave.

I posted the photo with that caption then opened up the blank document I had for book three. I took a gulp of wine and started the story with my main character getting on the Eurostar to Paris after having hit rock bottom in her love life.

This was a novel but there was no doubt that part of me was in this character. Like me, my leading lady was about to arrive in Paris lost and believing that love no longer existed. Then she would meet a French man who would show her all Paris had to offer and slowly her broken heart would heal. I knew writing that part wouldn't be as easy as the start when I knew exactly how she felt. But I also wasn't quite in that same place any more. Paris had helped already. Ethan had showed me that I didn't want to let go of happy ever afters.

By the time my character was meant to leave Paris, she needed to believe in love again. She needed to fall for her Frenchman. And maybe decide to move to the City of Love to be with him. I couldn't fathom taking such a leap of faith after being so burnt by my last relationship, but I told myself not to worry about that. I just needed to start the story and hope that by the time I got to that part, I would be able to write it.

At least the idea of it all wasn't filling me with the dread it would have done five days ago.

I took a breath and my fingertips found my laptop keys.

And then I started to type.

22

I was startled by Juliette's apartment doorbell ringing in the afternoon. I got up stiffly from the writing desk, rolling my neck, which ached after being in a hunched position over my laptop for the first time in months. Pulling open the door, I was surprised to see Ethan standing outside. 'Oh, I lost track of time,' I said, then I broke into a smile.

'You seem happy about that?' Ethan asked, looking amused.

'Well, it's been a long time since I've had a burst of writing like that. I managed to write three chapters, and time slipped away in the best way possible.'

'That's great. How do you feel writing again?'

'Good, I think. I feel rusty from not writing for a while but I actually enjoyed it. It's so fun taking my main character to Paris. I feel like I really set the scene well, being here myself. Shall we go out? I definitely need some fresh air.'

'Let's go.'

Ethan waited as I got my jacket and bag, then we left the apartment to walk to a row of homeware shops he thought I would like. 'It's great hearing you sound so enthusiastic about writing,' Ethan said as we strolled side-by-side. He touched my hand and our fingers entwined easily. 'I was reading more of your book that I bought on our course lunch break. You're really talented, Tessa.'

My cheeks heated up from his praise. 'That means a lot that you think that.'

'Well, it's true.'

'Thank you. And when we're back in London, I can't wait to try the food at your restaurant. I know it will be delicious.'

Ethan gave me a cute smile. 'I will make all your dishes personally.' Ethan steered us towards a shop. 'This is one of my favourites. It's all made in France. Unique to this place. So you'll be the only one who has a piece if you buy one.'

'That sounds great. Very different to the high-street stores at home! Juliette's guest room is so beautiful; I love how she's styled it. I feel like it's inspiring me. Right now, my Putney flat is basically a white box.'

Ethan held the shop door open for me and we walked in. 'That's how mine was when I moved in too. But I'd picked up a lot when I lived here for a year so once all my things were in there, it felt so much more like home.'

'I suppose because I lived for six months with Joe, and I haven't bought anything since I moved into my own flat, I've sort of lost what I like when it comes to home décor. His flat was so... plush. And he didn't want anything changed or moved. I felt like I could never relax,' I found myself saying as we looked at the vintage-style furniture.

'Joe's place never felt like home then?' Ethan asked me quietly.

'I was nervous to use his fancy TV, and the white carpet was terrifying when it came to doing my makeup. He gave me one drawer and one part of the walk-in wardrobe... I'm sorry,' I said. 'We keep ending up mentioning him.'

'It's hard not to,' Ethan said quietly. 'I hope we can find some things you like. You deserve your flat to feel like home.'

I paused by a writing desk that was very similar to the one I had been sat at all morning. I ran my hand over the ornate wood. 'Wow.'

'You wouldn't have writer's block if you were sat at that,' Ethan said, watching my reaction.

'It would fit perfectly by the window in the living room; I could look out at the river from it,' I mused, picturing my flat back in London. It felt very far away right now but I wouldn't be able to avoid going home forever. I glanced at the price. It wasn't as bad as I had feared. 'How would I get it home though?'

'Let me sort that,' Ethan said, walking over to talk to the shop owner in his fluent French. I watched him, touched he cared and wanted me to have this piece. It made me worry less about extending my trip here.

I pulled my phone out of my bag and sent a message to Carly.

> Things feel weird between us, and I really don't want that. I wrote three chapters this morning and now I'm shopping for things for my flat with Ethan. I know you're worried but I'll be okay. I am really enjoying being here.

Carly replied a couple of minutes later.

> I'm sorry for what I said. I'm just trying to look out for you. I don't want you to get hurt again. I'm glad you're writing. I can't wait to read it. Call me soon!

I smiled with relief.

> I hope you're looking after you and baby!

She messaged in return:

> Don't worry about us.

I did miss my friend and it was strange to not be with her when she had just found out she was pregnant. But I knew it wouldn't be for long, and this felt like where I should be for now.

Ethan came back and said there was a way to ship the desk over, so I bought it along with a small ornate mirror and a gold clock for my mantelpiece.

At the next shop, I found a chess set that I knew would look great on one of the few pieces of furniture I had in my flat – a distressed oak coffee table.

'I don't have my own. I didn't have anyone to play with when I moved to London,' I said.

'Are you telling me you're actually rusty at playing chess?' Ethan asked, tutting. 'That makes me feel even worse at how easily you've beaten me so far.'

I grinned. 'Maybe I should get this set then so we can keep practising in London?' I avoided looking at him, suddenly worried that had been too presumptuous a question. I had no idea if he was thinking about us spending time together once we left Paris or not.

'I think you should,' Ethan said close to my ear.

I was able to look at him then; he was smiling. I felt my heart lift a little bit. He really was cute when he smiled at me like that. 'It would look good with everything we've bought so far,' I said, picking it up. I could picture us playing it together in Putney, and although I knew I was in danger of getting carried away again, the image was just too enticing for me not to buy the set.

We went to a few more shops and I got a couple more prints of Paris to match the one Ethan had bought me, thinking I'd get gold frames for them all once I was back in London. Ethan picked up a couple of vinyl records. It was a fun afternoon.

When we left the last shop in the row, the sun was setting. I turned to Ethan and spontaneously gave him a kiss on the lips.

'What was that for?' he asked, looking surprised.

'Today. But also the last few days,' I said, holding on to him as we stood on the quiet Paris street together. 'I might not have been able to write anything of my next book if we hadn't been here at the same time.'

'I think Paris deserves more credit than me,' Ethan replied. 'I'm glad we are here together though.' He leaned in and gave me a longer kiss, lingering on my lips, holding me close.

I had never been into PDA but if you couldn't kiss a man you liked in public in Paris, then where could you?

We leaned back from one another, smiling happily.

'I'm so glad you're staying longer,' Ethan said.

'Me too. Honestly, I feel so different already to how I felt when I first got here. I feel like maybe I will be okay, you know?'

'Of course you will,' he replied. 'I knew that as soon as we met. You're stronger than you think you are. And that heart of yours won't let you give up on love.' His voice dropped on the word 'love'.

'I hope not,' I said. 'So, what now?'

'Shall we wander over to Cinq? It's not far from here. We can have a drink before we eat.'

'Good idea.' I was looking forward to going to Juliette's restaurant again. I had had such a good time there before Ethan was not much more than my accidental roommate. Now, he was so much more.

'This was really fun,' I said as we approached Cinq. Ethan opened up the door to the restaurant for me and we walked through. I turned to him in the lobby area. 'Thank you. My flat is going to look so much better with these new things in it; maybe it will start to finally feel like home.'

'I hope it will,' Ethan said, taking hold of my hand and entwining our fingers together. 'You need a place to call home.' He leaned in and brushed my lips with his. Smiling, we drew apart and turned to find Juliette only a few feet away with a man, both of them staring at us.

'Bonjour...' The greeting died on Ethan's lips as we both noticed that Juliette was standing with someone we both knew. 'What...?'

My eyes widened as Ethan spluttered in confusion. Juliette raised her eyebrows and looked furious but the man next to her was smiling like he was enjoying shocking the three of us.

And I thought he probably was.

Instinctively, I let go of Ethan's hand as I looked at the man I hadn't seen for two months. The man who had made me think love just didn't exist. His best friend had started to make me think it did again but now my heart spluttered as the man turned to me.

'Tessa, what an unexpected pleasure,' Joe said.

23

My stomach turned over as I faced Joe again. Two months ago, he had broken my heart and now he was smiling at me like we were old friends reunited.

'What are you doing in Paris?'

'Exactly!' Juliette cried, unable to stay silent any longer. 'I said that when he walked in!' She glared at Joe, who looked unruffled by her greeting.

'You didn't say you were coming to Paris,' Ethan said to Joe, but then he glanced at me and I saw his eyes drop to his now empty hand. I felt bad for dropping it but it had felt too weird holding in front of my ex. I wondered if he had seen me kiss Ethan or not. I had no idea if I wanted him to have seen it. My mind was racing and my heart was thumping. He was the last person I had expected to see in Paris.

Am I having an out of body experience?

'It was an impromptu decision. So I thought I'd pop in here in case Juliette knew where you were,' Joe said with a casual shrug.

'Why didn't you just call Ethan to ask him?' Juliette asked, putting her hands on her hips. It was a good question.

Joe fidgeted on the spot then, the first visible sign that he wasn't completely comfortable. 'I didn't just come to see Ethan,' he replied, his dark eyes locked on mine. 'I want to talk to Tessa.'

I stared back in shock, frozen and unable to speak or react. I thought about how he had been trying to get hold of me and meet up with me. I hadn't agreed to it so, what, he had come to Paris to force me to speak to him?

'*Merde!*' Juliette cried, making me jump. 'You...' she began, her hand in the air, then she slipped into a stream of French flung at Joe, who stood there nonplussed.

'Juliette,' Ethan said firmly. She glared at him. 'Why don't you show Joe to a booth and we'll get us some drinks and come over? Tessa?' Without looking at me, Ethan strode towards the bar.

'Fine. You, come on,' Juliette said, sighing, pointing with her finger for Joe to walk on ahead towards one of the red booths. Then she looked back at me and spoke more gently. 'Tessa, you don't need to do anything either of these men want you to, okay?'

I blinked and made myself move. I followed Ethan to the bar, seeing how tense his shoulders were as he got a tray and started to pour red wine into glasses on it. 'Ethan?' I said, tentatively.

Ethan took a quick swig of the wine then looked at me. 'Did you tell Joe to come here?' he asked, his tone harsher than I'd ever heard it.

'What? No, of course not!'

'Well, he asked you to meet him yesterday when he messaged you, and suddenly here he is!'

'Why would you think I'd do that and not tell you?' I asked, hurt that he thought I'd make plans with my ex like that after how we had been naked together last night.

Ethan must have seen the truth in my eyes because he slumped, leaning against the side of the bar. 'I'm sorry, I'm just so shocked to see him. And we were having such a good time. What does Joe want to talk to you about?'

'I have no idea.' My eyes involuntarily looked over as Joe slid into a booth and Juliette marched away from him towards us. Joe caught me looking so I quickly turned back to Ethan. 'Maybe he's just here to apologise. Not that I will accept it.'

'I've never known Joe to apologise for anything,' Ethan replied darkly.

Juliette came up to us then. 'He wants to eat here,' she said, shaking her head. 'I told him that depends whether my two good friends who are dating want him to or not,' she said, looking pleased with herself.

'You said we were dating?' Ethan asked her.

'Are you not?' she flung back. 'He should know he lost someone amazing!'

I was touched she felt that way about me. 'What did he say?' I asked her, wondering what I was hoping Joe's reaction had been.

'He said he would only stay if you two were okay with it.' Juliette folded her arms across her chest. 'Which I suppose was the right thing to say.'

'Are you okay with it?' Ethan asked me.

'Why is it all up to me?' I snapped back. I saw a flicker of hurt cross his face. 'Sorry, this is just very weird. I have no idea what to say or do.'

'You could tell him to leave,' Juliette said hopefully.

'Or you could hear him out,' Ethan said.

I glanced back at Joe. I couldn't help but feel a tiny bit flattered he was here. In Paris. He had come to see me. In another country. It was effort he hadn't made when we were together. It was a grand gesture. And I wished I could pretend that didn't make me feel a little bit better after how rejected I had felt when he had watched me leave our flat and not tried to persuade me to stay. He had chosen Rachel that night but if they were still happy together, why was he here? Curiosity made me think about sitting down with him because if they weren't happy, I kind of wanted to know. 'I suppose he has come a long way,' I said. 'Maybe I could just hear him out. But will you come too?' I asked Ethan. I didn't want to be alone with Joe. And Ethan's presence was calming. It had been since he had made me that first cup of tea in our Airbnb.

'If that's what you want,' Ethan said, picking up the drinks tray. 'Let's go then.'

'I'll go to the kitchen and order meals for you three. I hope you know what you're doing, Tessa,' Juliette said, leaving us with a look that told us she plainly thought we were crazy.

Ethan paused. 'Are you really okay with Joe knowing we're dating?'

'I know we haven't labelled it… but it's fine with me. If it is with you.' I thought then about what Carly had asked me on the phone – was I with Ethan to make Joe jealous? I knew I wasn't, but Joe was here now and had found out about us. I couldn't help but feel pleased that seeing someone else with me might make him realise that I could be good enough for someone. Even if I hadn't been enough for him.

'You want him to see what he's missing?' Ethan asked me.

I honestly wasn't sure what to say, but Joe had lied to me for so long, I didn't want to be anything like him – I never wanted to lie to Ethan. 'Maybe just a little bit.'

Ethan let out a puff of air. 'I guess I can't blame you after what he did to you. And maybe I kind of want him to know that I can get a beautiful, smart woman too,' Ethan confessed. He started to walk again with the drinks and I followed him, wondering if this was a terrible idea or not.

Both Ethan and I had admitted to one another that we did care about what Joe thought about us. I wasn't sure if this meant Carly had been right that we were moving too quickly. Were we trying to prove something to Joe? And was that more important than how we felt about each other?

We reached the booth then and sat opposite Joe. Ethan handed around a glass of wine each. Joe took a sip of his then raised an eyebrow. 'I didn't think I'd see you two still together after you were so annoyed to find Tessa in your apartment, mate,' he said casually to Ethan.

'Juliette said she told you we are dating,' Ethan replied. It was strange to hear those words. We hadn't once discussed labelling what had been happening between us the past few days but now Joe was here, it had been labelled. It made me uneasy. Like Ethan only wanted to date me to show Joe that he could. Or that I was only going along with it to show Joe I was desirable even if he didn't want me.

God, this is complicated. How the hell do I handle this?

'Yeah, she said something like that,' Joe said, turning to me. 'Paris seems to suit you, Tessa. You look really well. That's okay for me to say, isn't it?'

'I suppose so,' I replied tightly.

'I was even more surprised when you said you were staying on here, but now things make more sense.' He eyed us as he sipped his wine again. 'I couldn't wait to talk to you back in London so I thought why not take a few days' break in Paris and see why you are loving it here so much.'

'You're staying here?' I repeated.

Joe smiled that dazzling Disney-prince smile of his. 'We have a lot to talk about, baby.'

24

Joe's sentence settled in silence for a moment.

I was flabbergasted.

Joe was still smiling.

Ethan leaned forward. 'She's not your baby,' Ethan snapped at him.

Joe's smile didn't falter an inch. 'Isn't she?'

Juliette arrived with the first course then, stopping by the table suddenly when she heard the conversation. She looked over at me. 'Are you okay?' she mouthed while Joe and Ethan stared at one another as if locked in a silent battle.

Juliette shook me out of my silence. 'Can you both stop?' I pleaded. 'This is crazy. You're best friends. Look, Joe, I'm confused why you're here. I needed to get away after everything and I've been having a good time.'

'I don't want to ruin that,' Joe promised. 'I am so proud of you, coming to Paris alone and setting your new book here. I bet it's amazing.'

I tried to not let on that anything was wrong. 'So, why are you here?'

'We didn't get a chance to talk that night... You left our flat in such a hurry, and we were both angry and upset. Now we've had a chance to have some space and think, I thought we needed to get... closure, I suppose.'

'Oh.' He was right that everything moved so fast. One minute, I was at his works do trying to meet his colleagues and prove to him I could be the kind of girlfriend he wanted, and the next I found out he'd been seeing another woman, and then I was moving out of our flat.

'Why couldn't that wait until Tessa's trip was over?' Juliette broke in then. She made another excellent point. I was so glad she was here. Joe was so charming, it was hard sometimes to think he could be capable of what he had done to me. I supposed that was how he had been able to get away with it for six months.

'Because I also have something important to talk to Ethan about. So I thought why not come and spend some time with two of my favourite people?' Joe said. 'Food looks great, Juliette.'

'Oh, yes.' She placed our plates down, flustered. I knew the feeling. Joe was being very disconcerting. He seemed relaxed and happy and polite, like nothing was wrong right now. Like we hadn't had a bad breakup or I hadn't just been kissing his best friend. Whereas me, Ethan and Juliette were tense and confused and snapping not only at him, but also at each other. I envied Joe's confidence and ease like I always had. Maybe I had hoped it might rub off on me if we spent enough time together.

It hadn't though.

'Yeah, I have something to tell you that you're really going to want to hear,' Joe offered to Ethan.

'What the hell are you on about?' he replied heavily.

'Well, I'd rather talk about it just us two. No offence, Tessa or Juliette,' Joe said, smiling at us. He tasted the first course Juliette had bought. I wasn't even paying attention to what it was. 'This is great. Anyway, yeah, Ethan, it's something my dad has been keeping a secret. You'll want to hear it, trust me.'

'Can I trust you?' Ethan replied.

'I wasn't able to,' I added quietly.

'How about this for an idea...' Joe said, ignoring Ethan's question and my response easily. 'I'll meet you for a coffee tomorrow morning, Ethan. I was thinking of taking Tessa somewhere she wanted to go when we planned this trip. I think it would help with your book. So, I could meet you after I speak to Ethan, Tessa. What do you both think?' he asked.

Ethan looked at me. I had no idea what to say. 'You're playing games with us, Joe.'

Joe held up his hands. 'I'm not. I just want to make amends. To both of you, okay? While I'm here in Paris. Will you let me do that, please?'

'Why should they?' Juliette asked him.

'It's a fair point, Juliette. As I said, Ethan will want to hear my news. And you'll be pleased about it too. I know what you two always dreamed about...' He let that tantalising thought hang in the air before looking at me again. 'And, Tessa, as I said, we have a lot to say to each other, don't we? Let me take you out and if nothing else, it'll be inspiration for your novel. But hopefully, it will give the closure that I bet you've been looking for. I know you; you haven't been able to move on properly, have you?'

I could feel all their eyes on me. I hated that he knew he was still on my mind. He maybe didn't realise how much he had shattered my trust and hope in love, but he guessed enough to know I must have been struggling to come to Paris alone, and not want to return home yet. If this was my chance to finally put me and Joe in the past and move on then I had to take it, didn't I?

'I want closure,' I said, making sure he knew that was all this was. 'I'll hear you out but then that's it. After tomorrow, you'll go home again?'

'Mate?' Joe turned to him.

Ethan sighed. 'Fine. I'll hear you out too.'

'Neither of you will regret it.' He stood up quickly. 'I'll message you both where and when to meet me. The starter was great, Juliette, but I need to make a call so I'll leave you all to it. It's on me though.' He waved his credit card. 'Goodnight!'

I watched him go and realised he hadn't replied to me asking if after tomorrow, he would go back to London.

'This is a very bad idea,' Juliette said, and neither Ethan nor I could disagree with her.

* * *

The next morning dawned dry and bright, the promise of a new season in the air.

I woke up early at Juliette's, restless after our encounter with Joe at her restaurant. When he had left, Juliette had joined us and we had picked at her lovely food before deciding we all needed an early night. Ethan and I had shared an awkward goodbye, only a hug, not a kiss, before going to our separate apartments to sleep. I hated that Joe's arrival had forced a pause in our time together. If he hadn't turned up, maybe we would have spent last night together. Instead, I looked out of Juliette's guest bedroom window at the way the sun peeked through the Parisian rooftops, casting the city in a golden glow.

Juliette had stayed out last night with her older man and so her apartment was quiet. I made myself a cup of tea and grabbed a croissant and took both to her writing desk, deciding the only way I could put the fact Ethan was meeting up with my ex, and I soon would be, out of mind was to work on my book before I needed to have a shower and get ready.

I had finished chapter three with my leading lady meeting a French man in a café in Paris on a rainy night and, after too much wine, confessing she had given up on love. He had made her promise to let him show her she shouldn't give up on it. I started the next chapter with them meeting the next day and him taking her to The Wall of Love.

Writing about it brought back the day Ethan had taken me there. It was the first moment that I had felt hope that I would believe in love again. I was so grateful to Ethan for that. I lost myself in writing, using my experience of seeing all the ways you could say 'I love you' in the story, and when my characters had a moment by the wall, the first spark between them showing up, I stopped writing to think about how there had been a spark between Ethan and me when we had gone there. I had no idea when I'd gone to the wall with him that we'd end up kissing, or that my writer's block would finally clear while I was in Paris. I was still a long way from where I had been before I met Joe, but I knew I was so much closer than I would have been if I had stayed in London.

Checking the time, I closed my laptop and went to the bathroom to get ready. Ethan had promised to get in touch after his coffee with Joe before my own meeting with him so I would know what he had told him. I hadn't heard anything yet though. I was anxious about my ex and the man I had been kissing meeting up without me. What if Joe put Ethan off me somehow? Or Ethan decided his friendship with Joe meant more than whatever we had started? Joe had seemed to take us seeing one another in his stride, but I had no idea if that had been a front and if he might beg Ethan to stop seeing me. My anxious mind was overthinking hard as I got ready.

After my shower, I put on jeans and a white shirt along with my trainers as it was a lovely day. I pulled my hair into a ponytail and put on some light makeup. As I glanced in Juliette's mirror, I realised this outfit was really me. Back when I was with Joe, meeting him like this would probably have worried me because he would think I was too casual, not dressed 'girly' enough for his tastes. But we weren't together now. I could dress exactly how I liked. That helped calm my nerves at seeing him again and hearing what he had to say to me. This meeting was for closure, he had said, and I needed that. I hoped after this, I would finally move on from our time together and get my old spark fully back. I would be able to finish my novel, and whatever was happening with me and Ethan could carry on as if he hadn't interrupted us.

It was time to head to the spot Joe had asked to meet me at. I checked my phone again but there had been no contact from Ethan. I bit my lip, hoping that wasn't a bad sign.

So I sent a quick message.

> Are you okay? What happened with Joe? I'm just about to meet him...

I waited five minutes but there was no reply and I needed to leave or I would be late. Maybe Ethan would be there with Joe and would tell me face-to-face. I tried to hope for that as I left Juliette's apartment, but my stomach swirled with nerves regardless.

25

I met Joe near the River Seine. Paris was bustling thanks to the sunshine, but I spotted him easily. A group of younger women were looking over at him as I approached. He wore a smart beige jacket with matching trousers and a white shirt with shiny shoes. His hair despite the slight breeze was styled to perfection and in his hand was a bunch of red roses.

I stopped walking, my heart racing. He made for a very handsome sight and I had to remind myself that his looks were deceiving.

Joe turned and saw me, a smile forming on his face as he waved.

Taking a deep breath, I went over to him, hoping this would be a quick meeting and I could get back to my Paris trip. 'Hi,' I said.

'Morning, Tessa. These are for you. You look lovely.' Joe greeted me, planting a kiss on my cheek, the compliment he gave me surprising me enough that I didn't duck away when he made the move to kiss me. His aftershave hit me, a musky scent that took me back to being in his arms. I tried to shake off the memory but it was impossible. He handed me the roses then gestured behind him at the river. 'I remembered that you really wanted to take a boat trip on the Seine so I thought we could do that while we talk,' he said.

I looked at the waiting boat. It was a small one, clearly hired just for us. I had really wanted to do that but it had slipped my mind while I was here. I was surprised he remembered that. 'Oh, okay then,' I said, not wanting to turn down the opportunity even if it meant doing it with Joe. I would have preferred to do it with Ethan. As we went over to the boat, I checked my phone again but there had still hadn't been a response to my message from Ethan. 'Um, so how was coffee this morning?' I asked Joe, hoping he would tell me what they had talked about so I could stop worrying.

'Oh yeah, it was good. Ethan went straight to talk to Juliette afterwards,' Joe said, holding out a hand to help me onto the boat.

I frowned, wondering why Ethan went to talk to her but not tell me what had happened. I couldn't ask anything else though as the boat driver greeted us and we sat at the back.

My mind quietened a little as we set off along the water at a gentle pace. The river glistened from the sunshine and as we approached a bridge, I could see the Eiffel Tower stretching up into the cloudless blue sky. I smiled despite the current situation.

'What a view, huh?' Joe said, looking across at me, seeing me smile. 'I knew you'd love this. Remember when we took that boat trip in London? Champagne under the stars.'

'That was beautiful,' I agreed. Joe had been very good at romantic dates like that, but now I questioned them all.

'Speaking of...' Joe reached behind him and pulled out a bottle of champagne from a bucket and two glasses. 'We have to continue the tradition.'

'I'm not sure that...' I started to protest, but he handed me a glass and I thought maybe it would make this situation less awkward, so I took a sip. Then I looked at him. 'What is this all about, Joe?'

'What do you mean?'

I waved the glass. 'The boat trip, the champagne, turning up here in Paris...'

Joe sighed. 'I've missed you,' he said.

I looked away. 'You can't say that.'

'It's true. I kept seeing all these photos on social media of you here; you looked so happy and I thought, why am I not there with her?'

'Why?!' I turned back to him incredulously. 'Because you cheated on me; you chose another woman over me.'

'No,' he said firmly.

'You're denying it?'

'No,' he said, softer. 'I did cheat. But I cheated on Rachel, not you.'

'What are you talking about?' I snapped, confused. I gulped down my champagne in the hopes it might help make this conversation a tiny bit more bearable.

'I was with Rachel first, on and off for a long time; she's a family friend,' Joe said. 'When I met you, I tried hard to ignore my attraction to you but I couldn't stop thinking about you. I wanted you to be mine. And these past two months, I've missed you, Tessa. Seeing you walking in that restaurant with Ethan was like a gut punch. My best friend has been sleeping with my girlfriend!' Joe shook his head.

I stared in shock. Was he serious? 'I'm not your girlfriend!' I cried, struggling to keep calm. 'How can you say that? You cheated on me. The whole time we were together. You haven't spoken to me for two months. We are not together. You are my ex.' I wasn't about to tell him Ethan and I hadn't had sex – it was none of Joe's business. 'You didn't want me,' I added, trying not to let him see how much his rejection had affected me.

'I did,' he argued. 'You have no idea how much I wanted to be with you. I know I screwed us up. I screwed a lot of things up. I swear the last thing I wanted to do was hurt you.'

I looked away from him again. The sights of Paris rolling past the river didn't help this time. All I could think about was how he had broken my heart. 'What is the point of this? You did hurt me, Joe. You really hurt me.'

Joe looked crushed. 'This isn't going the way I was hoping.'

'What were you hoping?' I asked, confused as to what he was expecting to happen here.

Had he thought I'd leap into his arms?

'I hoped that you had missed me too,' he said, confirming my thoughts. He moved a bit closer on the boat bench. 'Tessa, I know what I did was wrong, but you have no idea the pressure I've been under. My family expects a lot of me. My father especially… They love Rachel. She's a family friend. Our fathers are in business together, for God's sake. It's been expected we'd get married since we were teenagers.'

'So why did you start something with me?' I asked pointedly.

'Because I don't love her. No, I do… but I'm not in love with her. When I saw you in the park that day, I was desperate to get to know you and every day we spent together confirmed that what I have with Rachel isn't the real thing.'

'You can't believe what we had was the real thing,' I said, startled that he was being so open with me after all this time. It made me hesitate. Had he actually loved me? I felt confused and just like I had felt when I was him – unsure what was real and what wasn't.

'Of course it was! We fell in love, didn't we?' Joe asked, his lips curving into that devastating smile of his. 'I know we were happy. That you wanted me. That when I held you in my arms, it was real.'

'Only because I had no idea I wasn't the only woman you were holding.' I shook my head.

'I never held her like I held you, I swear. Tessa, I made a huge mistake. But Rachel was the mistake. You never were.'

'I thought you said you came to give us closure.'

'I came to get you back,' he replied matter-of-factly.

26

Joe's words hung in the air as the boat continued on down the River Seine. I stared at Joe as he watched me.

I came to get you back.

'I know you have missed me too,' Joe said then. He reached out and touched my cheek. 'Haven't you?'

My skin warmed to his touch, the familiarity of it confusing me for a moment. Looking into his eyes on this romantic boat trip was seductive. Like the past two months could be erased if I leaned into him. But did I actually want them erased? I thought about Ethan then and I leaned away from Joe's touch. 'I've been here with Ethan,' I said, avoiding answering his question directly.

'Well, Ethan has always wanted everything that I have,' Joe said. 'He has really low self-esteem. He's always been jealous of me. Has he said anything about you two carrying on after Paris?'

'Um...' I didn't know what to say. We hadn't exactly made any promises to each other. I knew Ethan had compared himself to Joe in the past, he'd admitted it and questioned whether he could be my type after I'd been with Joe. But I knew our kisses had been real. He wasn't with me because of Joe.

I really hope not anyway.

'Besides,' Joe said, carrying on when I failed to respond. 'It's not like you'll get much time together when he moves here, and you're in London.'

'Why would Ethan move to Paris?'

'To open a restaurant with Juliette,' Joe said with a shrug. 'Here.' He held out the champagne and re-filled our empty glasses.

'What do you mean?' Whenever they had talked about it, neither Ethan nor Juliette had mentioned their restaurant would be in Paris, and besides that, I knew Ethan didn't want to do anything about opening their own place until he'd paid back the money Joe's father had lent him to study to be a chef.

'That's what I came to tell Ethan,' Joe said. 'I wasn't lying, I did need to talk to him but I decided to come to Paris instead of call him so I could see you too. Ethan told my dad that he wanted to pay back the money he'd lent him years ago and my dad had been thinking about it. He finally told me the full story and said I could tell Ethan.' Joe paused to sip his champagne, and I did the same. 'Ethan's mum inherited money from her parents and put some of it into an account for Ethan without him knowing. When she became ill, she went to my dad and asked him to take the account over and use it if he needed it. She didn't want Ethan to spend it and end up in financial trouble like his father had done. She was adamant Ethan shouldn't know about it until he turned thirty when my father could hand it over, and he'd be responsible enough to handle it.'

'Oh,' I said, thinking Ethan must have been shocked to hear this. 'So, your father dipped into it when Ethan said he wanted to study to be a chef?'

'Exactly. So when Ethan said he wanted to pay the money back before he could open his own restaurant, my father decided to come clean about the whole thing. The money left in the account is more than enough for Ethan to do what he wants.'

'Wow. What did Ethan say?' I asked, wishing he had replied to my message and told me all of this himself. He could finally make his dream come true. I was so happy for him. And Juliette too.

'He rushed off to tell Juliette the news. He was already talking about quitting his job in London so they can get started. Maybe he'll work at her family's place until they find their own place.'

'So they want to open somewhere here in Paris?'

'I thought he would have told you that.'

I slipped into silence. When Ethan and Juliette had talked about it, neither had said where they wanted the restaurant to be. I had no idea why I had assumed it would be in London when Juliette's life was here in Paris. Suddenly, it seemed Ethan and I could never be anything more than a holiday thing.

'Tessa, isn't this, just us two here, good? We could have this all the time.'

And it was good. A romantic boat trip in Paris. Us two with champagne. Joe, handsome and charming, paying me attention and making me feel special. This had been why I had moved in with him after only six weeks. Why I had fallen so quickly and hard for him. Why Carly said I'd been so impulsive after meeting him. 'But this isn't real life,' I said. 'We had romantic dates but you didn't let me into your life. You didn't want me to meet your friends, you would never bring me home to your family, I was kept away from your colleagues. We were in this little bubble of us two because you knew if you let me into your life, I'd realise I wasn't the person you were planning to have a future with.'

Joe reached for me then but I pulled back. He sighed but didn't try again. 'I kept you away from people who might tell you about Rachel. Like Ethan. He gave me so much shit... but he doesn't get it. What it's like to have all this pressure to do what your family wants. I won't let them make me be with someone I don't want to be with though. Rachel and I are over. I promise, Tessa.' He took my hand in his and squeezed it. 'You are who I want a future with.'

He was saying things I had longed for him to say. The night I saw him with Rachel, I had been so angry and upset but I had hoped he might follow me and beg me to stay, to say he chose me not her, but he hadn't. 'Why are you saying this now?'

'Because now I know what it's like to lose you,' Joe replied.

Oh God, the way he is looking at me...

The boat driver called behind him then to say the trip was almost over and he steered the boat back towards where we had got on it earlier. My head was spinning with everything Joe had said along with the glasses of bubbly. My heart was starting to remember falling for Joe. And I really didn't want it to.

When we climbed out of the boat, Joe took my hand but he didn't let it go as we stood by the edge of the river together. He turned to face me. 'Do I have any chance of getting you to forgive me? Of making things up to you? Of us trying again? We can't let those six months go, can we?'

I hesitated as I looked into his eyes. I tried not to think about the good times or how it had felt to be in his arms. I tried to remember the hurt, but him looking at me like that, the boat trip, the fact we were in Paris and the disappointment in my chest thinking that there was no chance of me and Ethan really starting something made me unsure what to say to Joe right now.

Joe reached out to touch my cheek and this time, I didn't pull away. He kept his eyes on mine and moved down to touch my lips. 'I really did miss us, Tessa,' he said.

'I have missed us too,' I admitted then. I had missed what I thought we had.

Can we actually have it for real this time with Rachel out of the picture?

Joe smiled, looking pleased, and he leaned down. I was rooted to the spot, confused and unsure, but I was also curious what it would feel like to kiss him again. He moved his hand to the back of my head, drawing me closer, and his lips found mine. Muscle memory crept in. My mouth knew what his felt like. My body responded to his touch like there hadn't been a two-month gap and I found myself kissing him back, losing myself for a moment.

Just when I realised what I was doing and was starting to pull back, Joe abruptly leaned away from me. 'Oh, hi mate,' he said, letting me go as he spoke to someone behind me.

I turned around and my stomach dropped to see Ethan standing right by us, shock and pain on his face.

27

'Ethan! What are you doing here?' I cried, my cheeks turning pink. I quickly stepped back from Joe but I knew it was too late. Ethan had seen us kiss.

'I came to see you,' he replied tersely. 'Joe said this was where you would be. Did you plan this, Joe?'

I turned from Ethan to Joe.

Joe held up his hands. 'Of course not. Why would I? Tessa was mine to kiss a long time before you decided to pursue her, mate.' The word 'mate' was heavy with bitterness.

'You lost her a long time ago, mate,' Ethan replied, copying his tone. 'What are you really doing here?' he said, walking right up to us. 'I don't buy that you came to tell me what your father said; you could have phoned me.'

'I wanted to see Tessa. I miss her,' Joe said, throwing me a smile.

'You've got some nerve,' Ethan said then. 'Seriously, Joe, you cheated on her!'

'Well, she said she's missed me too,' Joe said with a triumphant smile. 'I don't blame her after days with you. She doesn't want second best any longer.'

My mouth fell open. That was such a low blow, and it was untrue too. I shook my head. 'Can I speak now?' I said, exasperated by the both of them.

'You know what, Joe? I stayed quiet when I realised that you were stringing both Tessa and Rachel along because we've known each other since we were kids, but you're taking the piss now,' Ethan said, ignoring me, an edge to his voice I hadn't heard before.

Joe stepped closer to Ethan. 'What the fuck has it got to do with you? You're nothing to Tessa. You've known her a few days; we were together for six months. We were in love. She doesn't want you. And for trying to take my girlfriend from me, you can think again about being part of my family any more.'

Ethan flinched and I knew that had hurt him. But to Joe, he shrugged. 'Good. I don't want to be part of it any more. I have always been so grateful for everything your family has done for me but Jesus, you like to remind me about it at every opportunity. You make me feel crap because I have a different background than yours. But as I see it, I'm happier than you've ever been so I don't know why you're so superior with me all the time. It's not friendship, what we have. Not any more.'

'What are you talking about?' Joe asked with a laugh like he couldn't believe Ethan was talking to him like this.

'I'm done with us. And if you think Tessa would ever go near you again—'

'I can speak for myself,' I reminded Ethan sharply. I was tired of being stuck in between the two of them like this.

He looked at me and shook his head. 'Shit, I know, I'm sorry, but him thinking that you might take him back...' His blue eyes flashed in anger.

'Now Tessa knows I want her back, she'll never go near you again,' Joe replied with such confidence, I stared at him, stunned.

'You want her back?' Ethan asked in a quieter voice. His chest sagged like a deflating balloon, the fight going out of him.

Joe wrapped an arm around me. 'We're working things out, mate. I'm sorry.'

Before I could say anything, Ethan spun around and walked away. I watched him go for a second but I knew I couldn't leave things like this, so I rushed after him, ignoring Joe calling my name.

'Ethan!' I managed to catch up with him and took his arm, forcing him to stop. Reluctantly, he turned to face me. 'We need to talk.'

'What's the point, Tessa? Joe is back.' He was avoiding my eyes.

'What about us?'

'Be honest, would you have ever looked twice at me if we hadn't been forced to spend time together in that apartment?'

I didn't know what to say. I shifted on the spot. 'But we did spend all that time together and you know I enjoyed it and...'

'Joe is your type and I'm not.' Ethan shrugged.

I knew he had admitted to being jealous of Joe and having low self-esteem so I could see that witnessing my kiss with Joe had really hurt. 'Joe's kiss took me by surprise.'

'You kissed him back; I saw.'

'I was just about to pull away,' I protested.

'Were you?' Ethan sighed. 'Look, you clearly want to talk to Joe and try to sort things out, and I have a lot to deal with too. Joe's father says I have the money for mine and Juliette's restaurant after all.'

'Why didn't you tell me?' I asked him, hurt he hadn't contacted me after their coffee chat. 'What Joe had said, I thought I'd hear it from you. Instead, he was the one to tell me.'

'I needed to tell Juliette; we've been talking about this for years.'

I nodded. I did get that. 'I am happy for you; I just wish things with us were different,' I said, thinking about how he soon would be building a life here in Paris. I wasn't sure I could ever be part of it and I was too scared to ask if he thought I could be.

'Me too, Tessa. Look, I need to go, and you should go back to Joe,' Ethan said with a sigh.

'So...' I trailed off, feeling suddenly like I could cry. 'That's it then?' I asked, wondering how just yesterday we had felt so close, and now I felt like this was the last time I was going to see him.

Ethan looked at me once before avoiding my gaze again. He nodded. 'Goodbye, Tessa.'

I couldn't think of anything else to say to prolong this conversation.

Ethan slipped his hands into his pockets and turned to go. Then he looked back at me for a moment. 'We'll always have Paris, right?'

'Right,' I choked out as he turned and walked off, slouching away into the Parisian crowds. I watched him go with a heavy heart.

'Tessa.'

I jumped as Joe appeared beside me.

'Why did you tell Ethan we were working things out?' I asked him.

'Aren't we?' Joe asked, eyebrow raised.

'I don't know. This has all come out of the blue. I'm confused. I haven't heard from you in two months; it's a lot to take in. And Ethan—'

'Isn't the right man for you,' Joe broke in. 'You need a romantic hero, Tessa.'

'Like you?' I enquired with a raised eyebrow.

He missed the sarcasm though. He grabbed my hand with his. 'Yes,' he said fiercely. 'I'm the man you write about, aren't I?'

'You're the *type* of man I have written about,' I acknowledged. Handsome, charming and rich. Joe was like the love interests in my books. But then he had broken my heart. 'But a lot has changed since we met.'

'You haven't changed,' he replied confidently.

Haven't I?

'I know you can love me again. Why don't we go home and see what happens? You don't want to stay in Paris now, surely?'

Joe's question hung in the air.

I had been so excited to stay in the city longer – to work on my book and spend more time with Ethan. But everything had changed. Suddenly, I wondered if Carly had been right all along and I had made another bad decision about my love life – falling into something so quickly with Ethan. My priority should be my book. But once again, my impulsive heart had pulled me into something that I wasn't ready for. Joe arriving again had shown that. I had let him kiss me. Part of me had wanted him to. Although I was having a good time with Ethan. The problem was, I wasn't sure I trusted either Ethan or Joe, and I definitely didn't trust my heart. I was confused and lost. And coming to Paris had seemed to be the answer, but now I had no idea what the answer was.

'Maybe I should go home,' I said both to myself and to Joe.

28

'What are you doing?' Juliette demanded from the doorway of her guest bedroom. I had sent her a message after Joe had walked me back to her apartment and told her I was planning to leave Paris today. She had rushed from Cinq to catch me, and I had heard her throw a disgruntled greeting to Joe, who was waiting for me in the living room.

'Um... packing my things,' I said, pausing as I folded a T-shirt into my case. I was becoming a pro at packing at this point.

'But why are you leaving? I thought you wanted to stay!' Juliette said, shaking her head.

'Things have changed,' I replied, going back to the task in hand. 'You and Ethan have lots to sort out and I need to do the same in London.'

She leaned in closer. 'Don't tell me you mean you and that *man* in there,' she said, practically spitting the word 'man'. 'Ethan told me he saw you kissing!'

'It's complicated,' I said, lowering my voice in case Joe could hear us. 'I was with Joe a long time, we lived together, I loved him. He is sorry, he's not with the other woman any more...'

'But what about Ethan?'

'What about him?' I snapped back, my heart aching at the thought of him. 'He didn't try to stop me leaving. He has future plans that don't involve me. We hardly know each other after all.'

'*Non*. That's not true. I've seen you together,' she argued. 'You're making a mistake getting back with Joe.'

'You're just like my friend Carly. Can everyone stop telling me what's best for me please?' I threw my hands up in the air. I was so confused. Everyone seemed so sure I was doing something wrong all the time. Was it any wonder I was terrified of making another mistake?

'What about your writing though?' Juliette asked.

'I have spent enough time here to be able to write the book. There is no way I'm going to make my deadline anyway so I need to speak to my publisher.' I bit my lip; that thought was terrifying. I wanted to put it off for as long as possible. The same way I wanted to avoid any more decision making. 'Paris has been fun but this isn't real life. I can't stay on holiday forever.'

'I thought you liked it here,' she said quietly. I could see our conversation was upsetting her but I didn't know what to do. I was just as upset by the thought of leaving but how could I stay and watch Ethan and her make their dreams come true and know I wouldn't be part of it?

Ethan doesn't want me to stay anyway.

Him walking away from me earlier would hurt for a long time, I knew. There was nothing left for me in Paris.

'I'm sorry, Juliette. I am so grateful we met.' I zipped up my case and pulled it upright. 'Maybe we'll see each other again sometime.'

Juliette came over and gave me a tight hug. 'Do not forget you are amazing, okay?' she said softly into my ear. 'You deserve to be loved for exactly who you are.'

A lump lodged itself in my throat. I gave her a quick squeeze back, fighting the urge to lie down on her guest bed and cry. 'Thank you for everything,' I choked out before grabbing my things and leaving her.

'Ready, baby?' Joe asked, jumping up from the sofa when I walked through.

'Yep,' I said, trying to smile.

'Got us all booked on the next Eurostar. Let's go home.'

I followed him out, glancing behind me before I walked out of Juliette's front door, a wave of sadness washing over me. I couldn't stay here now that Ethan and I were over, but it was a wrench to leave at the same time.

'You're doing the right thing,' Joe said, seeing my face. He led me out of Juliette's building and into a waiting taxi to take us to the train station. Joe was always confident and decisive. It was nice to just let him organise everything so I didn't have to think. I ignored the prickling feeling in the back of my mind that being with someone who didn't want you to think wasn't a good thing.

As we arrived at the station and had all our documents checked for the Eurostar, I looked at my phone. There was nothing from Ethan. He clearly didn't care that I was leaving, I almost sent a message to Carly to tell her I was heading home but decided I couldn't face it. She would want to know why and I knew she would be like Juliette and think I was crazy to be leaving with Joe, for even entertaining the idea of trying again with him. So I was a coward and put my phone away.

We soon boarded the waiting train. Joe stowed our bags and we sat down next to one another.

'I am so happy you're giving us a second chance,' Joe said, reaching over to squeeze my thigh.

'I didn't say that,' I corrected him. 'We have a lot to talk about.'

'You're coming home with me; that's enough to show me that you do still love me. We are meant to be. So why did you decide to come to Paris on your own?'

'I needed a change of scenery,' I told him. The train started up then and I looked out of the window as we left Paris still bathed in sunshine. I had felt like Paris had been good for me but now I wasn't so sure. It suddenly seemed like I was back to exactly who I was when I had first sat on the Eurostar fleeing London. I crossed my legs so that Joe's hand slipped off my knee.

'I'm glad you got it out of your system. I was so shocked when Ethan said you'd come on our trip. I thought, that's not like my Tessa...' Joe grinned at me. 'Now you're back where you belong.'

I forced out a smile and Joe pulled out his phone to check his emails. I leaned back in my seat, glad of the silence. I should have felt happy that Joe wanted me back, that I was going home. But I couldn't feel it. I told myself to shake it off. My chapter in Paris was over. Like I said to Juliette, it had just been a holiday. Holidays have to end after all. I needed to focus now on the future.

Turning to Joe, I said, 'I have started writing my next book. I'm setting it in Paris but—'

'Sorry, baby, I need to just focus on this for a bit. Why don't you read or something?'

I didn't answer but I reached into my bag and pulled out my Kindle. On the way here, I hadn't been able to read the book my publicist Stevie had given me, *First Impressions* by Liv Jones, because I'd felt so betrayed by love. I thought about how Ethan had been reading my book in Paris. Joe didn't even want to hear about my writing. I believed in love again but I knew that was thanks to Ethan and not the man sitting beside me. Everything felt all upside down suddenly. I shut out the feeling that things had gone completely wrong and tried to lose myself in someone else's love story.

29

We arrived in London at dusk. Predictably, it was raining in my home city, a far cry from the spring-like day I'd left behind me in Paris. I hoped it wasn't a bad omen. Joe needed to see his father so he suggested that I go round to his flat in the morning and we'd have brunch. I felt almost in a trance as I agreed to it and let him give me a quick kiss on the lips. I didn't feel anything when his lips touched mine, but I told myself I was just shattered from such a long day and all the upheaval, not to mention the train journey. Joe put me in a taxi with my things and I exhaled heavily as I was finally left alone.

The taxi took me from St Pancras to my flat in Putney. We drove over the bridge and I looked at the familiar River Thames welcoming me home. The rain was coming down in sheets by the time we reached my building. I paid the driver and rushed inside, but I was soaked when I walked through the door.

I propped up my suitcase and switched on the lights in the living room. I'd found this flat in a mad panic after moving out of Joe's. Carly and Luke had wanted me to move into theirs, but they had one bedroom and I didn't want them to deal with my heartbreak more than they were already. I'd taken the first flat I'd found that wasn't extortionate rent. It was further out in London than I'd ever lived but it was close to the river. I could hear birdsong here and not just traffic and the view out of the small window in the living room showed trees and not just buildings as far as the eye could see.

I looked around now. I'd barely done anything other than unpack my things. It hadn't been furnished and I had only bought the bare minimum to make it liveable. So it felt empty compared to the Paris Airbnb and Juliette's place. I opened up my case and pulled out the print Ethan had got me and the things I had bought with him in Paris. I would have to wait a while for the furniture that was being shipped. I carried everything through and placed it in the living room, and instantly it felt homelier.

I put the chess set on my coffee table with a heavy heart. It inevitably reminded me of Ethan, and playing our games in the Airbnb together.

I won't have anyone to play chess with now.

My phone beeped then and I checked to see an email had come through from Gita, my editor. An uneasy feeling spread through me as I read it.

Hi Tessa,

    Just checking in as we get close to your deadline. How's the book coming? Do you have a title for me yet? I'm excited to read it. I hope you had a fabulous trip. Let me know...

    All the best,

    Gita.

'Oh God,' I said aloud to my empty flat. I had no idea what she would say when I confessed I only had a few chapters written. I had been hoping to get more done on my extended stay in Paris but now I was home, I didn't know how well I would be able to write. After all, I had been so stuck before I went away.

Telling myself I would deal with everything tomorrow, I went into my bedroom. In theory, it was far too early to go to bed but I needed to change after getting wet in the rain, so it made sense to pull on my pjs. I was tired, it was dark and my flat had nothing in so I let myself crawl under the covers and block it all out for just one more night.

* * *

The following morning, I decided to walk to Joe's flat even though it took about an hour. I picked up a takeaway tea on the way. The morning was dry but breezy, but I needed that to clear my head. I had slept for hours and I felt bleary-eyed today.

It had been a crazy twenty-four hours.

One minute, I had been homeware shopping with Ethan and scared that Carly was right and I was rushing into things with him, then Joe had turned up and everything had changed. Ethan would be waking up ready to start making plans with Juliette for their restaurant in Paris while I was here in London walking to meet my ex who wanted me back. Definitely something I hadn't seen coming.

I approached Joe's building with caution. I had moved in there in such a hurry when I'd had to leave my flat suddenly.

'You're moving in with him?' Carly and Luke had exchanged an uneasy look when I had gone round to tell them Joe had asked me to stay at his.

'I know it's quick...'

'How well can you know someone after only six weeks?' Carly said.

'It does feel quite sudden,' Luke added, more diplomatically.

'I'm happy,' I had replied. I was so head over heels for Joe that I didn't want to listen to my friends. If anything, I felt kind of smug that I'd had a whirlwind romance whereas theirs was a stable, comfortable relationship. Looking back, that was one of the only times Carly had given me unsolicited advice, and I'd ignored it. The second time was being worried about me staying in Paris with Ethan in case I rushed into something for the second time and ended up with a broken heart again.

As I looked up at the building I had shared with Joe for six months, I knew Carly would be even more worried about this. This time, I wouldn't be surprised by her worry. I would expect it. And that was why I hadn't told her yet. I knew deep down that hiding something from your best friend because you knew they wouldn't approve meant you knew it wasn't quite right. But I remembered how upset I had been when I saw Joe with Rachel, how much I had loved him and wanted him to love me the same. I had felt so rejected that night but now Joe wanted me again.

Two months ago, I would have been desperate for this reunion. But today, I hesitated on the doorstep before ringing his flat and being buzzed in.

I got in the lift and went up to his top-floor flat, the door swinging open before I could knock.

'There you are,' he said, stepping back to let me inside, closing the door behind us. Then he reached for me, pulling me towards him and pressing his lips against mine.

The same thing happened again as it had in Paris. I leaned in for a moment and returned the kiss, but then I didn't know if I wanted it or not. Luckily, he kept it brief and pulled away with a grin.

'Welcome home,' Joe said.

I looked around. The flat was unchanged since I was last in it. With my things gone, it was as if I had never been here. I'd lived here for six months but he hadn't changed anything except giving me a drawer and part of his wardrobe. It was all plush carpet, white walls, leather furniture and gadgets. The ultimate bachelor pad. I'd said nothing about it though. I hadn't tried to make my mark on it. But instead of that making him want me more, he had let me leave.

'I've ordered us brunch; I thought we probably would want to stay in and talk… and make up,' Joe said, throwing me a grin. 'I ordered from our favourite place.'

He meant his favourite place, of course. I walked over to the island where brunch was laid out along with glasses of Bucks Fizz. I ignored his comment about making up. I definitely wasn't ready for anything like that. I had only recently been in someone else's arms. I told myself to stop thinking about Ethan, but it was so hard when I looked at the brunch and knew that Ethan could have cooked me something even more delicious himself.

'Oh, and I got you something…'

I turned to see Joe bringing over a box. He laid it on the island and opened it up. Peering inside, my heart sank to see a silky black dress inside.

'So I can take you out tonight somewhere fancy.'

'With your father?' I asked, looking away from the dress, knowing I would hate having to wear it.

'Huh?' Joe sat at one of the stools and took a sip of Bucks Fizz. 'Sit. It's getting cold.'

I slid onto the stool next to him but knew even though I hadn't had dinner, I wouldn't be able to eat anything; it all just felt… off. I felt off being here again. I looked around. It had never felt like home, I realised now. 'I just wondered if I'd meet your family now you're not with Rachel. They can know about me now, right?'

Joe shifted on the stool. 'Sure, at some point. But we both want it to just be us for a while, right? Make up for the time we lost...' He reached over and squeezed my thigh. 'You'll look so hot in that dress tonight, baby, and then you can stay over. I missed you in our bed.'

'This is all moving too fast. You only just told me you missed me,' I said, feeling a bit panicked at how he seemed to think we would just go back to how we were two months ago before I knew about Rachel.

'What more is there to say?' Joe asked.

'Well, what about Rachel?'

'What about her?' He sighed as if annoyed.

'You still work with her. What if she wants you back?'

'She doesn't,' Joe said. 'Can we stop talking about her?' He was tucking into the brunch like this conversation didn't matter.

I was feeling increasingly like I shouldn't be here. 'Hang on,' I said. 'What did Rachel say when she found out about me? She saw me pour that wine over you...' I glanced at my glass of Bucks Fizz.

Joe sighed. 'She ended it. But only because she could see I was still in love with you...'

'When?'

'A couple of weeks ago.'

'So, you came to Paris because she dumped you; you wouldn't have done otherwise?' I asked, it all becoming clear. Joe didn't want me over Rachel; he just didn't want to end up with no one.

Joe reached for me. 'Baby, I'm your romantic hero, remember?'

It would be so easy to crawl back into his arms, but I realised looking at Joe, I was wrong. Paris *had* changed me. I no longer fit in his arms or his flat, if I ever really ever had done in the first place. Which I didn't think I had.

I pulled away from him. 'A romantic hero doesn't hide his heroine away like he's ashamed of her; he makes her feel loved and wanted and special, he cares about her, is kind to her and takes an interest in her life and the people she loves, and he sure as hell doesn't lie or cheat or be a complete coward who can't tell his family who he really loves.'

Joe's eyes widened in shock at my outburst. 'I told you I missed you.'

'But did you really miss me? Because you make me feel like I'm not good enough for you.' I jumped up off my stool and pointed to the dress he had bought me. 'Why did you buy me this?'

'Because you'll look hot in it,' he said.

'But you know I hate wearing dresses.'

'We can't go to this fancy restaurant with you looking casual like that,' Joe said, gesturing to my outfit of jeans, a thin jumper and boots.

There it is.

'You always want to change who I am but these past few days in Paris, I've realised that I quite like who I am. And other people like her too.'

Joe frowned. 'God, you're not talking about Ethan, are you? He was only with you to screw me over. He's always wanted what I have. He's so jealous of me, it's pathetic. He doesn't give a shit about you, Tessa. He didn't want you to stay in Paris, did he?'

I flinched, his words hurting me. 'Even if that's true, I don't want to be with you.' I said the words quickly before I could stop myself. Ethan had shown me what being with someone who liked the real me could be like. I didn't want to go back to something with Joe and end up feeling crap about myself again. It had taken leaving Paris and losing Ethan to make me see that I'd rather be alone than feel second best like Joe made me feel.

I wasn't sure who my romantic hero was in real life, but I knew for sure – it wasn't Joe.

I moved away from the island, further from him. 'I was so broken when I found out about Rachel. I felt like I couldn't write romance any more. You made me question love and happy endings and whether I could ever find a relationship in real life like the ones I write in my books. You made me not want to write about love any more. I thought you breaking my heart meant it was all bullshit. But I am not letting you ruin love and romance and relationships for me any more. And I sure as hell am not going to let you ruin my career for me either.' I took a deep breath and looked him right in the eyes. 'We are over, Joe. For good.'

Joe let out a laugh. 'Well, good luck finding a man to put up with you, Tessa. And listen to you talk about your nonsense career. Your books are worthless. Silly, girly books about love. It's embarrassing. Maybe I did you a favour if you can't write them now – give it up and get a proper job.'

I stared at him. I had no idea how I had believed myself to be in love with a man who thought so little of me and what I did for a living. Who thought so little of anyone but himself.

'I'm leaving now, Joe.' I turned around and walked out of his flat and vowed I'd never go back in there again.

30

I jumped into the lift and went downstairs, hurrying through the lobby until I was back out in the fresh air again. I slumped against the wall outside and closed my eyes. My hands were shaking. I had told Joe exactly what I thought. I wasn't sure I had ever really done that with anyone before, particularly people who had hurt or upset me or treated me less than I'd deserved. It was kind of exhilarating. I had spent so much time in this sad limbo but going to Paris had snapped me out of it, and I knew I couldn't let myself go back there. I had to carry on facing everything.

I started walking towards where Carly and Luke lived. They had been sure that Paris would help to heal me. It had helped me close a chapter of my life. My six months with Joe and the damage they had done, the way I had lost sight of who I was and what I wanted, and the hurt I had felt when we had ended. Paris had shown me that I would get back to myself. It wouldn't happen overnight, I still had scars on my heart, but I had let go of Joe for good. And I would find myself again.

When I reached their flat, I knocked nervously, hoping Carly would be pleased to see me. We hadn't spoken since she questioned me staying in Paris, apart from exchanging a message, and I missed her.

Carly opened the door and did a double take. 'Tessa! What the hell?' She broke into a wide smile and grabbed me, pulling me into her arms.

'I'm back,' I said, clinging on to my best friend gratefully.

'Why didn't you tell me?'

'I was too scared to.'

She pulled back and frowned. 'Why? Come in! This sounds like a wine chat but we got rid of all alcohol in the flat so is tea okay?'

'Perfect.' I went on through and sat down on the sofa while Carly made us both a cup of tea. Luke was out at work, she said, and she had been trying to work herself but had been thinking about me.

'And then you turn up!' she said, joining me on the sofa, handing me a cup of tea and nursing one herself. 'I missed your face,' she said.

'Me too. I'm sorry about our call in Paris. I know you were only looking out for me. And I should have listened.'

'And I should butt out unless you ask my advice. I'm sorry too.'

'How are you? How's everything with the baby?' I asked her.

'Good, I think. I have a doctor's appointment later this week. I'm so excited but it is a weird feeling. Like abstract?' She looked down. 'I forget there is someone growing inside me sometimes. I suppose it'll be more real when I get a bump or feel it kicking. If all goes smoothly, of course.'

'You guys will make wonderful parents. You both have basically parented me since we were teenagers.'

She laughed. 'We used to joke you were like our little sister even though we're all the same age. Dreamers need practical people to help them navigate life while they are dreaming.'

I smiled. 'I'm glad I've always had you both. And I can't wait to be an auntie. You know I've always been unsure about my own feelings about motherhood but I'll be right by your side for your journey.'

'Good. Because I have a feeling there will be a lot of freak-outs, I warn you now.'

'Noted. I'm so happy for you guys,' I told her.

Carly eyed me over her mug. 'I feel like you're trying to get me to forget that you've just suddenly come back from Paris. What happened, Tessa?'

I took a breath. 'Okay. Well...' I launched into the full story. Everything that had happened between me and Ethan, and then Joe turning up and Ethan seeing us kiss.

'Oh my God, Tessa!' Carly cried. 'I'm really trying not to give unsolicited advice any more but...' She grimaced.

'I didn't tell you because I knew what you would say. But for a moment, I was tempted to go back with Joe,' I admitted. 'Ethan walked away from me in Paris, and I doubt I'll see him again. I just felt lost and Joe was saying all the right things. I was so hurt when we broke up. But being in his flat just now, I realise I don't feel that way any more. I still hate that I gave him six months but I'm glad that's all I gave him. It would have been a mistake to try again.'

Carly nodded vehemently. 'I hate that you even gave him six months. You've made the right decision. But I'm sorry about Ethan. You really don't think you'll see him again?'

'He wants to open a restaurant in Paris. And his face when he saw me kissing Joe...' I shuddered at the memory. 'Plus, I think you were right. It all moved so quickly; maybe I was making the same mistake of jumping in and being impulsive. I don't know if I trust my heart right now.'

'You have a really good heart though, Tessa. Well, despite how it ended, I can see Paris has been good for you. You seem more confident and decisive. I don't think you would ever have said those things to Joe before.'

I thought about that. 'That's true. I do feel good that I was finally able to tell him what I think about him. And you know, I've never been good at telling people what I think. I always think years later of things I could have or should have said!'

'Yes,' she said, nodding furiously as she sipped her tea.

'For once, I said exactly what I wanted to say. Maybe if Joe had turned up here before I went to Paris, maybe he would have charmed me or convinced me to try again. But I don't know, after these past few days, I guess I have more perspective. I realised that I never felt like myself when I was with Joe. He made me feel like I wasn't good enough.'

'He's the one who isn't good enough,' she scoffed.

I smiled. 'I realised I'd much rather be single than be with someone who doesn't love me for who I am, you know?'

'Amen to that!' Carly looked regretful. 'Maybe I was too hard on this Ethan. If this is the effect he's had on you...'

'He did make me feel like he really saw me, that he liked me for who I am. He even read one of my books. Something Joe never did.' I shook my head. 'I need to see it though for what it was – just a lovely few days. Paris helped heal me when I needed it. Now, I need to focus on writing my book and moving on.'

'I guess so,' Carly said. 'How is the book going?'

'I've finally written a few chapters, and I think it could be good. But there is no way I'll make my deadline so I'm going to go and see my editor and tell her everything. I've been putting it off for far too long.' I reached out and touched Carly's arm. 'Thank you, and Luke, for convincing me to go to Paris. It didn't end the way I was hoping, maybe, but you're right – I do feel different now.'

Carly smiled. 'I'm glad. Want me to come to your publishers for moral support?'

'No, it's fine. I can do it. I just hope they don't give up on me.' I leaned back against her sofa. 'It's crazy to think I was worried I wouldn't be able to write again. I can't believe I let Joe do that to me.'

'Don't beat yourself up. I always knew it would be a temporary block. You are a writer. You can't give that up. Especially not for a man.'

I smiled. 'I'm glad I have you in my corner.'

'Always.'

'Me too, okay?'

'I know that,' Carly assured me. She patted her stomach. 'We'll need you around a lot.'

'Same. I need you making me tea and passing me biscuits to get this book finished.'

'Deal.'

* * *

If you can tell Joe to go and fuck himself, you can tell Gita you need an extension on a deadline.

That was my inner pep talk as I approached my publisher's office from the Tube. I looked up at the tall, sleek modern building that housed Turn the Pages with a mixture of nerves and resignation. I knew that I should have talked to Gita way before now. I hoped she wouldn't be too disappointed in me but if she was, it was time to face the music.

I walked into the office and got into the lift to go up to the floor my publishers had in the building. It opened to show the reception area complete with floor-to-ceiling bookshelves. Feeling like a fraud when I saw my titles they had published amongst the books on there, I greeted the receptionist and asked to see my editor. Gita soon strode out wearing an elegant suit, her dark hair in a sleek bun.

'Tessa, what a lovely surprise,' she said, kissing me on the cheek. 'Is everything okay?'

'Do you have time to talk, please?'

'Of course. Let's go into the boardroom.' She led me through the double doors and across their open-plan office. I recognised most of the faces and waved and smiled at people that I passed. I spotted Stevie on the phone at her desk by the window, who mouthed she would come and see me in a minute. I nodded, hoping she would still want to speak to me once she found out I would be missing my deadline.

Gita stood back to let me go into the boardroom in front of her and I turned down her offer of coffee, so we sat down at one end of the long table. 'What's wrong, Tessa?' she asked, studying me from the chair opposite.

I took a deep breath. 'I haven't exactly been truthful about where I am with the new book.'

She took a beat to respond. 'Okay. Where are you with it?'

'I've only just started it.'

I watched her eyebrows shoot up.

'Let me explain...' I quickly told her the story as briefly as I could. Everything that had happened with Joe, us breaking up and me having to find a new flat in a hurry then me finding myself in the midst of writer's block. 'Honestly, the last thing I wanted to do was to write about two people falling in love.'

'Well, I got that. I'm sorry, Tessa, that's such a horrible thing to go through. I understand why it's been hard for you to write. I wish you had told me what was going on; I wouldn't have pushed you for a synopsis or got Stevie to set up the book tour. I know now though so what are you thinking about it?'

'As you know, I went to Paris and it really helped.'

A look of relief passed over her face.

'I have started writing. I still think the idea I sent you has legs. A woman thinking she hates love but Paris opens her heart again.'

'I love the idea,' Gita agreed enthusiastically. 'And it sounds like you can use your trip as inspiration. You seem so much... calmer than when I last saw you.'

'I do?'

'You were rushing off to meet your boyfriend and you seemed, I don't know, nervous. Now I know why.'

I let that sink in. I supposed I had never felt comfortable in my skin during our six months together. 'You are right. I thought I had lost my hope in love, but I am not going to let Joe ruin romance for me. I love writing love stories and even if I'm not in love right now, even if I don't find my own happy ever after, I can still write one. I love reading romance whether I'm single or not, so I can write it whether I'm single or not too. Joe did leave me feeling bitter, I'm not going to lie, but I can use that for the start of this book.' I unwittingly thought about Ethan. 'Plus, Paris was a huge inspiration. Going there really helped me. I am sorry that I will need more time though as I've only got a few chapters down.'

Gita nodded. 'Of course. I always make sure my deadlines have room for life emergencies and it sounds to me like this could be a perfect Valentine's Day book. Let me talk to the team but if we move publication from the autumn to early in the New Year, that will give you time to write the first draft and we can do lots of activity around Valentine's for it. What do you think?'

My face almost cracked from how widely I smiled at her. 'Oh, Gita, I'm so relieved. I thought you'd tell me you didn't want to publish me any more.'

'Tessa,' she admonished. 'As if! You're one of our most talented and popular authors. We need to do some juggling, sure, but I'd much rather that than we publish something neither of us are fully happy with. Your fans will wait. I think this could be even bigger than your last book. And you're in luck: Deborah Day has sent in her book early so she can take your slot and the autumn tour. I'll speak to Stevie about it.' Gita stood up. 'I'll be back in a bit.'

I sank back into the chair as she went out and five minutes later, Stevie came into the boardroom. She was a gorgeous blonde who always wore a headband and a smile.

'Stevie!' I jumped up as she hurried around the table and we hugged warmly. 'You look so happy,' I said, without envy because she was lovely and deserved to be happy.

She pushed back her hair, flashing the large diamond ring on her left hand. 'I really am, I can't lie. On that note, I had something for you but Gita just told me everything...' She shook her head. 'Can I be frank and say that Joe is a complete dick? How could he do that to you?'

'Thank you,' I said with a chuckle. 'And you're right, he is. I'm so much better off without him. He showed up in Paris to try to get me back.'

Stevie's eyes widened.

'I know. I told him there was no way.'

'Good,' she said firmly. 'He doesn't deserve you. I'm sorry he's made writing so hard. But I love your new idea and I think it'll be brilliant. And actually, I think moving to February is a much better plan; I just told Gita that.'

'I'm so relieved. I was so nervous to tell you all.'

'You know us, we care about our authors, we want you to produce your best work and we want to sell it as best we can,' Stevie said.

'Great. Thank you. So, what did you have for me?' I asked.

'Well, it doesn't feel appropriate now but I have an invitation...' she said slowly, biting her lip.

'For your wedding?' I reached out and grabbed it from her hand. 'You don't need to hide that. Oh my God!' I looked at the fancy cream envelope. Stevie got engaged to Noah last year. I was touched they had invited me.

'We really want you to come,' she said as I opened it. 'I put a plus one on there.'

'You're getting married in autumn,' I said, seeing the date.

'Our favourite season,' she confirmed with a smile. 'There is so much to do but I'm so excited. We have a bridesmaid fitting later. Gita and Emily from here, of course, Liv, and Georgina who used to work with Noah.'

'Oh, tell Liv I am really enjoying reading her book,' I said.

'You two should get coffee sometime. I'll pass on your details to her.'

'That would be great.' I put her invite in my bag. 'I'll be there, Stevie; I can't wait. You will make a stunning bride and I know you two will be really happy together.'

She grabbed me for another hug. 'Thank you, Tessa. I was so scared to trust Noah with my heart again but I'm so happy I did. You'll meet someone who will make it easy to trust them, I know it.' Stevie and Noah had dated before he broke up with her so when she started working here, she was stunned to find he was her new boss and wanted her back.

My mind flitted to Ethan. Maybe if we had trusted each other more, we might have had a chance.

Gita returned to join us. 'What are you still doing here, Tessa? You need to get writing,' she said, but she was smiling.

'You're right.' I picked up my bag and looked at them. 'I really do appreciate you moving things for me. I promise I'll write you a brilliant book.'

'I would never doubt that,' Gita said.

'You've got this,' Stevie added.

I left them feeling much more confident and so happy I had been honest with them. As I left the office, I wished I could tell Ethan what had happened. He had been so encouraging of me writing again. He would be rooting for me right now. But then I remembered our goodbye by the river and shook my head. It was so hard to think that was our last conversation. I would remember his final words to me for a long time.

We'll always have Paris.

And then it hit me.

That was the perfect title for my novel.

31

The next few days were spent in a writing haze.

I worked all the hours I could and it helped to stop me thinking about Ethan and Paris. But once I finished for the day, I lay awake in bed remembering our kisses and touches, and the look on his face when he saw me with Joe. It haunted me. I kept wondering what would have happened if Joe hadn't turned up in Paris like he had done.

And then my furniture I had bought with Ethan arrived. I put my new writing desk by the window in my living room so I could look out at the river view while I wrote. It fitted in perfectly.

'I love it,' Carly said when she came round to work with me on a bright Monday morning. There were signs that spring was on its way to the city, and I couldn't wait. The winter had been such a long one. 'You found such gems in Paris.'

I nodded as I looked at it. 'I did. Ethan knew some really great places. I told him this flat didn't feel like home yet so he took me out and helped me arrange to ship this all over.'

Carly looked across at me. 'Sounds like he cared about you, Tessa.'

'Maybe,' I said. 'But it was too complicated. And I messed up by kissing Joe. I don't think he'd ever forgive that. And even if he could, we live in different cities.' I shrugged but I was sad that he wouldn't know how good the furniture looked in my flat. 'It's really starting to feel like home,' I added, looking around.

'It really does.' Carly curled up with her laptop on my sofa to start work while I sat down at my new desk and opened up my manuscript. 'How's the book coming now?' she called over.

'Good, I think. My characters are just on a romantic night standing by the Seine looking up at the sparkling Eiffel Tower. It might be time for their first kiss.' I started to write. My leading lady had been on a journey since arriving in Paris, realising that even though she had believed love was over forever, it was right there in front of her again if she had the courage to open her heart to it.

> That was the thing about love. You could try to run or hide from it but it would always be there waiting until you were ready. This man beside me was the last thing I expected to find in Paris.
>
> But I had found him.
>
> But somehow, more than that, I had realised what I wanted out of my life. I had decided to follow my dream of moving to my favourite city. To start over. To listen to my gut. To open my heart to possibility.
>
> So, most of all, I had realised I needed to love myself. I had found me. And that was a love story that would never end.
>
> As we kissed under the glow of the Eiffel Tower, I knew whatever happened between us, I would be okay and I would not run away from love ever again. Because this moment was worth all the heartache that had come before Paris. And I wanted to be, I deserved to be, happy.

'Tessa, are you okay? You're crying,' Carly said, alarmed.

I looked over at her in surprise. I reached up and touched a tear that was rolling down my cheek. 'I hadn't realised. What I was writing did it. I think I finally see why I was attracted to Joe, why I stayed when I knew deep down it wasn't the right relationship... I think I didn't believe I deserved the kind of love I write about. That I didn't love myself enough to walk away from him. I thought I wasn't good enough, you know? Maybe I've always thought that a little bit.'

'Why?' Carly asked, looking shocked.

'I've always felt kind of different; you know how much I overthink and worry and how I live in these fantasy worlds I create – my imagination overworks a lot. I hate wearing dresses or doing housework, I hate cooking, I'm not sure I want to be wife or a mother, but instead of accepting that about myself, of loving who I am, I kept trying to earn the approval and love of these men the world sees as ideals. Because maybe then I would finally fit in and be accepted and be the kind of woman I'm supposed to be. But now I realise I can only be myself. And that's okay.'

'Of course it's okay, it's more than okay. You're amazing, Tessa. I admire your creativity, your style, your sense of humour, and your loyalty. You have been such a good friend to me. I had no idea you didn't feel accepted. You've always been accepted by me.' She got up from the sofa to come over to my desk and pulled me into her arms. 'I love you for exactly who you are. So does Luke. And all your friends in Paris. And what about your readers? They love your stories. You make people feel better with your words. You inspire people. When I thought I might be pregnant, I called you instead of telling my husband first!'

I chuckled through my tears. 'Thank you.'

'Thank *you*. You're my best mate and you deserve everything. You are more than good enough, you're the best.'

I hugged her tightly. 'So are you.'

'I've always seen exactly who you are and I love you.'

I nodded. 'I love you too.'

Loving myself was the first step in letting go of my fears. Because if you loved yourself and realised you deserved love then it didn't matter if someone walked away from you like Joe had done. They weren't the right person for you. You would be okay. Because you knew you were good enough. Relationships would come and go, people too, like Carly had said, but you always had yourself.

'Let's go out for dinner and celebrate your book, and you, and us,' Carly said, gesturing to her stomach. 'We've been working so hard, we deserve it.'

I grinned. 'Okay, I like that idea.'

'Where do you fancy? We'll get Luke to take us; it can be his treat.'

'Poor Luke.' I thought about it. I knew that I needed to forget my time in Paris with Ethan but I was still so curious about him. What was he doing in

Paris? Did he think about me? What was happening with him and Juliette? I kept going to message her but I knew she'd talk about Ethan, and I was worried how that would make me feel. But I could do something they wouldn't know about. 'Why don't we try Bon Appétit!'

Carly frowned. 'Isn't that where Ethan works?'

'Ethan is in Paris.' Joe had said the plan was for Ethan to quit working in the London restaurant and work at Juliette's Cinq while they got their own restaurant going. 'I'd like to try his dishes there. See where he worked. I don't know, it just seems fitting after writing this scene.' I thought about my first kiss with Ethan in Paris. It had been incredible. There was no doubt he was inspiring my novel even though he was miles away right now.

'As long as it doesn't upset you. I could go for fancy French food. I'll book us a table.'

I wondered if I should tell Ethan I was going to eat there, but we'd had no contact since that last day in Paris so I chickened out. Maybe I would tell him what I thought after the meal instead.

* * *

That evening, I pulled on my outfit – leather-look leggings, a striped T-shirt – and sat on my bed to do my makeup. I curled my hair and put in a pair of hoop earrings. I stepped into my boots and added my black leather jacket before standing in front of the mirror to look at my reflection. If I was honest with myself, I felt confident and pretty. If I had been going out with Joe, I would have felt like I needed to wear a dress and that would have made me feel uncomfortable, so I would have spent most of the evening watching the clock for when I could be home and relaxed again. I wished I had realised those feelings were not something to ignore. I wished I had realised he wasn't making me feel good about myself. But I had stuck my head in the sand, telling myself he was the kind of man any woman would want to be with. I just forgot to make sure that *I* wanted to be with him.

I was determined not to make that same mistake again. My phone beeped telling me my Uber was here, so I grabbed my coat and bag, then headed out and jumped in the car for the short drive to Bon Appétit.

As soon as I walked in, I instantly knew the restaurant Ethan worked at was very different to Juliette's family's place in Paris. There were round, white tableclothed tables, a cream carpet and pale chairs with white walls and a chandelier hanging from the ceiling. The glasses sparkled and the cutlery was polished to perfection. There was a pianist in the corner. We were led to our table by a straight-faced waiter dressed all in black. It all felt perfect but almost cold. Whereas Juliette's family's restaurant, Cinq, had felt warm and I had been welcomed like an old friend.

Carly and Luke waved to me from the table they were already seated at close to the window and near to the kitchen, so I hurried over and after we'd hugged, I joined them.

The waiter came over and took our drinks order and suggested we try the tasting menu, which we all went for. I looked at it, wishing I knew exactly which dishes Ethan would have created or would have been preparing for us in the kitchen had he been here.

'I'm starving,' Carly said. 'I hope we get big portions.'

'I think it might be too fancy for that,' Luke told her.

'Joe told Ethan this place was too fancy for me, which was why he never brought me here,' I said then.

Luke stared at me. 'Why?'

'I think he thought Ethan might tell me about Rachel if I spent too much time with him,' I said.

'What a dick,' Carly said. 'I hope neither you nor Ethan have to see him again.'

'I definitely won't but he and Ethan have been best friends for so long, I wonder...' I trailed off as I heard someone behind me say Ethan's name. I turned around to see the waiter telling the table they could pass the compliments to their chef himself.

Following his gaze, I saw the kitchen's double doors swing open.

My breath caught in my throat as a man came out and headed for the table behind us, a smile wide on his face, his blue eyes catching in the lights.

'Oh my God,' I said.

'What's wrong?' Luke asked as Carly twisted in her seat to see who I was staring in shock at.

'Ethan's here,' I said, frozen as I watched him walk past our table without noticing me to speak to the people wanting to compliment him. I blinked, doubting my eyes, but there he was. Just a few feet away from me.

Ethan wasn't in Paris after all.

'Ethan?' Caily cried.

She said his name so loudly, he heard and turned to look over at our table. His eyes found mine and our gazes locked, the shock on his face mirroring mine as he registered that I was in his restaurant.

Before either of us said anything, the kitchen doors opened again, and out came Juliette. She saw me instantly. 'Tessa!' she said, stopping short. She looked over at Ethan then back at me. '*Quelle surprise.*'

That's an understatement.

32

Ethan finished greeting the table behind us then walked over as Juliette did the same. I couldn't stop staring at them both being here in London. I was so confused. My pulse sped up as I looked at Ethan. I was still so attracted to him, and seeing him again made my heart ache.

'Oh, are you Carly?' Juliette said after she leaned down to kiss me. I was so dumbfounded, I barely returned it. Juliette gave me a funny look. 'Bonjour! I'm Juliette, Tessa's French friend.' Carly and Luke introduced themselves to her as I was still speechless.

When Ethan joined us, they did the same with him. I watched, waiting for Ethan to look at me, but he seemed not inclined to do so. I couldn't bear this. It was so awkward. We had felt so close for a moment; now we weren't even speaking.

I snapped myself out of my silence and stood up, turning to Ethan. 'Can we talk?' I asked him. Our friends stared at us but I tried to tune them out.

Finally, Ethan faced me. His blue eyes met mine and I drank them eagerly as I had been sure I'd never look in them again. 'I'm at work...' he said gruffly.

'You can take a ten-minute break,' Juliette said. 'Go into the office; I'll keep Carly and Luke company,' she added, sitting down in my seat.

Ethan looked at her like she was paining him, but he sighed. 'Okay, fine.'

He turned around and set off towards the double doors he had just come out of. I glanced at our friends. Juliette gave me an encouraging wave of her hand, Luke looked concerned and Carly gave me a small smile. With a deep breath, I took off after Ethan, my heart thumping in my chest. I never expected to find him here at Bon Appétit but now I had, I was desperate to clear the air between us. We'd never be as we were in Paris, but maybe one day we could be friends.

Ethan led me into the small office to the side of the kitchen, which was hot and noisy and smelled delicious. I walked in and he closed the door behind us so we were suddenly in a quiet bubble together. 'What are you doing here, Tessa?' Ethan said, leaning against the desk and folding his arms across his chest. 'Is Joe coming too?'

'What? No...' I shook my head, hovering awkwardly between Ethan and the door behind me. 'I just wanted to try your food, to come here, as I never had. But what are you doing here?'

Ethan raised an eyebrow. 'I work here. Why would you not expect to see me?'

I was thoroughly confused now. 'Because I thought you were in Paris.'

'My course finished so I came home. And Juliette joined me so we could keep working on our restaurant plans.' Ethan sighed. 'As much as I enjoy this chit-chat, I am at work so...' He made to get off, leaning against the desk.

I shook my head. 'But Joe said you were staying in Paris. I honestly didn't think you'd be here tonight.'

'Sorry to disappoint you,' Ethan huffed.

'I didn't say it was a disappointment; I'm just surprised and confused.' I thought about everything Joe and Ethan had said in Paris. 'And you didn't disagree when I said I thought you were staying in Paris to work on the restaurant with Juliette. Joe told me you two are opening one there so I assumed you'd be staying on.'

'I never said I was staying in Paris beyond my course. Look, Tessa, is there any point in going over that last day in Paris? We said goodbye then, and I don't really feel the need to do it again. If Joe is coming, you better get back to the table anyway.'

I frowned. 'Why do you think Joe is coming?'

'You left Paris with him, I saw you kissing – you're back together!' Ethan cried.

'No,' I said, shaking my head. 'I won't lie that for a minute I was tempted, but I told him that we were over. He doesn't make me happy. I don't feel good when I'm with him. He isn't the man for me. I don't want to be with him,' I said, all in a rush. There might not be any future for us but he needed to know that I hadn't chosen Joe.

Ethan's chest sagged and he un-crossed his arms. 'You aren't back together?' he asked. I couldn't tell if he looked more confused or relieved. My heart thumped a little bit harder to think there might be some relief inside him. I couldn't help it.

'Definitely not. And you're not moving back to Paris? Joe said you'd always planned to open your restaurant with Juliette there...'

'He did? No, that was never our plan. Juliette has always wanted to do it here in London with me. Where a French bistro might have a unique selling point. And she wants to do it on her own, away from her family...'

I definitely felt relief. It rushed over me like something I couldn't stop. I exhaled unsteadily. Knowing Ethan would be in London too felt like huge news. Then I shook my head. 'Why did Joe tell me that then? He told me about the money your mum left you and how you could now make your dream come true, and that you'd be in Paris. It made me think that...' I trailed off, not wanting to admit it had upset me to think we'd be living in different countries, that there would be no future for us. It felt too honest after not seeing each other since our awkward encounter by the Seine.

'Joe is a liar,' Ethan replied simply. 'He told me after you two left that you were going to try again; that's why I didn't get in contact with you. After we said goodbye at the river, I thought about finding you and asking you to stay, but when he messaged me that, I knew there was no point. I assumed you were back together.'

'What a dick,' I burst out.

Ethan's mouth twitched. 'I think you're right. I guess he tried to manipulate the situation to stop... well, us.'

The word 'us' made me smile.

'It worked though,' Ethan added.

My smile faded instantly.

'We let him do it, didn't we? So, whatever we had just wasn't strong enough.'

'But we didn't know he was lying,' I said, hating that Joe had made us doubt each other so much. So easily. *That wasn't our fault.*

'We could have talked to one another though, found out the truth.' He sighed. 'Tessa, I was so jealous when I saw you and Joe kissing by the river. It reminded me that you loved him first. He's the kind of man you are looking for. A million miles away from me. I hated that you had chosen him over me. It hurt. A lot. I can't get the image out of my head…'

Shit. I hated to hear the pain in his voice. 'But I wouldn't have kissed him if I didn't think you were making all these future plans that wouldn't include me. You said you'd tell me what Joe told you after you met him; I even messaged you but you didn't reply. You went to tell Juliette and not me. So when Joe told me your plan, I believed it. I thought you didn't care enough to talk to me about it all,' I said, pain creeping into my voice too.

'I wanted to tell you face-to-face,' Ethan said. 'I told Joe that, so he said where to meet you both. Oh…' He trailed off and left the desk to pace in front of me a little bit. 'He wanted me to come and find you after the boat, to see you together. He probably even planned to kiss you so I would see it.'

I stared at Ethan, shocked. I thought back to that day by the Seine. How the romantic boat trip, coupled with Joe's promises that he wanted me and knowing Ethan would be staying in Paris, had made me wonder if I should get back with Joe. And when he'd leaned in to kiss me, I had let him. It had just been for a moment but Ethan had been there to see it. I remembered then the look on Ethan's face when he saw the kiss. He had looked crushed.

Did Joe make sure Ethan would see us?

33

For a second, I almost protested that Joe couldn't be *that* manipulative, but he had fooled both me and Rachel for six months. He was a liar, and he was selfish. He didn't want Ethan to have me so did all he could to come between us. I felt sick. 'I'm so pissed off I let him manipulate me like that!' I cried.

'We both did,' Ethan said quietly.

'I just felt so rejected when he did what he did that knowing he wanted me back... I got swept up in it for a moment,' I said, hating that Joe making me feel like I was never good enough made me want to go back to him because finally, he did. How pathetic was that?

'And you didn't trust me.'

I looked at Ethan. He was right. 'I was worried I was getting carried away with you, with us... I rushed into things with Joe and look at what happened. So when he told me you would be moving to Paris, that just confirmed that I was getting carried away thinking we could be something after our holiday. I was so impulsive with Joe, moving in with him so quickly, what if I just keep making bad decisions when it comes to relationships? I was scared, I think.'

'I was scared too. I felt like I was second best compared to Joe. I think he did manipulate us, but we clearly weren't ready for what was happening between us.'

'I wished we hadn't let him,' I said quietly. 'When it was just us two in that apartment...' I trailed off, hoping he would know what I meant. Hoping he had felt the same pull to me as I had to him.

Ethan nodded. 'I know. But we did let him, didn't we?'

We looked at one another. There was still the same connection between us now that we'd had in Paris, but our time alone together in that apartment was over. We had crumbled once we left it, and I had no idea if we could ever get past that. Joe had come between us far too easily.

'You don't trust me,' Ethan said then.

'Nor do you,' I replied defensively. Ethan had easily believed I'd chosen Joe over him; he couldn't have thought I had any real feelings for him. But I knew I had. When he had kissed me and touched me, I felt closer to him than any man before him. Had he felt any of that too?

'Tessa...' Ethan began. I really hoped he would tell me that he could trust me, trust us, one day. He started to say more but the office door swung open suddenly behind me, making us both jump.

'I'm sorry, but Carly needs you,' Juliette cried at me from the doorway.

'What do you mean?' I asked, seeing the panic in her eyes.

'She is bleeding,' Juliette said. 'They are trying to get an Uber but it's all busy.'

'Oh no,' I said, moving towards the door instantly. 'I'll try mine,' I said, pulling out my phone to open the app.

'I have my car,' Ethan said from behind me.

I turned around. 'What?'

'My car is outside; let me drive you all to the hospital,' Ethan said. 'Juliette, will you cover?'

'No, I'm coming. I will tell Marco...' She disappeared again.

Ethan sighed but turned to me. 'I'll just change, then we can go.'

I hesitated but I knew Carly and Luke would be worried sick and desperate to get to the hospital quickly, so Ethan's offer to drive us would be very welcome. 'Okay, thank you,' I said gratefully, hurrying out of the office. I glanced back and he gave me a reassuring smile. It reminded me of how calm he could be and how much I had liked that about him. I felt a tiny bit better as I hurried out of the restaurant to find Carly and Luke pulling their coats on and looking worried.

'Ethan's going to drive us,' I told them as I hurried over to our table.

'Oh, thank God,' Luke said.

Ethan appeared in record time, changed out of his work clothes and clutching his car keys.

Luke turned to him. 'Thanks for this, mate.'

'It'll be okay,' I said to Carly. I really hoped I wasn't lying to her. She looked really pale and I took hold of her arm, wanting to help in any way I could.

'Let's go,' Juliette said, rushing from the kitchen.

'Juliette, you don't have to...' I began as Luke took Carly's other arm and we started off after Ethan as he led us out of Bon Appétit.

Juliette glared at me. 'I am your friend. They are your friends. So we are all friends. Yes?'

She was so fierce, I didn't dare raise any more objections. '*Oui*,' I said, glancing at Ethan, who smiled at me. I smiled back, and for a second, it was like our connection had returned.

We all hurried out of the restaurant and piled into Ethan's car, Carly in the front, the rest of us squished together in the back. Ethan set off across London to the nearest hospital. There was a lot of traffic as usual and we were in a tense silence the whole way. I looked at Carly. Her hands were folded in her lap and she was biting her lip. I wished I could say something to make her feel better as she had helped me so much, but I knew it was pointless. We were getting her to people who would help, and that was all we could do for now.

'Okay,' Ethan said as the hospital finally came into view. 'I'll drop you at the front then find somewhere to park,' he added, still so calm. He pulled into the drop-off point. Luke jumped out to help Carly, who turned to look at me.

'Will you come too, Tessa?'

'Of course,' I said, also getting out. I followed Carly and Luke inside as Ethan and Juliette stayed in the car and went off to park.

'Isn't it crazy?' Carly said to me as Luke rushed to reception to find out what we should do. 'I was so freaked out by the thought of being pregnant and now I'm freaked out that something is wrong...'

'Of course you are,' I said. 'It's a life-changing thing; it would be crazy if you weren't freaked out.'

Carly raised a smile. 'That makes no sense but it makes perfect sense.'

'This way,' Luke said, coming back. We headed to where we'd been sent and a nurse came over to find out what was going on. She said she'd arrange a scan and sent us to another area where we sat down to wait to be called in.

I had a message from Ethan to say he and Juliette would go and get a coffee and to keep him updated. I promised I would.

'How was it seeing Ethan again?' Carly asked, watching me as I responded to him on my phone.

'That's so unimportant right now,' I told her.

'No, it'll take my mind off all this...' she said, giving me a pleading look.

'Well, I don't know,' I said. 'We realised that Joe did all he could to keep us apart, which was crap. But we let him do it. So maybe we weren't as close as I thought we were. Or could be...' It all felt so confusing.

'You still fancy him though?' she asked.

'Well, yeah,' I admitted. 'But I think it's too complicated with everything that happened with Joe. I don't know if I'll ever trust that Ethan really likes me, and he will always wonder if I'd prefer to be with his best mate. Or former best mate anyway... Plus, as you said, I can't even trust my own heart when it comes to love. Ethan might be an even worse decision than Joe was,' I added with a sigh. I knew deep down that wasn't true though. Ethan had always been honest with me. Joe was a liar.

But there still seemed to be many more reasons for me and Ethan to try to not be together than there were reasons to try.

'We're ready for you.' A sonographer came out to call Carly and Luke in for an ultrasound then.

'Tessa, you have to come too,' Carly begged me as they got up.

'Are you sure?'

'Of course,' Luke said, waving me after them. I got up too and we went into the small room. Carly laid down on the bed and Luke sat beside her. I stood nervously by the door, hoping they would be okay whatever happened next. I watched as the sonographer got everything ready, putting gel on Carly and setting it all up. Luke was gripping Carly's hand and they looked at each other and not at the screen. I kept my eyes on it though as the woman started the scan.

There were a few excruciating seconds when everything seemed too quiet, the screen too blank, but then I heard a noise and something showed up.

The woman smiled. 'We have a heartbeat. Wait...'

'What's wrong?' Carly asked, finally looking over. 'Have I lost the baby?'

'No,' the sonographer said, peering at the screen. She moved the scanner over again then turned to Carly and Luke. 'The babies are fine.'

'Sorry?' Carly asked, frowning.

'What do you mean?' Luke demanded.

I stepped forward in shock as I looked at the screen and could make out two blobs on there.

'You're having twins,' the woman replied.

34

The sonographer left us alone to find a doctor as Carly's pregnancy was now considered higher risk and she would need more monitoring. The three of us stared at the picture of the scan she had left in the room.

'Twins,' Luke said for maybe the tenth time in a row. He shook his head. 'Actually, my grandfather was a twin...'

Carly snapped her head around to glare at him. 'And you didn't think to mention that in all the years we've been together?'

'He died before I was even born,' Luke protested.

'This is good news,' I said. 'Not only is the baby fine but now you have two.' I saw their faces. 'No?'

'It's just a lot to take in...' Carly said. She touched her stomach. 'And now I'm classed as higher risk. I hope everything will be okay. And I was just getting my head around becoming a mother. But to two at once? I mean, how will I cope?'

'How will *we* cope,' Luke corrected. 'I'm here. And we've always been a team, right? We can handle this. I promise.'

Carly looked at it and smiled. 'I guess you're right.'

Luke leaned in to give her a kiss. 'Tessa, tell my wife she will be an incredible mother, please.'

'Definitely,' I said firmly. 'You've always looked out for me.'

There was a knock on the door and we called out to whoever it was to come in. Ethan and Juliette walked inside. I had sent them a message to give them an update.

'All okay then?' Ethan asked as they edged into the room.

'Look!' Carly held up the scan. 'Twins. We can't believe it.'

'Congratulations,' Ethan said as Juliette looked at the scan picture. 'We'll wait outside until you're ready and I'll give you all a lift home.' He turned from the bed to glance over at me.

'Thanks, Ethan,' I said, giving him a shy smile. The last hour had been dramatic and it meant our conversation in his office had ended abruptly. I wanted to talk to him more, but I didn't know if he felt the same. We looked at one another for longer than was strictly necessary.

Juliette made a tutting sound, making us turn away from each other. 'Carly must be thirsty and hungry; you didn't have dinner. You two...' She pointed at Luke and Ethan. 'Go and get us some supplies while we wait for the doctor.'

'Juliette, you can't keep bossing...' Ethan began.

'Actually, I would like some food and drink,' Carly said, cutting him off. She turned to Luke. 'You know what I like.'

He nodded and got up. 'No point arguing, mate; I've learnt that through the years,' Luke said to Ethan. 'Let's go.' Ethan let himself be led out of the room, leaving us three ladies alone.

'You are very impressive,' Juliette said to Carly. 'I can't imagine one baby, let alone two, but you'll be fine, I can sense it.' Juliette gestured to me. 'Tessa, I'm not so sure.'

Carly nodded. 'I know what you mean.'

'Huh?' I looked at them. 'Why are you both ganging up on me? This is why you shouldn't introduce friends to one another.'

'You and Ethan,' Juliette said. She said something in French. When she saw our blank faces, she sighed. 'You are both being... how you say it? Stupid.'

Carly barked out a laugh. I glared at them both. 'Sorry, Tessa, but Juliette has a point. The way you two just looked at one another. It was like no one else was in the room. Is this what they were like in Paris?'

Juliette nodded. 'I could see the chemistry instantly. Lots of sparklers.'

'Sparks,' Carly corrected. 'I can see that.'

'You told me I was rushing into things!' I reminded her.

'Yeah, I was worried about that. But things have changed,' she replied. 'You finally told Joe to fuck off. You've realised that you deserve to be loved for exactly who you are. And if Ethan does that, then I am not as worried. And what happened here tonight... it could have gone very differently. Life is short. Finding love in whatever form is precious, right?'

'Who said anything about love?' I said, panic setting in that I could end up with another broken heart.

'Okay, not love yet, but there is something between you two, right?' Carly pressed me.

'I don't know. Joe was able to break us apart pretty easily...'

'That man,' Juliette spat out. 'I hate him, I think. He loved to make Ethan feel bad about himself, and it sounds like he did the same to you, Tessa. I think if you let him win then you are both fools.'

'Exactly,' Carly agreed.

I looked at them both. They were so clear that we shouldn't give up on us. 'I'm scared of getting hurt. And so is he...' I said quietly.

'Of course you are,' Carly said to me gently. 'It won't be easy to trust each other but will it be easy to walk away and forget one another?'

'*Non*,' Juliette answered for me. 'Ethan has been miserable without you. And I saw how happy you were to see him tonight.'

'He was?' I asked, hope rising in my heart. I thought about letting Ethan go forever. It felt alien. Ever since I walked in and found him in my Paris apartment, we had become linked in a way I never expected. Being apart since I came back to London showed me that I did want him in my life. I just wasn't sure that he wanted me in his still.

The doctor came in then to check Carly over and explain what would happen now, and soon after, Ethan and Luke returned with food and drinks for us all. We left Carly and Luke with the doctor and waited outside until they were ready to go home.

We all piled back into Ethan's car but this time, Carly wanted to be with Luke so I ended up in the passenger seat beside Ethan. The evening had turned chilly and drizzly. Ethan's headlights reflected off the puddles in the road as we drove to Carly and Luke's flat. Carly was half-asleep on her husband's shoulder. We were all quiet in the car again. I looked out of the window, conscious of how close Ethan was to me, but not knowing what to say to him with the others in the back.

'Here we go,' Ethan said when he reached their flat.

'I can't thank you enough, Ethan,' Carly said when Luke roused her. 'You're my hero for tonight.'

I could see Ethan duck his head, embarrassed. 'You're very welcome.'

'Look after her,' Juliette said sternly to Luke.

'I will,' he promised.

'Goodnight, guys,' I called as they climbed out of the car.

'Drop me at my hotel next,' Juliette said as Ethan set off again. I saw him glance at her in the rear-view mirror. 'Tessa lives near you, doesn't she?' she asked.

Ethan looked over at me. 'Yeah, that's right.'

I had forgotten for a minute that we were neighbours in London. I carried on looking out at the rainy city as Ethan drove to Juliette's hotel to drop her off. I was nervous to be alone with him again. It had been such a long day, I felt shattered too. But equally, I didn't want to leave things this awkward between us. We had to clear the air one way or another.

Juliette leaned forward to kiss us goodbye once we reached her hotel. She said she'd be in touch with Ethan in the morning as they had a potential restaurant venue to look at and suggested we all have dinner. Neither of us agreed to that but she got out, waving cheerfully, like we had. Ethan quietly asked for my address and I gave it, so we set off in silence again.

'Is it near your flat?' I asked after a moment, desperate to say something.

'Round the corner,' Ethan replied. 'In fact, I can probably see your building from mine.'

I absorbed that news. I kind of liked it. 'The furniture we bought together arrived and it looks great. I love my new desk; I've been doing lots of writing at it already. My publisher gave me an extension too,' I added.

Ethan looked across at me. 'That's really great, Tessa.'

I finally turned to him. 'So, how do you feel about being able to work on your own restaurant now?' My question skirted close to the subject of Joe, but I wanted to make sure Ethan was happy.

He smiled in the dim light. 'It's really exciting. We thought it was years away. Finding out about my mother's money... it was such a shock. It's sad that she won't be able to see what I do with it though.'

'She would be really proud of you,' I said. We approached my building. 'Do you want to come in for a coffee and see the furniture?' I winced inwardly at such a lame offer, but the thought of Ethan leaving me now suddenly panicked me.

Ethan took a moment to respond. I thought he might say no. And then I would have to resign myself to not having Ethan in my life any more. But he nodded. 'Sure.'

I hoped he didn't see how wide my smile was.

35

Ethan parked in my space that I never used as I didn't have a car, and I led him up to my flat, opening the door and switching on the lights. He would be the first man in here apart from Luke. 'Come in,' I said, closing the door behind us as Ethan wandered through to the open-plan living area.

'Honestly, thank you for tonight,' I said as I followed him. 'It was really kind of you to drive us to the hospital like that. I'm glad you were there.'

'Yeah?' He turned to look at me. 'I'm glad I could help. And it all turned out okay.'

'Me too. Carly and Luke are going to make great parents. I still can't believe it's twins.' I shifted on my feet. 'So, shall I make coffee?'

'Do you have coffee?' he asked with a smile.

'Oh, shit.' My cheeks flamed as I realised I had invited him back for coffee but I only drank tea and didn't have any in the flat.

'Tea is fine, Tessa,' he said. 'Oh, wow, the desk looks so good.' Ethan went over to look at the new addition, so I ducked into the kitchen area to put the kettle on, feeling embarrassed but relieved he hadn't used it as a reason to make a quick exit.

'I'm sorry we didn't get to eat at your restaurant in the end,' I called out as I made our tea.

'You'll have to come back. But to be honest, it's not how I would run my own place. Going back there after two weeks in Paris just showed me all the things I want to do differently. So you could just wait to eat at mine and Juliette's hopefully sometime soon.'

'That's a long time to wait without eating your delicious food. I've missed it,' I said, carrying over the two cups of tea.

'I'm happy to cook for you anytime,' Ethan said as I handed him one of the mugs. Our fingers brushed for a second. I felt warmth travel all through my body, like he had given me an electric shock. Ethan seemed to realise what he had said and cleared his throat. 'Well, uh, yeah, I mean...' He trailed off awkwardly.

I was quite pleased he seemed as nervous as I felt. I turned to the desk – an easy thing to talk about. 'It does look good in here, doesn't it? The flat already feels so much homelier now.'

'I'm glad,' Ethan replied. 'Are you writing at this desk? How is it going?'

'I am. And good, I think. I'm sending my editor the chapters as I go. Setting it in Paris was such a good idea. I'm including all my favourite spots.' I looked away shyly. 'Like the ones you took me to.'

'I'm so happy you're enjoying writing again. I knew you would,' Ethan said, pride unmistakable in his voice. 'I finished your book *A Love Like Ours* and I really did love it, Tessa. You're so talented.'

'Thank you.' I walked over to the sofa and sat down with my cup of tea, suddenly tired from the night. I gestured to the coffee table. 'The chess set looks good, doesn't it?' I hesitated. 'Have you played since I left Paris?'

Ethan shook his head. He looked over at the mantelpiece and the print he had bought me in Paris propped up there. He sighed. 'It seems like so long ago.'

'I was so happy when you bought me that,' I said softly.

Ethan came over and sat down on the sofa, but he left a big gap between us. 'I was happy too,' he said. 'I'm sorry I was so distant back at Bon Appétit. It was such a shock to see you, and I assumed you and Joe were back together. Honestly, the thought of that made me so jealous, I could barely see straight.'

I sucked in a breath. 'You don't need to be jealous. I meant what I said – we are over for good.'

'I still hate that you loved him first though. And that you almost did go back to him.'

'We both made mistakes that day in Paris. I felt rejected by you, and that brought back how much what Joe did to me had hurt.' I put my cup down on the coffee table and twisted to face him. 'But thinking that you didn't care I was leaving Paris and we'd never see each other again hurt so much more than what Joe did. Because he never cared about the real me, but you always seemed to.'

Ethan put his cup down and faced me too. 'I do care about you, Tessa. And you know I like you for exactly who you are.'

'That's how I feel.'

Ethan looked hopeful, but he sighed. 'What if neither of us can trust how the other one feels though? We didn't in Paris.'

'I know. But think about all the time we spent together before Joe showed up. I felt so close to you. Can't we feel that way again? Or... even more?' I asked him, putting my heart on the line. I was terrified. I had put my trust in the wrong man before and I was scared to follow my heart again. But Carly and Juliette had been right tonight that I could miss out on something that was potentially really special by being scared. I had been too impulsive before and made bad decisions, but Paris had shown me that I didn't want to give up on love. And that meant taking a leap sometimes.

I just didn't know if Ethan was willing to take a leap along with me.

'I want that,' Ethan said. 'So badly.'

'Ethan, you reminded me how much I love to write, you showed me Paris and inspired me with it, and you made me want to open my heart again. In fact, I think you prised my heart open with your fingers. You made me fall in love with Paris. You gave me back my writing spark. And stopped me believing that love was dead.'

Ethan shook his head. 'If I did any of that, it's because you inspired me. When I walked out of the bathroom in that apartment and saw you, I couldn't stay away from you. Everything about you made me want to stay by your side, to try to make you smile, to make you happy again.'

'I think you have more of a way with words than me, damn it,' I said, his words sending a thrill through my body. I smiled. 'I'm sorry for walking away from you in Paris.'

'No, I'm sorry for making you walk away from me.' Ethan reached out and touched my hand. 'Is this okay?' he asked as his fingers interlinked with mine.

'I wanted to touch you all night,' I replied simply. 'So, what now?' I asked, wondering what the next step for us should be.

Ethan made a pained expression then.

'What's wrong?' I asked nervously.

'I'm trying really hard not to say what I want to say,' he replied.

That didn't sound good. 'You better just say it,' I told him, bracing myself for another obstacle to be put in our way.

'You remember when you begged me to kiss you in Paris?' he asked gruffly. 'I'm trying really hard not to beg you to let me kiss you now.'

36

I smiled; I couldn't help it. I wanted him to beg me. I wanted him to kiss me. 'Hmm. Quite the conundrum,' I teased.

'Is it too soon?' Ethan asked, smiling back at me.

'I like the idea of you begging me, I can't lie,' I confessed. It had been too long since his lips had been on mine. I watched his eyes flick to my lips and I cleared my throat. 'Eyes on my eyes, Taylor,' I said sternly. He lifted them immediately. 'We should take this slowly,' I said, enjoying the fact he wanted me as much as I wanted him.

Ethan nodded. 'Okay. Yeah, you're right.'

'Am I? Or do I just enjoy torturing you?'

'I know you do. Remember that night in Paris when you stripped naked in front of me when I was trying to be a gentleman?' he asked, rubbing his thumb against my hand still linked with his.

I grinned at the memory of that night. 'I was very impressed you stayed on the bed.'

'Maybe next time, I'll do the same to you,' Ethan suggested playfully. 'See if you can keep your hands off me.'

I cleared my throat. 'We should change the subject or you should kiss me because I am slowly dying.'

'I'm enjoying turning the tables and torturing you now,' Ethan replied.

'If you like that sort of thing, I have some handcuffs somewhere.'

Ethan spluttered.

'Carly's hen do,' I explained with a shrug.

Ethan closed his eyes again and breathed. 'God's sake, now I really want to see them.'

I grinned. 'I bet. How about you kiss me and then maybe I'll go and find them?'

'Tessa, I've wanted to kiss you since I saw you in Bon Appétit. But are you really sure this is what you want? That I am who you want?' He looked unsure again. I realised it would take time to trust this thing between us, but I really wanted us both to.

'Yes, Ethan. Am I who you want?'

'So much,' he whispered.

'Then kiss me. Please.'

'I thought I was begging this time?' He smiled and moved closer, letting go of my hand. His fingertips touched my cheek then my lips. 'Tessa Elliot,' he said softly. 'The woman of my dreams. Will you let me kiss you? Please, sweetheart?'

The term of endearment tore away any remaining concerns I had. I needed to kiss him. 'Yes, Ethan Taylor. Man of my dreams.'

God, you have no idea how much I mean that.

His eyes lit up as he leaned in and brushed my lips gently with his. I whimpered and he drew me in for a deeper kiss. He reached for the back of my head, tangling his fingers in my hair as his tongue found mine. I wrapped my arms around him and kissed him back, thinking that we would have been crazy to have let this go. Ethan's lips fit mine so perfectly, it was like we were two puzzle pieces coming together.

Ethan leaned back to look at me then. 'Tessa,' he said in a low voice. 'Are you really sure about us?'

I leaned in closer so I almost touched his ear as I whispered, 'I'm all in.'

'God, so am I,' Ethan said. 'But we can take things slowly. Maybe I should go.'

'I don't want you to,' I said instantly. 'We've been apart too long.'

'I know what you mean.' He brushed my lips with his again. 'I love kissing you.'

'Don't stop then,' I pleaded with him. 'Why don't you stay? Back in a one-bed apartment together...'

Ethan chuckled. 'God, I have missed that place. But I meant what I said. I don't want to mess this up.'

I climbed off the sofa and held out my hand. 'You won't. I want to be with you tonight. If you want to be with me?' I bit my lip, hoping he would want to stay.

'There is nothing I want more.' He got up and took my hand.

'Finally, spending the night together,' I said, leading him towards my bedroom.

'We already have,' he teased.

'You know what I mean.'

We walked into my bedroom and I turned on the bedside lamp, then went to draw the curtains as Ethan stepped towards my bed. He turned to watch my movements.

'You have no idea how much I've wanted you,' Ethan said to me. 'That first night we slept in the same bed together, God, when you started to ask me what the French word was for kissing, you almost killed me.'

My breath hitched. 'You have no idea how hot it was when you told me to beg you if I really wanted to kiss you.'

'Hmm. So, do you do like to beg?' Ethan asked, his eyes darkening.

'Hold that thought...' I ducked out of the room, smiling as I heard him protest. I hurried to the hall cupboard and rooted through the cardboard box of junk in there that I kept meaning to sort out. I smiled to myself when I found what I was looking for, grabbed them, and hurried back to Ethan in the bedroom.

'Speaking of begging... I found the handcuffs I got for Carly's hen do. They're pretty flimsy but they might come in useful,' I said, holding up the fluffy leopard print pair. I went over and gave them to Ethan.

He dropped them onto the bed, then his hands slid up to my waist. 'There are a thousand possibilities running through my head, but what do you want, Tessa?'

'You,' I said simply. 'It's been torture thinking about writing a sex scene in my book but not being able to re-enact it with you.'

Ethan pulled me towards him and our lips met in a soft kiss. He leaned back and cupped my cheek in one hand. 'I am here for that anytime you want,' he said huskily. He brushed my hair back off of my shoulders, his fingertips lingering on my warm skin. 'So soft. So beautiful. So...' He leaned in to whisper, 'Naughty. You are perfect.'

I pulled back and looked into his eyes, pupils as dark and dilated as I knew mine were. 'I take back ever calling you sweet,' I said, more turned on than I had ever been.

'You want me to be sweet, I will be. But if you don't...' He trailed off.

'You agree we don't have to move slowly?' I asked, my voice turning breathless as I thought about what we could do on my bed.

'Definitely not. We are going to move very slowly and you're going to love every minute of it.'

37

I raised an eyebrow at Ethan telling me we were going to move slowly tonight. There he went surprising me again. Ethan might just have been the king of foreplay at this point. My whole body was lit up like it was catching fire from the slowest, sweetest burn.

Ethan smiled back like he knew exactly what he was doing to me. Our lips met again but this time, we kissed with abandon. Our lips met frantically, desperate to erase our time apart.

I moved closer as Ethan's hands slid down my back to my bum, cupping it. Wrapping my arms around his shoulders, I met his tongue eagerly with my own. When I gave a contented sigh, Ethan broke away and reached for my chin, tilting it up so our eyes were locked. 'How did I meet someone like you?'

'Babe, can we finally stop talking?' I reached out for the buttons of his shirt. 'I feel like I'm going to go crazy,' I half growled at him as I desperately undid the buttons and slipped it off his shoulders, taking in his defined chest, running my fingertips down it, enjoying the way his body trembled underneath my touch.

'Did you just call me babe?' Ethan's eyes flashed at me as he pulled my T-shirt over my head. He pushed my hair off my shoulder and leaned down to kiss me there and across my collarbone and then up my neck towards my ear, making me shiver.

'Yes,' I gasped as his hands stroked me over my chest. His lips found mine and he kissed me as he reached behind me and undid my bra, pulling it off quickly, his mouth moving to my exposed breasts.

'Am I really driving you crazy?' he murmured before sucking on one of my nipples, which were already hard and desperate for his mouth.

'Yes,' I gasped again, moving closer, arching my back to bring him even closer. I couldn't get close enough to him. He ran his tongue over my nipple and I shivered again.

Ethan stepped back. 'Take your jeans off, sweetheart.'

I reached for my jeans and slowly unbuttoned them as his eyes watched me, dark and hooded. He let out a loud exhale when I slipped my thumbs inside my waistband and pulled them down, stepping out of them so I was in front of him just in my thong. 'What about you?' I asked, raising an eyebrow.

Eyes still on me, Ethan slid his jeans off and I could see that he was straining through his underwear.

'Hmm,' I said approvingly.

'I need you on the bed now, please,' he said. I backed up and climbed onto the bed, Ethan following, leaning over me as I lay down. He reached out to touch my lips with his fingertips as he propped himself over me. 'Take your thong off,' he said huskily, staring down at me. I bit my lip and he watched as I slipped it off. 'You have no idea how incredible you look right now,' he said, his eyes tracing me from head to toe then back up again.

My breath was fast and desperate as I noticed the way he was looking at me. No man had looked at me like that before. Like they wanted me that badly. Lusted after me. Needed me. Was hungry for me and only me. It turned me on even more.

'Ethan, please,' I begged him.

'I didn't even have to ask,' he said playfully. He ran a hand down the centre of my chest to my stomach and then paused, eyeing me.

'Ethan,' I said, arching towards him again.

'You want me to touch you?'

'Yes,' I breathed, trembling in anticipation. I propped my legs up either side of him and he gently parted them open. 'Please.'

'You want me to taste you?'

'Yes, please,' I said, practically writhing beneath him.

'God, I love it when you beg me,' he whispered, his hand finally dropping to where I ached for him. His fingers moved, teasing me, as I gasped at his touch.

When he slid his fingers inside me, Ethan grunted in approval. 'So ready, aren't you?'

I gasped out a 'yes'. I was losing all train of thought now.

He leaned down and trailed kisses where his fingertips had been all down my body. When his mouth reached between my legs, I cried his name like it was a prayer. His tongue worshipped me like I had never been before. My hand slid down and I ran my fingers through his hair.

This is so much better than the sex in my books.

As Ethan devoured me with his tongue, I clutched his hair, tipping closer to the edge. 'It's too good. I need to come,' I cried then, my legs trembling either side of him.

Ethan lifted off me suddenly, leaving me confused. His eyes met mine. 'Hold on,' he said, reaching down to run his tongue over my nipple so gently and softly.

I writhed under him as I teetered back from the edge. 'What...'

'Trust me,' he whispered, drawing my nipple into his mouth and sucking it. I gasped. My body was tingling; the throbbing between my legs had built to a level that was half pleasure, half agony. When he slid his hand down to touch me again, I let out a moan. 'It's going to be so good. Can you come with me inside you?' he asked as he brushed me gently, keeping me right at the edge.

'Yes,' I breathed, watching him smiling down at me. 'God, Ethan, I need you inside me. Please,' I begged again.

He let go of me and I watched him lean over the bed to find his jeans and pull out his wallet to find a condom.

I reached over and held up the handcuffs. 'Want to use these?'

Ethan came back to me and raised an eyebrow. 'They are too flimsy to actually hold you.'

'We can pretend.' I lifted my hands above my head and locked my wrists together.

Ethan watched me. 'Jesus, you're ruining me for anyone else ever,' he said, sitting up to click the handcuffs on my wrists.

I smiled. 'Good. I want to ruin you.' I wriggled my hands. I could get out of them but I wouldn't. I quite liked the feeling of being out of control and Ethan being in control. I bit my lip. 'What are you going to do to me now?'

Ethan leaned back on his knees, his eyes raking over me. 'I'm going to make you come so hard on my cock,' he said, pulling on a condom.

I always thought I'd find dirty talk in real life embarrassing, but Ethan is too good at it to not find it just incredibly hot.

I sucked in a breath. 'Yes,' I begged him again.

He reached down and stroked himself. 'I don't think I've ever been this hard before. Are you ready for me, Tessa?'

'I'm so close,' I replied, watching him eagerly, my hands tied up above my head. As he settled between my legs and slid inside me slowly, so slowly, I whimpered again. He settled in deep and then began slow, gentle thrusts that made heat build inside me rapidly. My whole body was thrumming with want and need. I tried to move faster against him but he placed a hand on my hip and put pressure on, slowing me down again. I groaned. 'Ethan, what are—'

'I need you to come harder than you have with anyone else,' he said urgently, still moving slowly but deeply inside me. 'It's going to be so good, I promise.' He leaned down to kiss me.

'You're so big,' I gasped as he moved his mouth to my breast and sucked on my nipple. 'You fill me up perfectly.'

'You have no idea how incredible you feel – so wet, so tight, so perfect for me,' Ethan said, lifting to look at me. He propped himself up and I slipped a leg over him and we both gasped as he moved in even deeper.

I gazed up at him. 'Can I come yet?' I asked, letting out a moan when I moved against him, matching his slow, steady rhythm as pleasure built inside me to a dizzying level.

Ethan looked down at me. 'Beg me first,' he commanded gruffly, his tone sending a shiver through my body.

I was now completely on fire. My skin was hot and sticky, and I throbbed with the need to release. Ethan's slow and steady thrusts were sending me into a frenzy. I could only moan in answer to his question. But he told me to beg him again.

'Please,' I managed to choke out. 'It's too good... Ethan... babe, I'm going to come so hard.'

'Yeah, you are.' He finally moved faster, thrusting harder, sending me wild. I dipped into the mattress, matching his change of pace.

'Come on my cock, sweetheart,' Ethan said, leaning down to kiss me once more before he reached out and hooked my other leg around him too. He pushed into me even deeper and our thrusts lost all sense of rhythm as we rocked together frantically. My moans were so loud, they sounded like they were coming from someone else. Ethan joined in and that sent me finally and beautifully over the edge.

'Ethan.' I cried his name as my release came hard and fast, sending pleasure shooting through every nerve in my body. I gasped and shuddered beneath him. Wave after wave rolled over me as I completely let myself go for what felt like the first time in my life.

'Tessa, fuck, that was so hot,' Ethan said as he watched me come apart beneath him. He pumped into me two more times than let out a guttural groan as his release came, crying my name out before pressing his lips to mine, caressing me with his tongue as his thrusts slowed to a stop and he gently pulled out, flopping down beside me with a satisfied grunt.

I pulled my hands free of the cuffs and let my arms come down, knowing they would be aching like hell tomorrow. But God, I didn't care one little bit.

Ethan rolled over to face me then so I twisted round to look at him as we lay side-by-side on my bed.

I was still breathless and his skin was slick with sweat. My whole body throbbed with aftershocks of pleasure. We stared at each other, our chests rising with our fast heartbeats in perfect harmony, unable to speak for a couple of minutes.

'I'd say the phrase "worth the wait" is pretty unclimactic after that but I can't think of another one,' he said, before wrapping his arms around me, pulling me towards him and kissing me gently like I was something precious.

'I've never...' I said, my voice breaking. A tear squeezed out of my eye and rolled down my cheek.

Ethan looked at me alarmed. 'Shit, are you okay?' He reached out to stroke the tear away.

'Yes. That was really something,' I said, embarrassed for getting emotional.

He touched my lips and smiled. 'It really was. No regrets then?'

I shook my head, unable to speak.

'I don't know what you unleashed in me but God, I fucking loved it,' he said, arching an eyebrow.

'Me too,' I said, smiling. I didn't think he would ever really understand what it had meant to me to feel like I could be myself with him, to enjoy it fully and not be worried about anything while we were together – to be present and embrace the moment without overthinking like I usually did.

Ethan watched me as if he was trying to figure out what was going on. 'It's pretty special being with someone like that, isn't it?' he said softly then, like he knew exactly what I was feeling right now.

'Yes.' I leaned in to kiss him, hoping my lips would be enough when words had failed me spectacularly. I kissed him passionately and he murmured against my mouth, pulling me closer into his chest. When we finally leaned back, we both smiled. 'Really special,' I agreed in a whisper. 'So, what now?'

Ethan twirled a strand of my hair in his fingers. 'I have an idea.'

38

I didn't expect Ethan to leave my bedroom and return with the chessboard we had bought together in Paris. I laughed as he climbed onto the bed wearing just his jeans, his chest and feet bare, his hair tousled from our activities, his face flushed, looking extremely delicious, and set it up between us. 'This is what you want to do now?'

'I'm thinking while you're distracted, I might just be able to win,' he said, smiling as he placed the pieces on the board.

'Oh, you think I'm distracted?' I had pulled my thong back on, but my top half was naked under the covers so I sat up, letting the duvet fall off me, revealing my bare chest. 'Two can play that game.'

Ethan stopped what he was doing to look at me. 'You have to put a top on; that's blatant cheating.'

'There's no referee here. You first,' I said, a smile playing on my lips.

Ethan's breath hitched. He shook his head but forced his eyes down onto the board. 'Fine. I can do this. And when I win, I will claim my reward,' he said, reminding me of the reward he'd given me back in Paris. A very satisfying reward. My breath hitched this time and I saw him smile when he heard it as he moved his first pawn.

'What if I win, I also get a reward?' I asked, reaching for my first piece and moving it forwards.

'Loser decides what it is,' Ethan said. He looked up and our eyes met. 'Really struggling to keep my eyes up,' he said softly.

'Good.' I leaned forward and took his pawn. 'I'm actually getting chilly.' I grinned at Ethan, who groaned.

'Nope, not looking,' he said, focusing on the board. I saw him adjust himself and I bit my lip. 'Stop it, Tessa.'

'No idea what you're talking about,' I said innocently. Then I watched as he took a knight from me. 'Hey!'

After that, we lapsed into silence, concentrating on the board, trying not to look at one another until only a few of our pieces remained.

'Check,' I said in triumph when I moved my queen. I looked up at him then.

Ethan frowned and sat for a moment but then I saw his lips curve into a smile. 'Actually...' He moved his queen. 'Checkmate.' Only then did he meet my eyes.

I stared at the board in shock. 'How did I not see that? That was a sneaky manoeuvre, Taylor.'

'I actually won,' he said in disbelief.

'No one likes a gloater,' I said sulkily.

'And now I can look...' His eyes drank in my naked top half. 'I really deserve a reward for getting through that with you in front of me looking that sexy. Look at you.' He shook his head.

'Okay, I might let you off for wining,' I said, my body humming from his words and attention.

'I have a confession to make,' he said, lifting the board off the bed and placing it on the floor. He crawled across the bed towards me. I laid back down as he leaned over me on his elbows.

'What's that?' I asked, my mind already rolling through ideas for his reward for winning that game.

'I've taken a few chess lessons online,' he said, looking sheepishly down at me.

'What?' I squealed. I grabbed his arms and rolled us over. Laughing, Ethan flopped against the pillow and I leaned over him. 'I got hustled?'

'I'm not sorry. I guess I thought if I ever was lucky enough to play you again, I wanted to be able to give you a good game,' he said, reaching up to push my hair off my face.

'God, that's actually so sweet,' I replied, thrilled that he had thought of me like that. 'Even though I left Paris?'

'Maybe I didn't think all was completely lost, I don't know,' he said. 'And we had a good game, right?' He moved his hand down my cheek and neck to my chest, moving slowly down to touch my breast.

'Hmmm,' I said, trying not to lose focus, but he started stroking me, and my nipples became even harder. 'But I might withhold your reward now.'

'That would be very mean, very unsportsmanlike behaviour,' he said huskily, pulling me towards him for a deep kiss.

I sighed against him and kissed him back, sliding my hands against his bare chest, moving them down like he had done to me, enjoying the curve of his muscles until I reached his jeans where I found him as excited as I now was.

'Hmm, you are very good at rewards,' he said, pulling away from my lips to look at me as I stroked him over the material.

'I decided on my reward,' I said, enjoying him writhing beneath me now. 'I want you in my mouth.'

'I'm not sure I can handle that,' he said breathlessly.

'You don't want it?' I asked, stopping touching him and leaning down to kiss his chest. I leaned over him and trailed kisses down towards his belly button.

'Fuck, I've never wanted anything more.' He gasped. 'Tessa...'

I looked up at him. 'Beg me,' I commanded.

Ethan reached down to touch my chin with his fingertips, his eyes dark, his breath short. 'I'll do anything you ask me to, sweetheart. Please, Tessa, God, I need to be in your mouth.'

I smiled, every part of my body alight with fire again. 'Why is this begging thing so hot? Is this now our kink?' I asked as I hooked my fingers into the waistband of his jeans and pulled them down.

'Hmmm. Along with half-naked chess,' he said, eyes fixed on every move I made, lifting his bum so I could strip him fully naked. 'And handcuffs.'

'Oh, that's a good idea.' I threw his jeans and boxers on the floor then bent down to find the discarded handcuffs. 'Arms up.'

'They didn't hold you; they won't hold me,' he said with a chuckle, but he still lifted his arms on the pillow above his head.

'Just pretend,' I said with a wink. I put them on him and moved down his body again. I eyed him. His chest was rising and falling rapidly beneath me. 'This is seriously hot, babe. I like being in control this time.'

'It's working for me, as you can tell,' he said, writhing beneath me again. 'You're driving me crazy.'

I smiled. 'Good. Beg me again.'

'Please, please, Tessa, I need your mouth on me.'

I slid down his body, enjoying how it made him gasp, ache building between my legs, which I knew he would take care of again soon. I had never felt this comfortable in bed with a man or as turned on. It was as if we had our own secret language together, and that was incredibly sexy. Hearing Ethan cry out my name or tell me, 'Yes, just like that, sweetheart,' drove me crazy and I knew I would soon be begging him to touch me again. This slow burn between us was now alight and sparkling and stronger than any flame I had ever ignited. I couldn't get enough of it. And Ethan seemed just as hooked as me.

Neither of us would be getting much sleep tonight.

And I didn't care one little bit.

39

When I woke up, I could see a glimpse of sun peeking through my bedroom window. I yawned, exhausted after staying up so late. We hadn't wanted to stop touching or kissing but finally, we'd been unable to stay awake any longer.

I turned to see Ethan beside me asleep on his back. Like me, he was only wearing underwear, and I eagerly snuggled against his bare chest. His arm came around my shoulder and he mumbled, pulling me closer.

God, I could get used to waking up beside him.

'Are you awake?' he asked sleepily, his eyes still closed.

'Yes but I don't want to move,' I said, placing a hand on his chest. It was warm and strong like him and as I stroked his skin, I marvelled how much had changed in such a short space of time. I would never have guessed I'd end up curled in his nook feeling like I had come home. 'I ache in places I didn't know I could ache.'

Ethan chuckled, and I felt the rumble through his chest. He leaned down to kiss the top of my head. 'Who needs the gym?' He tightened his arm around me and I sighed contently. There was a beat of silence. 'So, you're okay about last night?' he asked softly.

I lifted my head off his chest slightly to see his eyes had opened and he was looking at me. 'I have a feeling I won't be able to stop smiling today and everyone will be very annoyed with me.'

'I won't be.' He leaned down and brushed his lips against mine. 'I want to make you smile every day.' Then he looked at me so deeply, my heart started to speed up.

'I think you can easily do that,' I said, smiling happily.

He pulled me back for a kiss that turned hungry and frantic again. 'Ruined,' he gasped between kisses. 'I'm totally, utterly ruined and I couldn't be happier about it.'

'Me too,' I breathed as I shifted higher, pulling him closer, curving my body around him. Ethan grunted in approval, his free hand coming around to touch my face gently. I wrapped an arm around his neck and when our tongues met, my body was suddenly eager to carry on with last night. I was about to suggest that when his phone started to vibrate on the bedside table.

Ethan sighed as he pulled away. 'I remember Juliette saying something about seeing a venue today. And then us all having dinner together.'

I groaned. 'We have to leave this bed?'

'If I want to keep Juliette as my friend and restaurant partner.'

We looked at one another as his phone stopped vibrating then giggled.

'She doesn't mean that much to me,' Ethan added.

We kissed again then I leaned back. 'Knowing Juliette, she'd never let you cut her out,' I said.

'Good point.' Ethan leaned over to grab his phone and return her call, turning back to look and smile at me as he did so. Last night passed like a precious secret between us as Ethan arranged to meet her in an hour.

'I suppose we'll have to get up now,' I said. I sat up in bed and stretched. I eyed the handcuffs tossed on the floor with empty condom wrappers, and I shook my head. 'I can't believe we actually used the handcuffs.'

'You were very keen if I remember correctly,' Ethan said, leaning over to plant a kiss on my bare back. His hands rubbed my shoulders and then he moved my hair over to one side to press gentle kisses under my ear and down my neck.

'Don't,' I said, shivering. 'When you kiss me there…' My words disappeared as he trailed kisses down to my shoulder and then his hand moved up my side to cup one of my breasts. 'There isn't time.'

'There's always time,' he whispered, stroking my skin. 'So soft,' he said. I turned my head to smile, and he caught my lips with his. His fingers found my nipple and it hardened instantly under his touch. 'I don't how I'll keep my hands off you today,' he said, pulling back to give me a mischievous grin.

'Then don't,' I whispered, turning fully to face him. Hooking my arms around his neck, I pulled myself onto his lap. 'Will Juliette ask what's happened between us?'

'There is no doubt. If she asks if we're together, I want to say yes. What do you think?' Ethan asked me, looking seriously into my eyes, his hands firm on my waist as I sat astride him, feeling that he was just as aroused as I was.

I beamed at him. 'It's a yes from me too. It's yes to everything,' I managed to murmur as Ethan moved my thong to the side and eased two fingers inside me, curling them in a way that hit me exactly where I needed it. I let out a moan, and he grunted contentedly. 'We need to be quick,' I gasped as his mouth came down onto my nipple, sucking it deeply into his mouth.

'You know I don't like that,' he complained, flashing a grin up at me.

'Ethan,' I said breathlessly. 'Please?' I tried batting eyelashes at him.

He groaned but leaned over and grabbed a condom from the bedside table. 'I don't know how we've got ourselves into a situation that when you beg me, I have to do exactly what you want but...' He slipped it on and lifted me easily on top of him, both of us sighing when he slipped inside me. 'It feels so good.'

'Hmmm,' I agreed, rocking on top of him. 'So good.'

Ethan gripped my hips. 'No one else will make you feel this good.'

'I don't want anyone else,' I breathed. Ethan's hands moved up to stroke my breasts and I moved faster on top of him, both of us letting out an appreciative moan. I ran my hands through his hair. 'Are we really together now?'

His hand moved down to touch me, rubbing me exactly where I needed him, making me cry out with pleasure. 'Sweetheart, we were together as soon you begged me to kiss you; it just took us a while to figure it out,' he said huskily.

His words felt just as arousing as him inside me, touching me, looking at me reverently. The words rolled over me as pleasure built deep inside. This was fast and eager but still just as good as when we went slow. 'I'm so happy we're together.' I gasped as my release came suddenly, and I shattered on top of him, my body throbbing with satisfaction.

'I'll never get tired of watching you come,' he said, panting, thrusting into me. He cried out my name as he joined me, then rolled me down onto the bed and looked at me tenderly. 'This is real,' he promised me.

'I know it is.' I wondered how I had ever been unsure if this was real between us. Nothing had felt more real to me than this.

I could feel him trembling as he kissed me and we both held on to one another tightly as we came down from the sweetest high.

* * *

While Ethan and Juliette went to see a venue together, I got ready for the day and sat down at my writing desk to work on my book. I only had a few chapters left to write – my characters' sex scene, which I had been nervous to start but after my night with Ethan I now knew would be a breeze, and my leading lady deciding to move to Paris to start a new chapter of her life with the man she had fallen head over heels in love with.

My phone rang on the desk beside me, and I saw it was Gita, my editor.

'I finished reading the last chapters you sent me,' she said without preamble. 'I'm really loving this book, Tessa. It's romantic and compelling like all your books and your characters are so well drawn, their dialogue is perfect and Paris is like its own character. But most of all, I love the message about making sure you love yourself as well as being in love with someone else.'

'I'm so happy you're enjoying it,' I said, beaming from ear-to-ear. 'I only have a few more chapters to write.'

'I can't wait to read them. Did you have a think about a title so we can get working on a cover?'

'Actually, yes…' I said, explaining it to her.

'Oh, I love it,' Gita said. 'It's perfect. I'll get talking to your cover designer.'

'I'm sorry I had to push my deadline back,' I said then.

'Don't be. You did the right thing waiting to be able to write this. I think it will be your best book yet. And I think it's going to be a huge hit. You know Stevie will make sure it is.'

I laughed. 'I have every faith in her. I can't wait for her wedding in the autumn.'

'We will all raise a glass to your books, that's for sure. Now, let's speak after you send me the final chapters, and I'll keep you looped in with the cover. And Stevie will be in touch about promotion soon.'

'Thanks, Gita.'

I hung up and went back to my book. I started to write the sex scene, my mind going back to last night – and this morning. I had been so comfortable in bed with Ethan. I'd never felt like that before. I knew it was partly how comfortable I felt with him, and how special he made me feel, but it was also saying my final goodbye to Joe and the chapter we'd spent together. I knew that feeling I wasn't good enough for him had been wrong. It was him who wasn't good enough for me.

My time in Paris had shown me that it was okay to be me. No, not just okay. It was bloody fantastic to be me. To be myself.

Ethan and our friends had shown me that I was worthy of being loved. Maybe I even deserved love. In all the forms it came in. Because it wasn't just about romance, was it? The search for the one. Love was all around us. Love had all forms. And all of them were just as important, maybe even more so. Friendship, family, pets, yourself; hell, the love of life itself. So I had gone to Paris feeling like love was gone. That I'd never find it.

But I'd had it inside me all along.

I thought about what Gita had said about my novel, and its message about making sure you love yourself as well as being in love with someone else. It made sense that I had put that in my book as that was something I had realised in Paris and had come home changed by it. That was what helped me take the risk with Ethan. Because even if it didn't work out, although I had a sneaky suspicion it just might, I knew I wouldn't fall apart again.

I'm happy with who I am.

Looking out of the window of my flat, I spotted a blossom tree. There were beginnings of pink flowers on it. Signs that the new season had arrived. That even though winter could feel like it would last forever, it never did. Spring always arrived.

It was the same for life. Peaks and troughs. Ebbs and flow. The bad days followed by good ones. I had been stuck in winter for what had felt like forever. Letting myself wallow in hurt and disappointment, angry and bitter, thinking that betrayal meant that I'd been foolish to open my heart in the first place. But Joe had been the fool, not me. It was never a bad thing to let yourself fall. I knew now that I was able to get back up again.

And I always would get back up again.

40

That night, Ethan and I went for dinner with Juliette, Carly and Luke, and Juliette's older Frenchman Pierre, who was now officially her boyfriend, had followed her to London and seemed besotted.

We went to a small restaurant run by someone Ethan had trained with in a quiet corner of London, and all sat around a table with wine, and orange juice for Carly. Ethan sat beside me, his arm draped around the back of my chair, and we kept smiling at one another.

'The venue might actually be perfect,' Juliette told us. 'It's light and the perfect size and it's in a great spot near theatres for people looking to eat, right?' she asked Ethan, smiling happily.

Ethan nodded. 'It does feel pretty perfect. It was a catering college so can be easily changed into a kitchen and restaurant, and it's a listed building so would give us the cosy family feel we want for the French bistro. We want to do food that our parents made for us, recipes passed down, albeit with a slightly fancy twist.'

'It sounds great,' I said, feeling really proud of him. 'I love that you're making your dream come true.'

Ethan turned to me as the others fired more questions about the venue to Juliette. 'You helped inspire me to do it.'

'How?' I asked, liking the fact he'd dropped his arm to wrap around my shoulder. I loved how affectionate he was with me in front of our friends. Something again I hadn't experienced, particularly with Joe, who had told me he hated all public displays of affection. Although, I guessed it had been to make sure no one saw us who also knew Rachel. Now, I could just relax and enjoy Ethan's attention and touch. I felt just as comfortable here with him tonight as I had in bed with him.

'You came to Paris scared you couldn't write any more. You were blocked because of how hurt you were. But you didn't give up. You kept trying and now you've almost written your novel. You used what happened to you to write a brilliant story. Even though it meant reliving all your hurt, and being vulnerable, because writing is your dream. You inspire me, Tessa. I thought my dream would never come true, but I know I can do it because you did.'

'God, Ethan.' I leaned in to kiss him. 'I could only do it because of you. You took me to those romantic places in Paris, you encouraged me, you made me believe in myself – and love again.'

Ethan shook his head. 'You would have done it by yourself, I know you would have done. But I'm glad I was there to help a little bit.'

'More than a little bit,' I argued, but I smiled. I loved how he saw me.

We tuned back in to the conversation around us. Now, Juliette was telling Pierre our story in rapid French.

Ethan translated snippets for the rest of us. Then Juliette turned to me with a grin, so I asked Ethan what she had said.

'She said that she was out of the country when you got here so we had to share the one-bedroom apartment.'

'It was a very comfortable bed,' I told Pierre.

Juliette burst out laughing. 'I bet it was,' she said.

Ethan's hand found my thigh under the table and stroked it.

'I knew you couldn't give up on love,' Carly said, looking over at us with a smile that said she knew exactly what we had done last night.

'Being honest, I feel quite smug,' Luke said, nodding. 'It was my idea you should go to Paris for inspiration.'

'That's true,' I said. 'And I got more than I bargained for,' I said with a chuckle. I turned to Ethan, who was watching me with the kind of look I had always wanted someone to give me. 'I suppose it's true what they say – Paris is always a good idea.'

Ethan winked at me.

'God, get a room, you two!' Carly called over, making everyone laugh. She gave me a smile though, so I knew she approved really.

Juliette turned to us. 'Ethan, you better be good to Tessa.'

'Hey, shouldn't you be telling Tessa that; you were my friend first,' Ethan protested. He squeezed my thigh under the table and it sent warmth travelling up my whole body.

Juliette waved her hand. 'We are all friends now.'

As the others grilled Juliette about the venue they had looked at earlier, I turned to Ethan, who frowned at his phone. 'Are you okay?'

'Come outside with me?' he asked. I nodded as he got up. He asked the others to excuse us, and we walked outside the restaurant. He showed me his phone. Joe was calling him.

'Do you want to answer it?' I asked him.

Ethan looked down at the screen for a second then reached out and pressed the cancel button. He put his phone in his pocket and then wrapped an arm around my waist, drawing me closer to him. 'No. I will always have some fond memories of Joe when we were younger but right now, I want to focus on what's important to me. You, opening my own restaurant, the friends I love spending time with. I don't know what will happen in the future, but I feel better without him in my life right now.'

I nodded. 'I understand that. And I bet he does too. He may have hurt me, but he hurt you too. And if you're not ready to forgive him then you're not ready.'

'I don't know if I ever can. I hate that he tried to stop us being together. I can't help but wish we had met first.'

'Sometimes I do too, but I think we were meant to meet now. I had to go through what I went through with Joe to know what I want, to accept myself, to know that I'm okay just the way I am.'

'Of course you are!' Ethan looked shocked that I didn't already believe that. 'But maybe you're right. You gave me the confidence make this leap with the restaurant and Juliette.'

'I'm so happy we worked things out. It's a new chapter for both of us.' I grinned. 'Sorry for the writing pun.'

'No, I like it,' Ethan said, smiling back. 'It is a new chapter for both of us. Your book will be a smash hit, I know it.'

'You want to hear the title?' I asked, excited to tell him.

'Definitely.'

'It's going to be called *We'll Always Have Paris*. What do you think?'

Ethan looked taken aback. 'Are you serious?'

'What you said to me by the river, I kept thinking about it. It's perfect for the book, and for us. Whatever happens, I'll never forget our time in Paris.'

'Me too. We'll go back there together one day,' Ethan promised me. He drew me in to brush my lips with his again. 'I can't believe you're going to call your book that. I can't wait to read it. Tessa, you've changed everything for me.'

'You've done the same for me,' I told him.

Ethan leaned close to my ear to whisper, 'You know I'm falling in love with you, don't you?'

I turned my head to whisper into his ear. 'I'm falling for you too.'

We shared a deep kiss before we went back inside, arm-in-arm. I realised that I felt happy and content. I looked at our friends, who were listening to Luke testing out baby names for the twins with Carly, who hated all the ones he suggested, and I smiled. I loved my friends. I was enjoying writing again, which was and always would be my passion. And beside me was a man who I knew I was going to be head over heels in love with soon.

I couldn't wait to spend more time with Ethan. To be with someone who was honest with me, who I trusted, who told me how he felt and who saw a future with me and who I saw a future with. But most of all, someone who wanted me to be myself, who I could be myself with, and who had seen me before I saw myself clearly.

I knew one day we would go back to Paris together. It would always be our place. Where we met and where we first started falling for each other. The first chapter of our story, which I really hoped would continue for a very long time.

EPILOGUE
THE FOLLOWING FEBRUARY

It was Valentine's Day and I stood nervously in front of the packed room in Cinq in Paris. I knew that my book *We'll Always Have Paris* needed to be launched in the City of Love, and Juliette hadn't let me go anywhere but her family's restaurant for it.

I looked out at everyone as I read a passage from my novel. I didn't exactly enjoy events; I was still an overthinker at heart and panicked that no one would like the story, plus my imposter syndrome was high, but it helped to see familiar faces rooting for me amongst the strangers. Juliette and our Paris friends, Carly and Luke with their double pushchair, my parents, and everyone from my publisher Turn the Pages including Gita and Stevie. Then my eyes fell on a familiar face. I did a double take, smiling in surprise to see the person I was happiest to find here.

Ethan gave me a reassuring smile, and calmness rolled over me as it always did when I was around him. I took a breath and carried on, finishing the paragraph to an enthusiastic round of applause. I then sat down and Stevie organised a line of readers who wanted me to sign their books. I saw Ethan go over to her husband Noah and chat to him. They had got on well at Stevie and Noah's wedding last autumn.

'The story is so beautiful, I came to Paris because of it,' a reader said to me as I signed her book.

'Oh wow, that means so much to me,' I said.

She told me that she was enjoying the city. I still marvelled at how much my trip this time last year had changed things for me.

When everyone had had their books signed, I got up and went over to Ethan, eagerly leaning into him. He gave me a soft kiss that sent warmth from my lips down my body. 'What are you doing here?' I asked. 'You shouldn't have come; what about Amour?'

Amour was Ethan and Juliette's London restaurant. It had now opened and was generating great buzz. Juliette had wanted to keep the one-word tradition of her parents' restaurant and Ethan had suggested the French word for love to represent their passion for food, Paris, the City of Love, and because my gift for them when they found their venue had been a large print of The Wall of Love in Paris. That print was the first thing you saw when you went inside their restaurant, and it made my heart soar every time I walked past it.

I had never been prouder of someone before as I was of Ethan making his dream come true. But with Juliette here helping me organise my launch party, I had told Ethan I understood that he couldn't leave their place for the weekend to come to Paris too.

Ethan wrapped an arm around my waist, keeping me pulled in close to him. 'We show up for each other.'

I looked at him and smiled. 'I know we do. But what about your restaurant?'

'Pierre has it covered,' he replied. Juliette's boyfriend was their manager and ran it as a tight ship. 'Our sous chef deserved a chance to run the kitchen for the weekend too. It will all be fine. I had to celebrate your book with you.'

'It's really our book,' I replied. We smiled at one another.

'You were amazing up there doing your reading. As always.'

'I was so nervous.'

'You shouldn't have been; it went brilliantly,' Stevie said, coming over. 'Do you have time to film a video for social media?'

'Sure,' I said. I turned to Ethan and gave him another quick kiss. 'I'll see you in a bit?'

'We will celebrate in style.' He dropped me a wink and I watched him join Juliette and Oscar, still surprised he'd come to Paris for me. It meant a lot to me. But I knew he was right. That was what we wanted to do in life – show up for each other.

I went over to Stevie to do what she wanted for social media. Before this trip, I had gone to the Turn the Pages offices to meet with Gita and I had signed a new book deal with them. *We'll Always Have Paris* had become an instant hit, hitting the bestseller chart in the UK but also in America and around Europe, and a studio was interested in turning it into a film. I had signed on for four more romance novels with them and everyone was excited for what was to come next in my career.

When I finished what Stevie wanted me to do, I joined our friends and we all had a glass of bubbly. I leaned down to look at the twins with a smile. Carly and Luke were already amazing parents to their boy and girl. They had named their daughter Clementine, suggested by Juliette when Carly and Luke were unable to find one they both liked. She argued the babies were practically half French anyway, and Carly had been obsessed with drinking orange juice while she was pregnant. Then they had to choose a French name for their son too and Gabriel was picked as Carly loved *Emily in Paris* as much as me. Doted on by their parents and their auntie and uncles, the twins were currently sleeping peacefully in their pushchair while Carly and Luke managed to grab a glass of champagne for a rare evening out.

'I'm so glad you made it,' I told them.

'We wouldn't have missed it,' Carly said.

'We are all so proud of you,' Luke added.

'Don't, I might cry,' I said, looking at the people I loved most in the world all here to celebrate my book with me. It was more than I could ever have imagined when I came to Paris a year ago.

Ethan leaned in then. 'I have another surprise for you afterwards.'

'This was enough of a surprise,' I said, reaching out to take his hand.

Juliette raised her glass of champagne. 'To Tessa,' she said.

I smiled, embarrassed but touched as our friends toasted me. I glanced out of Cinq's window to see the Eiffel Tower sparkling in the distance.

Thank you, Paris.

Later, we left the restaurant, Ethan and I the last ones to leave walking out arm-in-arm, tired but happy.

'What a night,' I said as Ethan steered me in the direction of my surprise. 'I'm so happy you're here.'

'I don't want to be anywhere without you,' Ethan replied.

'You never have to be anywhere without me,' I promised, holding on to him tightly as we walked through the quiet streets of Paris. '*Toi et moi.*'

'You and me,' he murmured. 'You know, that's a very popular engagement ring design – two stones, one ring.'

I smiled. 'Juliette might have mentioned that a few times to me.'

'Hmm, did she now?' He gave me that amused look I loved. 'It's very sexy when you speak French, you know,' he said, echoing what I had told him when we had first met.

'I can speak more of it later if you like,' I said playfully.

'Let's walk faster,' he replied. We both laughed and turned into a street that I recognised.

'Is that…?' I looked and saw the apartment building ahead that housed the Airbnb we'd stayed in together a year ago.

'I booked it for us for the weekend as a surprise. Juliette moved all your things from her place without you knowing,' Ethan confirmed.

'Babe, that is so romantic!' I cried, so touched he had done this.

'Well, it's practically an anniversary trip as well as your book launch so where better to spend it than the place we fell for each other in?'

'I love the idea.'

We went inside and up to the one-bedroom apartment. Ethan let us in and turned on the lights. 'I'll open another bottle of champagne,' Ethan said. 'Why don't we have it on the balcony?'

'We have to play a game of chess later too,' I said, walking over to look out at the balcony, the twinkling lights of Paris ahead. We always had a game going in London. Ethan's chess lessons paid off so he could now beat me but only one in about five games, which was a constant source of irritation to him, and allowed me to be extremely smug.

We had left our flats and moved into one together, still overlooking the river in Putney. So now we only had one bed again and loved every minute of waking up and going to sleep beside one another. Pictures of Paris lined our walls and we loved nothing more than going home-décor shopping when we had the time. We dreamed one day of having a second home in Paris, but until then we wanted to come back as often as we could.

'We can play whatever games you like,' Ethan said, coming over to hand me a glass of champagne. He leaned down to drop a kiss on the spot on my neck that he knew would make me shiver with anticipation.

'Hmm, I have a few ideas,' I gasped.

Ethan lifted off me and pulled back with a grin. 'I can't wait to hear them. In French.'

'That's why you taught me all the dirty words first, isn't it?' I asked, raising an eyebrow.

'Guilty as charged.'

We stepped out onto the balcony. It was pleasantly warm for February. Spring had arrived early, so in our light jackets, we weren't cold. Ethan wrapped an arm around me and I leaned against him as we looked out at Paris together.

'This is perfect,' I said to him. *Je t'aime.*'

'I love you so much, sweetheart,' Ethan replied. He turned to me and gave me a kiss. 'Meeting you here was the best thing that ever happened to me.'

I smiled. 'I feel the same way.' Having someone by my side made everything sweeter. I loved and trusted Ethan, we made a great team, and I now knew that you could never plan who would be the perfect person for you. Ethan had been the best surprise. I was a better person for the time we had spent together in Paris last year. And I knew we had so many more years ahead of us too.

'A toast,' Ethan said. 'Before I take you inside and remind us how comfortable the bed is here...'

I giggled, already desperate to be on that bed with him.

Ethan looked at me with so much love in his eyes, my giggles died away. 'To Paris, for bringing us together. It will always be my favourite city because of that.'

'Me too,' I agreed. We clinked our glasses and took a sip as we smiled at one another.

Ethan reached out to touch my lip with his fingertips. 'I hope you are always by my side, sweetheart. *Pour toujours.*'

'*Pour toujours,*' I agreed.
Forever.
It sounds good to me.

ACKNOWLEDGMENTS

This is the first book I've set outside the UK – I was so excited to use the City of Love and I hope you enjoy coming to Paris with me! Thank you so much if you've picked up this book. I am always amazed by the lovely reviews and messages I see from readers, so thank you for supporting my books, it really does mean the world.

Thank you so much to Emily Yau, my fabulous editor, for being so supportive of this story and helping me make it the best it could be! As always, a huge thank you to my lovely agent Hannah Ferguson and the fabulous team at Hardman and Swainson for working so hard on all my books.

This is my third time working with the amazing Boldwood Books team so sending a huge thank you to you all! Special thanks to Niamh Wallace, Nia Beynon, Wendy Neale and Issy Flynn. Thank you so much to my copy editor Emily Reader, my proofreader Jennifer Davies, and Alexandra Allden for such a beautiful cover. And Geri Allen for reading my audiobooks so brilliantly.

A huge thank you to the lovely Anna Bell for looking over the French phrases in this book (any mistakes are definitely my own!!). Special thanks to Carly for letting me use your name and for thirty-plus years of friendship. Thank you so much and lots of love to my family and friends for all your support xx

PLAYLIST FOR THE PARIS CHAPTER

Bonjour Au revoir – Joyce Jonathan
    nuits d'été – Oscar Anton, Clementine
    Quelqu'un m'a dit – Carla Bruni
    La Vie en Rose – Ashley Park
    PS: Je t'aime – Christophe Willem
    Démons – Angèle, Damso
    Le reste – Clara Luciani
    Embrasse Moi – filous, Clementine
    Le temps passe – Emma Petes
    Pardonne-moi – Louane
    L'amour en Solitaire – Juliette Armanet
    Ces petits riens – Stacey Kent
    Don't break my... – Kenzie Cait
    Sacre Coeur – Tina Dico
    Secret – Louane
    Balance ton quoi – Angèle
    Under Paris Skies – Stacey Kent
    Ne t'en fais pas – Emma Hoet
    Un jour je marierai un ange – Pierre de Maere

Moonlit Floor – LISA
Mon Soleil – Ashley Park
From Paris With Love – Melody Gardot

ABOUT THE AUTHOR

Victoria Walters is the author of both cosy crime and romantic novels, including the bestselling Glendale Hall series. She has been chosen for WHSmith Fresh Talent, shortlisted for two RNA novels and was picked as an Amazon Rising Star.

Sign up to Victoria Walters' mailing list for news, competitions and updates on future books.

Visit Victoria's website: www.victoria-writes.com

Follow Victoria on social media:

- instagram.com/vickyjwalters
- facebook.com/VictoriaWaltersAuthor
- x.com/Vicky_Walters
- bookbub.com/authors/victoria-walters
- youtube.com/@vickyjwalters

ALSO BY VICTORIA WALTERS

The Love Interest

The Plot Twist

The Paris Chapter

LOVE NOTES
LOVE IN EVERY CHAPTER

WHERE ALL YOUR ROMANCE
DREAMS COME TRUE!

THE HOME OF BESTSELLING
ROMANCE AND WOMEN'S
FICTION

WARNING:
MAY CONTAIN SPICE

SIGN UP TO OUR
NEWSLETTER

https://bit.ly/Lovenotesnews

Boldwood

Boldwood Books is an award-winning fiction publishing company seeking out the best stories from around the world.

Find out more at www.boldwoodbooks.com

Join our reader community for brilliant books, competitions and offers!

Follow us
@BoldwoodBooks
@TheBoldBookClub

Sign up to our weekly deals newsletter

https://bit.ly/BoldwoodBNewsletter

www.ingramcontent.com/pod-product-compliance
Ingram Content Group UK Ltd.
Pitfield, Milton Keynes, MK11 3LW, UK
UKHW021044140125
453296UK00012B/5

9 781835 189689